A Woman of Thirty

Honoré de Balzac

A Woman of Thirty

The present edition is a reproduction of previous publication of this classic work. Minor typographical errors may have been corrected without note; however, for an authentic reading experience the spelling, punctuation, and capitalization have been retained from the original text.

ISBN: 979-8-88942-367-6

DEDICATION

To Louis Boulanger, Painter

CONTENTS

I

EARLY MISTAKES

It was a Sunday morning in the beginning of April 1813, a morning which gave promise of one of those bright days when Parisians, for the first time in the year, behold dry pavements underfoot and a cloudless sky overhead. It was not yet noon when a luxurious cabriolet, drawn by two spirited horses, turned out of the Rue de Castiglione into the Rue de Rivoli, and drew up behind a row of carriages standing before the newly opened barrier half-way down the Terrasse de Feuillants. The owner of the carriage looked anxious and out of health; the thin hair on his sallow temples, turning gray already, gave a look of premature age to his face. He flung the reins to a servant who followed on horseback, and alighted to take in his arms a young girl whose dainty beauty had already attracted the eyes of loungers on the Terrasse. The little lady, standing upon the carriage step, graciously submitted to be taken by the waist, putting an arm round the neck of her guide, who set her down upon the pavement without so much as ruffling the trimming of her green rep dress. No lover would have been so careful. The stranger could only be the father of the young girl, who took his arm familiarly without a word of thanks, and hurried him into the Garden of the Tuileries.

The old father noted the wondering stare which some of the young men gave the couple, and the sad expression left his face for a moment. Although he had long since reached the time of life when a man is fain to be content with such illusory delights as vanity bestows, he began to smile.

"They think you are my wife," he said in the young lady's ear, and he held himself erect and walked with slow steps, which filled his daughter with despair.

He seemed to take up the coquette's part for her; perhaps of the two, he was the more gratified by the curious glances directed at those little feet, shod with plum-colored prunella; at the dainty figure outlined by a low-cut bodice, filled in with an embroidered chemisette, which only partially concealed the girlish throat. Her dress was lifted by her movements as she walked, giving glimpses higher than the shoes of delicately moulded outlines beneath open-work silk stockings. More than one of the idlers turned and passed the pair again, to admire or to catch a second glimpse of the young face, about which the brown tresses played; there was a glow in its white and red, partly reflected from the rose-colored satin lining of her fashionable bonnet, partly due to the eagerness and impatience which sparkled in every feature. A mischievous sweetness lighted up the beautiful, almond-shaped dark eyes, bathed in liquid brightness, shaded by the long lashes and curving arch of eyebrow. Life and youth displayed their treasures in the petulant face and in the gracious outlines of the bust unspoiled even by the fashion of the day, which brought the girdle under the breast.

The young lady herself appeared to be insensible to admiration. Her eyes were fixed in a sort of anxiety on the Palace of the Tuileries, the goal, doubtless, of her petulant promenade. It wanted but fifteen minutes of noon, yet even at that early hour several women in gala dress were coming away from the Tuileries, not without backward glances at the gates and pouting looks of discontent, as if they regretted the lateness of the arrival which had cheated them of a longed-for spectacle. Chance carried a few words let fall by one of these disappointed fair ones to the ears of the charming stranger, and put her in a more than common uneasiness. The elderly man watched the signs of impatience and apprehension which flitted across his companion's pretty face with interest, rather than amusement, in his eyes, observing her with a close and careful attention, which perhaps could only be prompted by some after-thought in the depths of a father's mind.

It was the thirteenth Sunday of the year 1813. In two days' time Napoleon was to set out upon the disastrous campaign in which he was to lose first Bessieres, and then Duroc; he was to win the memorable battles of Lutzen and Bautzen, to see himself treacherously deserted by Austria, Saxony, Bavaria, and Bernadotte, and to dispute the dreadful field of Leipsic. The magnificent review commanded for that day by the Emperor was to be the last of so many which had long drawn forth the admiration of Paris and of foreign visitors. For the last time the Old Guard would execute their scientific military manoeuvres with the pomp and precision which sometimes amazed the Giant himself. Napoleon was nearly ready for his duel with Europe. It was a sad sentiment which brought a brilliant and curious throng to the Tuileries. Each mind seemed to foresee the future, perhaps too in every mind another thought was dimly present, how that in the future, when the heroic age of France should have taken the half-fabulous color with which it is tinged for us to-day, men's imaginations would more than once seek to retrace the picture of the pageant which they were assembled to behold.

"Do let us go more quickly, father; I can hear the drums," the young girl said, and in a half-teasing, half-coaxing manner she urged her companion forward.

"The troops are marching into the Tuileries," said he.

"Or marching out of it—everybody is coming away," she answered in childish vexation, which drew a smile from her father.

"The review only begins at half-past twelve," he said; he had fallen half behind his impetuous daughter.

It might have been supposed that she meant to hasten their progress by a movement of her right arm, for it swung like an oar blade through the water. In her impatience she had crushed her handkerchief into a ball in her tiny, well-gloved fingers. Now and then the old man smiled, but the smiles were succeeded by an anxious look which crossed his withered face and saddened it. In his love for the fair young girl by his side, he was as fain to exalt the present moment as to dread the future. "She is happy to-day; will her happiness last?" he seemed to ask himself, for the old are somewhat prone to foresee their own sorrows in the future of the young.

Father and daughter reached the peristyle under the tower where the tricolor flag was still waving; but as they passed under the arch by which people came and went between the Gardens of the Tuileries and the Place du Carrousel, the sentries on guard called out sternly:

"No admittance this way."

By standing on tiptoe the young girl contrived to catch a glimpse of a crowd of well-dressed women, thronging either side of the old marble arcade along which the Emperor was to pass.

"We were too late in starting, father; you can see that quite well." A little piteous pout revealed the immense importance which she attached to the sight of this particular review.

"Very well, Julie—let us go away. You dislike a crush."

"Do let us stay, father. Even here I may catch a glimpse of the Emperor; he might die during this campaign, and then I should never have seen him."

Her father shuddered at the selfish speech. There were tears in the girl's voice; he looked at her, and thought that he saw tears beneath her lowered eyelids; tears caused not so much by the disappointment as by one of the troubles of early youth, a secret easily guessed by an old father. Suddenly Julie's face flushed, and she uttered an exclamation. Neither her father nor the sentinels understood the meaning of the cry; but an officer within the barrier, who sprang across the court towards the staircase, heard it, and turned abruptly at the sound. He went to the arcade by the Gardens of the Tuileries, and recognized the young lady who had been hidden for a moment by the tall bearskin caps of the grenadiers. He set aside in favor of the pair the order which he himself had given. Then, taking no heed of the murmurings of the fashionable crowd seated under the arcade, he gently drew the enraptured child towards him.

"I am no longer surprised at her vexation and enthusiasm, if you are in waiting," the old man said with a half-mocking, half-serious glance at the officer.

"If you want a good position, M. le Duc," the young man answered, "we must not spend any time in talking. The Emperor does not like to be kept waiting, and the Grand Marshal has sent me to announce our readiness."

As he spoke, he had taken Julie's arm with a certain air of old acquaintance, and drew her rapidly in the direction of the Place du Carrousel. Julie was astonished at the sight. An immense crowd was penned up in a narrow space, shut in between the gray walls of the palace and the limits marked out by chains round the great sanded squares in the midst of the courtyard of the Tuileries. The cordon of sentries posted to keep a clear passage for the Emperor and his staff had great difficulty in keeping back the eager humming swarm of human beings.

"Is it going to be a very fine sight?" Julie asked (she was radiant now).

"Pray take care!" cried her guide, and seizing Julie by the waist, he lifted her up with as much vigor as rapidity and set her down beside a pillar.

But for his prompt action, his gazing kinswoman would have come into collision with the hindquarters of a white horse which Napoleon's Mameluke held by the bridle; the animal in its trappings of green velvet and gold stood almost under the arcade, some ten paces behind the rest of the horses in readiness for the Emperor's staff.

The young officer placed the father and daughter in front of the crowd in the first space to the right, and recommended them by a sign to the two veteran grenadiers on either side. Then he went on his way into the palace; a look of great joy and happiness had succeeded to his horror-struck expression when the horse backed. Julie had given his hand a mysterious pressure; had she meant to thank him for the little service he had done her, or did she tell him, "After all, I shall really see you?" She bent her head quite graciously in response to the respectful bow by which the officer took leave of them before he vanished.

The old man stood a little behind his daughter. He looked grave. He seemed to have left the two young people together for some purpose of his own, and now he furtively watched the girl, trying to lull her into false security by appearing to give his whole attention to the magnificent sight in the Place du Carrousel. When Julie's eyes turned to her father with the expression of a schoolboy before his master, he answered her glance by a gay, kindly smile, but his own keen eyes had followed the officer under the arcade, and nothing of all that passed was lost upon him.

"What a grand sight!" said Julie in a low voice, as she pressed her father's hand; and indeed the pomp and picturesquesness of the spectacle in the Place du Carrousel drew the same exclamation from thousands upon thousands of spectators, all agape with wonder. Another array of sightseers, as tightly packed as the ranks behind the old noble and his daughter, filled the narrow strip of pavement by the railings which crossed the Place du Carrousel from side to side in a line parallel with the Palace of the Tuileries. The dense living mass, variegated by the colors of the women's dresses, traced out a bold line across the centre of the Place du Carrousel, filling in the fourth side of a vast parallelogram, surrounded on three sides by the Palace of the Tuileries itself. Within the precincts thus railed off stood the regiments of the Old Guard about to be passed in review, drawn up opposite the Palace in imposing blue columns, ten ranks in depth. Without and beyond in the Place du Carrousel stood several regiments likewise drawn up in parallel lines, ready to march in through the arch in the centre; the Triumphal Arch, where the bronze horses of St. Mark from Venice used to stand in those days. At either end, by the Galeries du Louvre, the regimental bands were stationed, masked by the Polish Lancers then on duty.

The greater part of the vast graveled space was empty as an arena, ready for the evolutions of those silent masses disposed with the symmetry of military art. The sunlight blazed back from ten thousand bayonets in thin points of flame; the breeze ruffled the men's helmet plumes till they swayed like the crests of forest-trees before a gale. The mute glittering ranks of veterans were full of bright contrasting colors, thanks to their different uniforms, weapons, accoutrements, and aiguillettes; and the whole great picture, that miniature battlefield before the combat, was framed by the majestic towering walls of the Tuileries, which officers and men seemed to rival in their immobility. Involuntarily the spectator made the comparison between the walls of men and the walls of stone. The spring sunlight, flooding white masonry reared but yesterday and buildings centuries old, shone full likewise upon thousands of bronzed faces, each one with its own tale of perils passed, each one gravely expectant of perils to come.

The colonels of the regiments came and went alone before the ranks of heroes; and behind the masses of troops, checkered with blue and silver and gold and purple, the curious could discern the tricolor pennons on the lances of some half-a-dozen indefatigable Polish cavalry, rushing about like shepherds' dogs in charge of a flock, caracoling up and down between the troops and the crowd, to keep the gazers within their proper bounds. But for this slight flutter of movement, the whole scene might have been taking place in the courtyard of the palace of the Sleeping Beauty. The very spring breeze, ruffling up the long fur on the grenadiers' bearskins, bore witness to the men's immobility, as the smothered murmur of the crowd emphasized their silence. Now and again the jingling of Chinese bells, or a chance blow to a big drum, woke the reverberating echoes of the Imperial Palace with a sound like the far-off rumblings of thunder.

An indescribable, unmistakable enthusiasm was manifest in the expectancy of the multitude. France was about to take farewell of Napoleon on the eve of a campaign of which the meanest citizen foresaw the perils. The existence of the French Empire was at stake—to be, or not to be. The whole citizen population seemed to be as much inspired with this thought as that other armed population standing in serried and silent ranks in the enclosed space, with the Eagles and the genius of Napoleon hovering above them.

Those very soldiers were the hope of France, her last drop of blood; and this accounted for not a little of the anxious interest of the scene. Most of the gazers in the crowd had bidden farewell— perhaps farewell for ever—to the men who made up the rank and file of the battalions; and even those most hostile to the Emperor, in their hearts, put up fervent prayers to heaven for the glory of France; and those most weary of the struggle with the rest of Europe had left their hatreds behind as they passed in under the Triumphal Arch. They too felt that in the hour of danger Napoleon meant France herself.

The clock of the Tuileries struck the half-hour. In a moment the hum of the crowd ceased. The silence was so deep that you might have heard a child speak. The old noble and his daughter, wholly intent, seeming to live only by their eyes, caught a distinct sound of spurs and clank of swords echoing up under the sonorous peristyle.

And suddenly there appeared a short, somewhat stout figure in a green uniform, white trousers, and riding boots; a man wearing on his head a cocked hat well-nigh as magically potent as its wearer; the broad red ribbon of the Legion of Honor rose and fell on his breast, and a short sword hung at his side. At one and the same moment the man was seen by all eyes in all parts of the square.

Immediately the drums beat a salute, both bands struck up a martial refrain, caught and repeated like a fugue by every instrument from the thinnest flutes to the largest drum. The clangor of that call to arms thrilled through every soul. The colors dropped, and the men presented arms, one unanimous rhythmical movement shaking every bayonet from the foremost front near the Palace to the last rank in the Place du Carrousel. The words of command sped from line to line like echoes. The whole enthusiastic multitude sent up a shout of "Long live the Emperor!"

Everything shook, quivered, and thrilled at last. Napoleon had mounted his horse. It was his movement that had put life into those silent masses of men; the dumb instruments had found a voice at his coming, the Eagles and the colors had obeyed the same impulse which had brought emotion into all faces.

The very walls of the high galleries of the old palace seemed to cry aloud, "Long live the Emperor!"

There was something preternatural about it—it was magic at work, a counterfeit presentment of the power of God; or rather it was a fugitive image of a reign itself so fugitive.

And he the centre of such love, such enthusiasm and devotion, and so many prayers, he for whom the sun had driven the clouds from the sky, was sitting there on his horse, three paces in front of his Golden Squadron, with the grand Marshal on his left, and the Marshal-in-waiting on his right. Amid all the outburst of enthusiasm at his presence not a feature of his face appeared to alter.

"Oh! yes. At Wagram, in the thick of the firing, on the field of Borodino, among the dead, always as cool as a cucumber he is!" said the grenadier, in answer to the questions with which the young girl plied him. For a moment Julie was absorbed in the contemplation of that face, so quiet in the security of conscious power. The Emperor noticed Mlle. de Chatillonest, and leaned to make some brief remark to Duroc, which drew a smile from the Grand Marshal. Then the review began.

If hitherto the young lady's attention had been divided between Napoleon's impassive face and the blue, red, and green ranks of troops, from this time forth she was wholly intent upon a young officer moving among the lines as they performed their swift symmetrical evolutions. She watched him gallop with tireless activity to and from the group where the plainly dressed Napoleon shone conspicuous. The officer rode a splendid black horse. His handsome sky-blue uniform marked him out amid the variegated multitude as one of the Emperor's orderly staff-officers. His gold lace glittered in the sunshine which lighted up the aigrette on his tall, narrow shako, so that the gazer might have compared him to a will-o'-the-wisp, or to a visible spirit emanating from the Emperor to infuse movement into those battalions whose swaying bayonets flashed into flames; for, at a mere glance from his eyes, they broke and gathered again, surging to and fro like the waves in a bay, or again swept before him like the long ridges of high-crested wave which the vexed Ocean directs against the shore.

When the manoeuvres were over the officer galloped back at full speed, pulled up his horse, and awaited orders. He was not ten paces from Julie as he stood before the Emperor, much as General Rapp stands in Gerard's Battle of Austerlitz. The young girl could behold her lover in all his soldierly splendor.

Colonel Victor d'Aiglemont, barely thirty years of age, was tall, slender, and well made. His well-proportioned figure never showed to better advantage than now as he exerted his strength to hold in the restive animal, whose back seemed to curve gracefully to the rider's weight. His brown masculine face possessed the indefinable charm of perfectly regular features combined with youth. The fiery eyes under the broad forehead, shaded by thick eyebrows and long lashes, looked like white ovals bordered by an outline of black. His nose had the delicate curve of an eagle's beak; the sinuous lines of the inevitable black moustache enhanced the crimson of the lips. The brown and tawny shades which overspread the wide high-colored cheeks told a tale of unusual vigor, and his whole face bore the impress of dashing courage. He was the very model which French artists seek to-day for the typical hero of Imperial France. The horse which he rode was covered with sweat, the animal's quivering head denoted the last degree of restiveness; his hind hoofs were set down wide apart and exactly in a line, he shook his long thick tail to the wind; in his fidelity to his master he seemed to be a visible presentment of that master's devotion to the Emperor.

Julie saw her lover watching intently for the Emperor's glances, and felt a momentary pang of jealousy, for as yet he had not given her a look. Suddenly at a word from his sovereign Victor gripped his horse's flanks and set out at a gallop, but the animal took fright at a shadow cast by a post, shied, backed, and reared up so suddenly that his rider was all but thrown off. Julie cried out, her face grew white, people looked at her curiously, but she saw no one, her eyes were fixed upon the too mettlesome beast. The officer gave the horse a sharp admonitory cut with the whip, and galloped off with Napoleon's order.

Julie was so absorbed, so dizzy with sights and sounds, that unconsciously she clung to her father's arm so tightly that he could read her thoughts by the varying pressure of her fingers. When Victor was all but flung out of the saddle, she clutched her father with a convulsive grip as if she herself were in danger of falling, and the old man looked at his daughter's tell-tale face with dark and painful anxiety. Pity, jealousy, something even of regret stole across every drawn and wrinkled line of mouth and brow. When he saw the unwonted light in Julie's eyes, when that cry broke from her, when the convulsive grasp of her fingers drew away the veil and put him in possession of her secret, then with that revelation of her love there came surely some swift revelation of the future. Mournful forebodings could be read in his own face.

Julie's soul seemed at that moment to have passed into the officer's being. A torturing thought more cruel than any previous dread contracted the old man's painworn features, as he saw the glance of understanding that passed between the soldier and Julie. The girl's eyes were wet, her cheeks glowed with unwonted color. Her father turned abruptly and led her away into the Garden of the Tuileries.

"Why, father," she cried, "there are still the regiments in the Place du Carrousel to be passed in review."

"No, child, all the troops are marching out."

"I think you are mistaken, father; M. d'Aiglemont surely told them to advance——"

"But I feel ill, my child, and I do not care to stay."

Julie could readily believe the words when she glanced at his face; he looked quite worn out by his fatherly anxieties.

"Are you feeling very ill?" she asked indifferently, her mind was so full of other thoughts.

"Every day is a reprieve for me, is it not?" returned her father.

"Now do you mean to make me miserable again by talking about your death? I was in such spirits! Do pray get rid of those horrid gloomy ideas of yours."

The father heaved a sigh. "Ah! spoiled child," he cried, "the best hearts are sometimes very cruel. We devote our whole lives to you, you are our one thought, we plan for your welfare, sacrifice our tastes to your whims, idolize you, give the very blood in our veins for you, and all this is nothing, is it? Alas! yes, you take it all as a matter of course. If we would always have your smiles and your disdainful love, we should need the power of God in heaven. Then comes another, a lover, a husband, and steals away your heart."

Julie looked in amazement at her father; he walked slowly along, and there was no light in the eyes which he turned upon her.

"You hide yourself even from us," he continued, "but, perhaps, also you hide yourself from yourself—"

"What do you mean by that, father?"

"I think that you have secrets from me, Julie.—You love," he went on quickly, as he saw the color rise to her face. "Oh! I hoped that you would stay with your old father until he died. I hoped to keep you with me, still radiant and happy, to admire you as you were but so lately. So long as I knew nothing of your future I could believe in a happy lot for you; but now I cannot possibly take away with me a hope of happiness for your life, for you love the colonel even more than the cousin. I can no longer doubt it."

"And why should I be forbidden to love him?" asked Julie, with lively curiosity in her face.

"Ah, my Julie, you would not understand me," sighed the father.

"Tell me, all the same," said Julie, with an involuntary petulant gesture.

"Very well, child, listen to me. Girls are apt to imagine noble and enchanting and totally imaginary figures in their own minds; they have fanciful extravagant ideas about men, and sentiment, and life; and then they innocently endow somebody or other with all the perfections of their day-dreams, and put their trust in him. They fall in love with this imaginary creature in the man of their choice; and then, when it is too late to escape from their fate, behold their first idol, the illusion made fair with their fancies, turns to an odious skeleton. Julie, I would rather have you fall in love with an old man than with the Colonel. Ah! if you could but see things from the standpoint of ten years hence, you would admit that my old experience was right. I know what Victor is, that gaiety of his is simply animal spirits—the gaiety of the barracks. He has no ability, and he is a spendthrift. He is one of those men whom Heaven created to eat and digest four meals a day, to sleep, to fall in love with the first woman that comes to hand, and to fight. He does not understand life. His kind heart, for he has a kind heart, will perhaps lead him to give his purse to a sufferer or to a comrade; but he is careless, he has not the delicacy of heart which makes us slaves to a woman's happiness, he is ignorant, he is selfish. There are plenty of buts—"

"But, father, he must surely be clever, he must have ability, or he would not be a colonel—"

"My dear, Victor will be a colonel all his life.—I have seen no one who appears to me to be worthy of you," the old father added, with a kind of enthusiasm.

He paused an instant, looked at his daughter, and added, "Why, my poor Julie, you are still too young, too fragile, too delicate for the cares and rubs of married life. D'Aiglemont's relations have spoiled him, just as your mother and I have spoiled you. What hope is there that you two could agree, with two imperious wills diametrically opposed to each other? You will be either the tyrant or the victim, and either alternative means, for a wife, an equal sum of misfortune. But you are modest and sweet-natured, you would yield from the first. In short," he added, in a quivering voice, "there is a grace of feeling in you which would never be valued, and then——" he broke off, for the tears overcame him.

"Victor will give you pain through all the girlish qualities of your young nature," he went on, after a pause. "I know what soldiers are, my Julie; I have been in the army. In a man of that kind, love very seldom gets the better of old habits, due partly to the miseries amid which soldiers live, partly to the risks they run in a life of adventure."

"Then you mean to cross my inclinations, do you, father?" asked Julie, half in earnest, half in jest. "Am I to marry to please you and not to please myself?"

"To please me!" cried her father, with a start of surprise. "To please me, child? when you will not hear the voice that upbraids you so tenderly very much longer! But I have always heard children impute personal motives for the sacrifices that their parents make for them. Marry Victor, my Julie! Some day you will bitterly deplore his ineptitude, his thriftless ways, his selfishness, his lack of delicacy, his inability to understand love, and countless troubles arising through him. Then, remember, that here under these trees your old father's prophetic voice sounded in your ears in vain."

He said no more; he had detected a rebellious shake of the head on his daughter's part. Both made several paces towards the carriage which was waiting for them at the grating. During that interval of silence, the young girl stole a glance at her father's face, and little by little her sullen brow cleared. The intense pain visible on his bowed forehead made a lively impression upon her.

"Father," she began in gentle tremulous tones, "I promise to say no more about Victor until you have overcome your prejudices against him."

The old man looked at her in amazement. Two tears which filled his eyes overflowed down his withered cheeks. He could not take Julie in his arms in that crowded place; but he pressed her hand tenderly. A few minutes later when they had taken their places in the cabriolet, all the anxious thought which had gathered about his brow had completely disappeared. Julie's pensive attitude gave him far less concern than the innocent joy which had betrayed her secret during the review.

Nearly a year had passed since the Emperor's last review. In early March 1814 a caleche was rolling along the highroad from Amboise to Tours. As the carriage came out from beneath the green-roofed aisle of walnut trees by the post-house of la Frilliere, the horses dashed forward with such speed that in a moment they gained the bridge built across the Cise at the point of its confluence with the Loire. There, however, they come to a sudden stand. One of the traces had given way in consequence of the furious pace at which the post-boy, obedient to his orders, had urged on four horses, the most vigorous of their breed. Chance, therefore, gave the two recently awakened occupants of the carriage an opportunity of seeing one of the most lovely landscapes along the enchanting banks of the Loire, and that at their full leisure.

At a glance the travelers could see to the right the whole winding course of the Cise meandering like a silver snake among the meadows, where the grass had taken the deep, bright green of early spring. To the left lay the Loire in all its glory. A chill morning breeze, ruffling the surface of the stately river, had fretted the broad sheets of water far and wide into a network of ripples, which caught the gleams of the sun, so that the green islets here and there in its course shone like gems set in a gold necklace. On the opposite bank the fair rich meadows of Touraine stretched away as far as the eye could see; the low hills of the Cher, the only limits to the view, lay on the far horizon, a luminous line against the clear blue sky. Tours itself, framed by the trees on the islands in a setting of spring leaves, seemed to rise like Venice out of the waters, and her old cathedral towers soaring in air were blended with the pale fantastic cloud shapes in the sky.

Over the side of the bridge, where the carriage had come to a stand, the traveler looks along a line of cliffs stretching as far as Tours. Nature in some freakish mood must have raised these barriers of rock, undermined incessantly by the rippling Loire at their feet, for a perpetual wonder for spectators. The village of Vouvray nestles, as it were, among the clefts and crannies of the crags, which begin to describe a bend at the junction of the Loire and Cise. A whole population of vine-dressers lives, in fact, in appalling insecurity in holes in their jagged sides for the whole way between Vouvray and Tours. In some places there are three tiers of dwellings hollowed out, one above the other, in the rock, each row communicating with the next by dizzy staircases cut likewise in the face of the cliff. A little girl in a short red petticoat runs out into her garden on the roof of another dwelling; you can watch a wreath of hearth-smoke curling up among the shoots and trails of the vines. Men are at work in their almost perpendicular patches of ground, an old woman sits tranquilly spinning under a blossoming almond tree on a crumbling mass of rock, and smiles down on the dismay of the travelers far below her feet. The cracks in the ground trouble her as little as the precarious state of the old wall, a pendant mass of loose stones, only kept in position by the crooked stems of its ivy mantle. The sound of coopers' mallets rings through the skyey caves; for here, where Nature stints human industry of soil, the soil is everywhere tilled, and everywhere fertile.

No view along the whole course of the Loire can compare with the rich landscape of Touraine, here outspread beneath the traveler's eyes. The triple picture, thus barely sketched in outline, is one of those scenes which the imagination engraves for ever upon the memory; let a poet fall under its charm, and he shall be haunted by visions which shall reproduce its romantic loveliness out of the vague substance of dreams.

As the carriage stopped on the bridge over the Cise, white sails came out here and there from among the islands in the Loire to add new grace to the perfect view. The subtle scent of the willows by the water's edge was mingled with the damp odor of the breeze from the river. The monotonous chant of a goat-herd added a plaintive note to the sound of birds' songs in a chorus which never ends; the cries of the boatmen brought tidings of distant busy life. Here was Touraine in all its glory, and the very height of the splendor of spring. Here was the one peaceful district in France in those troublous days; for it was so unlikely that a foreign army should trouble its quiet that Touraine might be said to defy invasion.

As soon as the caleche stopped, a head covered with a foraging cap was put out of the window, and soon afterwards an impatient military man flung open the carriage door and sprang down into the road to pick a quarrel with the postilion, but the skill with which the Tourangeau was repairing the trace restored Colonel d'Aiglemont's equanimity. He went back to the carriage, stretched himself to relieve his benumbed muscles, yawned, looked about him, and finally laid a hand on the arm of a young woman warmly wrapped up in a furred pelisse.

"Come, Julie," he said hoarsely, "just wake up and take a look at this country. It is magnificent."

Julie put her head out of the window. She wore a traveling cap of sable fur. Nothing could be seen of her but her face, for the whole of her person was completely concealed by the folds of her fur pelisse. The young girl who tripped to the review at the Tuileries with light footsteps and joy and gladness in her heart was scarcely recognizable in Julie d'Aiglemont. Her face, delicate as ever, had lost the rose-color which once gave it so rich a glow. A few straggling locks of black hair, straightened out by the damp night air, enhanced its dead whiteness, and all its life and sparkle seemed to be torpid. Yet her eyes glittered with preternatural brightness in spite of the violet shadows under the lashes upon her wan cheeks.

She looked out with indifferent eyes over the fields towards the Cher, at the islands in the river, at the line of the crags of Vouvray stretching along the Loire towards Tours; then she sank back as soon as possible into her seat in the caleche. She did not care to give a glance to the enchanting valley of the Cise.

"Yes, it is wonderful," she said, and out in the open air her voice sounded weak and faint to the last degree. Evidently she had had her way with her father, to her misfortune.

"Would you not like to live here, Julie?"

"Yes; here or anywhere," she answered listlessly.

"Do you feel ill?" asked Colonel d'Aiglemont.

"No, not at all," she answered with momentary energy; and, smiling at her husband, she added, "I should like to go to sleep."

Suddenly there came a sound of a horse galloping towards them. Victor d'Aiglemont dropped his wife's hand and turned to watch the bend in the road. No sooner had he taken his eyes from Julie's pale face than all the assumed gaiety died out of it; it was as if a light had been extinguished. She felt no wish to look at the landscape, no curiosity to see the horseman who was galloping towards them at such a furious pace, and, ensconcing herself in her corner, stared out before her at the hindquarters of the post-horses, looking as blank as any Breton peasant listening to his recteur's sermon.

Suddenly a young man riding a valuable horse came out from behind the clump of poplars and flowering briar-rose.

"It is an Englishman," remarked the Colonel.

"Lord bless you, yes, General," said the post-boy; "he belongs to the race of fellows who have a mind to gobble up France, they say."

The stranger was one of the foreigners traveling in France at the time when Napoleon detained all British subjects within the limits of the Empire, by way of reprisals for the violation of the Treaty of Amiens, an outrage of international law perpetrated by the Court of St. James. These prisoners, compelled to submit to the Emperor's pleasure, were not all suffered to remain in the houses where they were arrested, nor yet in the places of residence which at first they were permitted to choose. Most of the English colony in

Touraine had been transplanted thither from different places where their presence was supposed to be inimical to the interests of the Continental Policy.

The young man, who was taking the tedium of the early morning hours on horseback, was one of these victims of bureaucratic tyranny. Two years previously, a sudden order from the Foreign Office had dragged him from Montpellier, whither he had gone on account of consumptive tendencies. He glanced at the Comte d'Aiglemont, saw that he was a military man, and deliberately looked away, turning his head somewhat abruptly towards the meadows by the Cise.

"The English are all as insolent as if the globe belonged to them," muttered the Colonel. "Luckily, Soult will give them a thrashing directly."

The prisoner gave a glance to the caleche as he rode by. Brief though that glance was, he had yet time to notice the sad expression which lent an indefinable charm to the Countess' pensive face. Many men are deeply moved by the mere semblance of suffering in a woman; they take the look of pain for a sign of constancy or of love. Julie herself was so much absorbed in the contemplation of the opposite cushion that she saw neither the horse nor the rider. The damaged trace meanwhile had been quickly and strongly repaired; the Count stepped into his place again; and the post-boy, doing his best to make up for lost time, drove the carriage rapidly along the embankment. On they drove under the overhanging cliffs, with their picturesque vine-dressers' huts and stores of wine maturing in their dark sides, till in the distance uprose the spire of the famous Abbey of Marmoutiers, the retreat of St. Martin.

"What can that diaphanous milord want with us?" exclaimed the Colonel, turning to assure himself that the horseman who had followed them from the bridge was the young Englishman.

After all, the stranger committed no breach of good manners by riding along on the footway, and Colonel d'Aiglemont was fain to lie back in his corner after sending a scowl in the Englishman's direction. But in spite of his hostile instincts, he could not help noticing the beauty of the animal and the graceful horsemanship of the rider. The young man's face was of that pale, fair-complexioned, insular type, which is almost girlish in the softness and delicacy of its color and texture. He was tall, thin, and fair-haired, dressed with the extreme and elaborate neatness characteristic of a man of fashion in prudish England. Any one might have thought that bashfulness rather than pleasure at the sight of the Countess had called up that flush into his face. Once only Julie raised her eyes and looked at the stranger, and then only because she was in a manner compelled to do so, for her husband called upon her to admire the action of the thoroughbred. It so happened that their glances clashed; and the shy Englishman, instead of riding abreast of the carriage, fell behind on this, and followed them at a distance of a few paces.

Yet the Countess had scarcely given him a glance; she saw none of the various perfections, human and equine, commended to her notice, and fell back again in the carriage, with a slight movement of the eyelids intended to express her acquiescence in her husband's views. The Colonel fell asleep again, and both husband and wife reached Tours without another word. Not one of those enchanting views of everchanging landscape through which they sped had drawn so much as a glance from Julie's eyes.

Mme. d'Aiglemont looked now and again at her sleeping husband. While she looked, a sudden jolt shook something down upon her knees. It was her father's portrait, a miniature which she wore suspended about her neck by a black cord. At the sight of it, the tears, till then kept back, overflowed her eyes, but no one, save perhaps the Englishman, saw them glitter there for a brief moment before they dried upon her pale cheeks.

Colonel d'Aiglemont was on his way to the South. Marshal Soult was repelling an English invasion of Bearn; and d'Aiglemont, the bearer of the Emperor's orders to the Marshal, seized the opportunity of taking his wife as far as Tours to leave her with an elderly relative of his own, far away from the dangers threatening Paris.

Very shortly the carriage rolled over the paved road of Tours, over the bridge, along the Grande-Rue, and stopped at last before the old mansion of the ci-devant Marquise de Listomere-Landon.

The Marquise de Listomere-Landon, with her white hair, pale face, and shrewd smile, was one of those fine old ladies who still seem to wear the paniers of the eighteenth century, and affects caps of an extinct mode. They are nearly always caressing in their manners, as if the heyday of love still lingered on for these septuagenarian portraits of the age of Louis Quinze, with the faint perfume of poudre a la marechale always clinging about them. Bigoted rather than pious, and less of bigots than they seem, women who can tell a story well and talk still better, their laughter comes more readily for an old memory than for a new jest—the present intrudes upon them.

When an old waiting-woman announced to the Marquise de Listomere-Landon (to give her the title which she was soon to resume) the arrival of a nephew whom she had not seen since the outbreak of the war with Spain, the old lady took off her spectacles with alacrity, shut the Galerie de l'ancienne Cour (her favorite work), and recovered something like youthful activity, hastening out upon the flight of steps to greet the young couple there.

Aunt and niece exchanged a rapid glance of survey.

"Good-morning, dear aunt," cried the Colonel, giving the old lady a hasty embrace. "I am bringing a young lady to put under your wing. I have come to put my treasure in your keeping. My Julie is neither jealous nor a coquette, she is as good as an angel. I hope that she will not be spoiled here," he added, suddenly interrupting himself.

"Scapegrace!" returned the Marquise, with a satirical glance at her nephew.

She did not wait for her niece to approach her, but with a certain kindly graciousness went forward herself to kiss Julie, who stood there thoughtfully, to all appearance more embarrassed than curious concerning her new relation.

"So we are to make each other's acquaintance, are we, my love?" the Marquise continued. "Do not be too much alarmed of me. I always try not to be an old woman with young people."

On the way to the drawing-room, the Marquise ordered breakfast for her guests in provincial fashion; but the Count checked his aunt's flow of words by saying soberly that he could only remain in the house while the horses were changing. On this the three hurried into the drawing-room. The Colonel had barely time to tell the story of the political and military events which had compelled him to ask his aunt for a shelter for his young wife. While he talked on without interruption, the older lady looked from her nephew to her niece, and took the sadness in Julie's white face for grief at the enforced separation. "Eh! eh!" her looks seemed to say, "these young things are in love with each other."

The crack of the postilion's whip sounded outside in the silent old grass-grown courtyard. Victor embraced his aunt once more, and rushed out.

"Good-bye, dear," he said, kissing his wife, who had followed him down to the carriage.

"Oh! Victor, let me come still further with you," she pleaded coaxingly. "I do not want to leave you——"

"Can you seriously mean it?"

"Very well," said Julie, "since you wish it." The carriage disappeared.

"So you are very fond of my poor Victor?" said the Marquise, interrogating her niece with one of those sagacious glances which dowagers give younger women.

"Alas, madame!" said Julie, "must one not love a man well indeed to marry him?"

The words were spoken with an artless accent which revealed either a pure heart or inscrutable depths. How could a woman, who had been the friend of Duclos and the Marechal de Richelieu, refrain from trying to read the riddle of this marriage? Aunt and niece were standing on the steps, gazing after the fast vanishing caleche. The look in the young Countess' eyes did not mean love as the Marquise understood it. The good lady was a Provencale, and her passions had been lively.

"So you were captivated by my good-for-nothing of a nephew?" she asked.

Involuntarily Julie shuddered, something in the experienced coquette's look and tone seemed to say that Mme. de Listomere-Landon's knowledge of her husband's character went perhaps deeper than his wife's. Mme. d'Aiglemont, in dismay, took refuge in this transparent dissimulation, ready to her hand, the first resource of an artless unhappiness. Mme. de Listomere appeared to be satisfied with Julie's answers; but in her secret heart she rejoiced to think that here was a love affair on hand to enliven her solitude, for that her niece had some amusing flirtation on foot she was fully convinced.

In the great drawing-room, hung with tapestry framed in strips of gilding, young Mme. d'Aiglemont sat before a blazing fire, behind a Chinese screen placed to shut out the cold draughts from the window, and her heavy mood scarcely lightened. Among the old eighteenth-century furniture, under the old paneled ceiling, it was not very easy to be gay. Yet the young Parisienne took a sort of pleasure in this entrance upon a life of complete solitude and in the solemn silence of the old provincial house. She exchanged a few words with the aunt, a stranger, to whom she had written a bride's letter on her marriage, and then sat as silent as if she had been listening to an opera. Not until two hours had been spent in an atmosphere of quiet befitting la Trappe, did she suddenly awaken to a sense of uncourteous behavior, and bethink herself of the short answers which she had given her aunt. Mme. de Listomere, with the gracious tact characteristic of a bygone age, had respected her niece's mood. When Mme. d'Aiglemont became conscious of her shortcomings, the dowager sat knitting, though as a matter of fact she had several times left the room to superintend preparations in the Green Chamber, whither the Countess' luggage had been transported; now, however, she had returned to her great armchair, and stole a glance from time to time at this young relative. Julie felt ashamed of giving way to irresistible broodings, and tried to earn her pardon by laughing at herself.

"My dear child, we know the sorrows of widowhood," returned her aunt. But only the eyes of forty years could have distinguished the irony hovering about the old lady's mouth.

Next morning the Countess improved. She talked. Mme. de Listomere no longer despaired of fathoming the new-made wife, whom yesterday she had set down as a dull, unsociable creature, and discoursed on the delights of the country, of dances, of houses where they could visit. All that day the Marquise's questions were so many snares; it was the old habit of the old Court, she could not help setting traps to discover her niece's character. For several days Julie, plied with temptations, steadfastly declined to seek amusement abroad; and much as the old lady's pride longed to exhibit her pretty niece, she was fain to renounce all hope of taking her into society, for the young Countess was still in morning for her father, and found in her loss and her mourning dress a pretext for her sadness and desire for seclusion.

By the end of the week the dowager admired Julie's angelic sweetness of disposition, her diffident charm, her indulgent temper, and thenceforward began to take a prodigious interest in the mysterious sadness gnawing at this young heart. The Countess was one of those women who seem born to be loved and to bring happiness with them. Mme. de Listomere found her niece's society grown so sweet and precious, that she doted upon Julie, and could no longer think of parting with her. A month sufficed to establish an eternal friendship between the two ladies. The dowager noticed, not without surprise, the changes that took place in Mme. d'Aiglemont; gradually her bright color died away, and her face became dead white. Yet, Julie's spirits rose as the bloom faded from her cheeks. Sometimes the dowager's sallies provoked outbursts of merriment or peals of laughter, promptly repressed, however, by some clamorous thought.

Mme. de Listomere had guessed by this time that it was neither Victor's absence nor a father's death which threw a shadow over her niece's life; but her mind was so full of dark suspicions, that she found it difficult to lay a finger upon the real cause of the mischief. Possibly truth is only discoverable by chance. A day came, however, at length when Julie flashed out before her aunt's astonished eyes into a complete forgetfulness of her marriage; she recovered the wild spirits of careless girlhood. Mme. de Listomere then and there made up her mind to fathom the depths of this soul, for its exceeding simplicity was as inscrutable as dissimulation.

Night was falling. The two ladies were sitting by the window which looked out upon the street, and Julie was looking thoughtful again, when some one went by on horseback.

"There goes one of your victims," said the Marquise.

Mme. d'Aiglemont looked up; dismay and surprise blended in her face.

"He is a young Englishman, the Honorable Arthur Ormand, Lord Grenville's eldest son. His history is interesting. His physician sent him to Montpellier in 1802; it was hoped that in that climate he might recover from the lung complaint which was gaining ground. He was detained, like all his fellow-countrymen, by Bonaparte when war broke out. That monster cannot live without fighting. The young Englishman, by way of amusing himself, took to studying his own complaint, which was believed to be incurable. By degrees he acquired a liking for anatomy and physic, and took quite a craze for that kind of thing, a most extraordinary taste in a man of quality, though the Regent certainly amused himself with chemistry! In short, Monsieur Arthur made astonishing progress in his studies; his health did the same under the faculty of Montpellier; he consoled his captivity, and at the same time his cure was thoroughly completed. They say that he spent two whole years in a cowshed, living on cresses and the milk of a cow brought from Switzerland, breathing as seldom as he could, and never speaking a word. Since he come to Tours he has lived quite alone; he is as proud as a peacock; but you have certainly made a conquest of him, for probably it is not on my account that he has ridden under the window twice every day since you have been here.—He has certainly fallen in love with you."

That last phrase roused the Countess like magic. Her involuntary start and smile took the Marquise by surprise. So far from showing a sign of the instinctive satisfaction felt by the most strait-laced of women when she learns that she has destroyed the peace of mind of some male victim, there was a hard, haggard expression in Julie's face—a look of repulsion amounting almost to loathing.

A woman who loves will put the whole world under the ban of Love's empire for the sake of the one whom she loves; but such a woman can laugh and jest; and Julie at that moment looked as if the memory of some recently escaped peril was too sharp and fresh not to bring with it a quick sensation of pain. Her aunt, by this time convinced that Julie did not love her nephew, was stupefied by the discovery that she loved nobody else. She shuddered lest a further discovery should show her Julie's heart disenchanted, lest the experience of a day, or perhaps of a night, should have revealed to a young wife the full extent of Victor's emptiness.

"If she has found him out, there is an end of it," thought the dowager. "My nephew will soon be made to feel the inconveniences of wedded life."

The Marquise now proposed to convert Julie to the monarchical doctrines of the times of Louis Quinze; but a few hours later she discovered, or, more properly speaking, guessed, the not uncommon state of affairs, and the real cause of her niece's low spirits.

Julie turned thoughtful on a sudden, and went to her room earlier than usual. When her maid left her for the night, she still sat by the fire in the yellow velvet depths of a great chair, an old-world piece of furniture as well suited for sorrow as for happy people. Tears flowed, followed by sighs and meditation. After a while she drew a little table to her, sought writing materials, and began to write. The hours went by swiftly. Julie's confidences made to the sheet of paper seemed to cost her dear; every sentence set her dreaming, and at last she suddenly burst into tears. The clocks were striking two. Her head, grown heavy as a dying woman's, was bowed over her breast. When she raised it, her aunt appeared before her as suddenly as if she had stepped out of the background of tapestry upon the walls.

"What can be the matter with you, child?" asked the Marquise. "Why are you sitting up so late? And why, in the first place, are you crying alone, at your age?"

Without further ceremony she sat down beside her niece, her eyes the while devouring the unfinished letter.

"Were you writing to your husband?"

"Do I know where he is?" returned the Countess.

Her aunt thereupon took up the sheet and proceeded to read it. She had brought her spectacles; the deed was premeditated. The innocent writer of the letter allowed her to take it without the slightest remark. It was neither lack of dignity nor consciousness of secret guilt which left her thus without energy. Her aunt had come in upon her at a crisis. She was helpless; right or wrong, reticence and confidence, like all things else, were matters of indifference. Like some young maid who had heaped scorn upon her lover, and feels so lonely and sad when evening comes, that she longs for him to come back or for a heart to which she can pour out her sorrow, Julie allowed her aunt to violate the seal which honor places upon an open letter, and sat musing while the Marquise read on:—

"MY DEAR LOUISA,—Why do you ask so often for the fulfilment of as rash a promise as two young and inexperienced girls could make? You say that you often ask yourself why I have

given no answer to your questions for these six months. If my silence told you nothing, perhaps you will understand the reasons for it to-day, as you read the secrets which I am about to betray. I should have buried them for ever in the depths of my heart if you had not announced your own approaching marriage. You are about to be married, Louisa. The thought makes me shiver. Poor little one! marry, yes, in a few months' time one of the keenest pangs of regret will be the recollection of a self which used to be, of the two young girls who sat one evening under one of the tallest oak-trees on the hillside at Ecouen, and looked along the fair valley at our feet in the light of the sunset, which caught us in its glow. We sat on a slab of rock in ecstasy, which sobered down into melancholy of the gentlest. You were the first to discover that the far-off sun spoke to us of the future. How inquisitive and how silly we were! Do you remember all the absurd things we said and did? We embraced each other; 'like lovers,' said we. We solemnly promised that the first bride should faithfully reveal to the other the mysteries of marriage, the joys which our childish minds imagined to be so delicious. That evening will complete your despair, Louisa. In those days you were young and beautiful and careless, if not radiantly happy; a few days of marriage, and you will be, what I am already—ugly, wretched, and old. Need I tell you how proud I was and how vain and glad to be married to Colonel Victor d'Aiglemont? And besides, how could I tell you now? for I cannot remember that old self. A few moments turned my girlhood to a dream. All through the memorable day which consecrated a chain, the extent of which was hidden from me, my behavior was not free from reproach. Once and again my father tried to repress my spirits; the joy which I showed so plainly was thought unbefitting the occasion, my talk scarcely innocent, simply because I was so innocent. I played endless child's tricks with my bridal veil, my wreath, my gown. Left alone that night in the room whither I had been conducted in state, I planned a piece of mischief to tease Victor. While I awaited his coming, my heart beat wildly, as it used to do when I was a child stealing into the drawing-room on the last day of the old year to catch a glimpse of the New Year's gifts piled up there in heaps. When my husband came in and looked for me, my smothered laughter ringing out from beneath the lace in which I had shrouded myself, was the last outburst of the delicious merriment which brightened our games in childhood..."

When the dowager had finished reading the letter, and after such a beginning the rest must have been sad indeed, she slowly laid her spectacles on the table, put the letter down beside them, and looked fixedly at her niece. Age had not dimmed the fire in those green eyes as yet.

"My little girl," she said, "a married woman cannot write such a letter as this to a young unmarried woman; it is scarcely proper—"

"So I was thinking," Julie broke in upon her aunt. "I felt ashamed of myself while you were reading it."

"If a dish at table is not to our taste, there is no occasion to disgust others with it, child," the old lady continued benignly, "especially when marriage has seemed to us all, from Eve downwards, so excellent an institution... You have no mother?"

The Countess trembled, then she raised her face meekly, and said:

"I have missed my mother many times already during the past year; but I have myself to blame, I would not listen to my father. He was opposed to my marriage; he disapproved of Victor as a son-in-law."

She looked at her aunt. The old face was lighted up with a kindly look, and a thrill of joy dried Julie's tears. She held out her young, soft hand to the old Marquise, who seemed to ask for it, and the understanding between the two women was completed by the close grasp of their fingers.

"Poor orphan child!"

The words came like a final flash of enlightenment to Julie. It seemed to her that she heard her father's prophetic voice again.

"Your hands are burning! Are they always like this?" asked the Marquise.

"The fever only left me seven or eight days ago."

"You had a fever upon you, and said nothing about it to me!"

"I have had it for a year," said Julie, with a kind of timid anxiety.

"My good little angel, then your married life hitherto has been one long time of suffering?"

Julie did not venture to reply, but an affirmative sign revealed the whole truth.

"Then you are unhappy?"

"On! no, no, aunt. Victor loves me, he almost idolizes me, and I adore him, he is so kind."

"Yes, you love him; but you avoid him, do you not?"

"Yes... sometimes... He seeks me too often."

"And often when you are alone you are troubled with the fear that he may suddenly break in on your solitude?"

"Alas! yes, aunt. But, indeed, I love him, I do assure you."

"Do you not, in your own thoughts, blame yourself because you find it impossible to share his pleasures? Do you never think at times that marriage is a heavier yoke than an illicit passion could be?"

"Oh, that is just it," she wept. "It is all a riddle to me, and can you guess it all? My faculties are benumbed, I have no ideas, I can scarcely see at all. I am weighed down by vague dread, which freezes me till I cannot feel, and keeps me in continual torpor. I have no voice with which to pity myself, no words to express my trouble. I suffer, and I am ashamed to suffer when Victor is happy at my cost."

"Babyish nonsense, and rubbish, all of it!" exclaimed the aunt, and a gay smile, an after-glow of the joys of her own youth, suddenly lighted up her withered face.

"And do you too laugh!" the younger woman cried despairingly.

"It was just my own case," the Marquise returned promptly. "And now Victor has left you, you have become a girl again, recovering a tranquillity without pleasure and without pain, have you not?"

Julie opened wide eyes of bewilderment.

"In fact, my angel, you adore Victor, do you not? But still you would rather be a sister to him than a wife, and, in short, your marriage is emphatically not a success?"

"Well—no, aunt. But why do you smile?"

"Oh! you are right, poor child! There is nothing very amusing in all this. Your future would be big with more than one mishap if I had not taken you under my protection, if my old experience of life had not guessed the very innocent cause of your troubles. My nephew did not deserve his good fortune, the blockhead! In the reign of our well-beloved Louis Quinze, a young wife in your position would very soon have punished her husband for behaving like a ruffian. The selfish creature! The men who serve under this Imperial tyrant are all of them ignorant boors. They take brutality for gallantry; they know no more of women than they know of love; and imagine that because they go out to face death on the morrow, they may dispense to-day with all consideration and attentions for us. The time was when a man could love and die too at the proper time. My niece, I will form you. I will put an end to this unhappy divergence between you, a natural thing enough, but it would end in mutual hatred and desire for a divorce, always supposing that you did not die on the way to despair."

Julie's amazement equaled her surprise as she listened to her aunt. She was surprised by her language, dimly divining rather than appreciating the wisdom of the words she heard, and very much dismayed to find what this relative, out of great experience, passed judgment upon Victor as her father had done, though in somewhat milder terms. Perhaps some quick prevision of the future crossed her mind; doubtless, at any rate, she felt the heavy weight of the burden which must inevitably overwhelm her, for she burst into tears, and sprang to the old lady's arms. "Be my mother," she sobbed.

The aunt shed no tears. The Revolution had left old ladies of the Monarchy but few tears to shed. Love, in bygone days, and the Terror at a later time, had familiarized them with extremes of joy and anguish in such a sort that, amid the perils of life, they preserved their dignity and coolness, a capacity for sincere but undemonstrative affection which never disturbed their well-bred self-possession, and a dignity of demeanor which a younger generation has done very ill to discard.

The dowager took Julie in her arms, and kissed her on the forehead with a tenderness and pity more often found in women's ways and manner than in their hearts. Then she coaxed her niece with kind, soothing words, assured her of a happy future, lulled her with promises of love, and put her to bed as if she had been not a niece, but a daughter, a much-beloved daughter whose hopes and cares she had made her own. Perhaps the old Marquise had found her own youth and inexperience and beauty again in this nephew's wife. And the Countess fell asleep, happy to have found a friend, nay a mother, to whom she could tell everything freely.

Next morning, when the two women kissed each other with heartfelt kindness, and that look of intelligence which marks a real advance in friendship, a closer intimacy between two souls, they heard the sound of horsehoofs, and, turning both together, saw the young Englishman ride slowly past the window, after his wont. Apparently he had made a certain study of the life led by the two lonely women, for he never failed to ride by as they sat at breakfast, and again at dinner. His horse slackened pace of its own accord, and for the space of time required to pass the two windows in the room, its rider turned a melancholy look upon the Countess, who seldom deigned to take the slightest notion of him. Not so the Marquise. Minds not necessarily little find it difficult to resist the little curiosity which fastens upon the most trifling event that enlivens provincial life; and the Englishman's mute way of expressing his timid, earnest love tickled Mme. de Listomere. For her the periodically recurrent glance became a part of the day's routine, hailed daily with new jests. As the two women sat down to table, both of them looked out at the same moment. This time Julie's eyes met Arthur's with such a precision of sympathy that the color rose to her face. The stranger immediately urged his horse into a gallop and went.

"What is to be done, madame?" asked Julie. "People see this Englishman go past the house, and they will take it for granted that I—"

"Yes," interrupted her aunt.

"Well, then, could I not tell him to discontinue his promenades?"

"Would not that be a way of telling him that he was dangerous? You might put that notion into his head. And besides, can you prevent a man from coming and going as he pleases? Our meals shall be served in another room to-morrow; and when this young gentleman sees us no longer, there will be an end of making love to you through the window. There, dear child, that is how a woman of the world does."

But the measure of Julie's misfortune was to be filled up. The two women had scarcely risen from table when Victor's man arrived in hot haste from Bourges with a letter for the Countess from her husband. The servant had ridden by unfrequented ways.

Victor sent his wife news of the downfall of the Empire and the capitulation of Paris. He himself had gone over to the Bourbons, and all France was welcoming them back with transports of enthusiasm. He could not go so far as Tours, but he begged her to come at once to join him at Orleans, where he hoped to be in readiness with passports for her. His servant, an old soldier, would be her escort so far as Orleans; he (Victor) believed that the road was still open.

"You have not a moment to lose, madame," said the man. "The Prussians, Austrians, and English are about to effect a junction either at Blois or at Orleans."

A few hours later, Julie's preparations were made, and she started out upon her journey in an old traveling carriage lent by her aunt.

"Why should you not come with us to Paris?" she asked, as she put her arms about the Marquise. "Now that the Bourbons have come back you would be—"

"Even if there had not been this unhoped-for return, I should still have gone to Paris, my poor child, for my advice is only too necessary to both you and Victor. So I shall make all my preparations for rejoining you there."

Julie set out. She took her maid with her, and the old soldier galloped beside the carriage as escort. At nightfall, as they changed horses for the last stage before Blois, Julie grew uneasy. All the way from Amboise she had heard the sound of wheels behind them, a carriage following hers had kept at the same distance. She stood on the step and looked out to see who her traveling companions might be, and in the moonlight saw Arthur standing three paces away, gazing fixedly at the chaise which contained her. Again their eyes met. The Countess hastily flung herself back in her seat, but a feeling of dread set her pulses throbbing. It seemed to her, as to most innocent and inexperienced young wives, that she was herself to blame for this love which she had all unwittingly inspired. With this thought came an instinctive terror, perhaps a sense of her own helplessness before aggressive audacity. One of a man's strongest weapons is the terrible power of compelling a woman to think of him when her naturally lively imagination takes alarm or offence at the thought that she is followed.

The Countess bethought herself of her aunt's advice, and made up her mind that she would not stir from her place during the rest of the journey; but every time the horses were changed she heard the Englishman pacing round the two carriages, and again upon the road heard the importunate sound of the wheels of his caleche. Julie soon began to think that, when once reunited to her husband, Victor would know how to defend her against this singular persecution.

"Yet suppose that in spite of everything, this young man does not love me?" This was the thought that came last of all.

No sooner did she reach Orleans than the Prussians stopped the chaise. It was wheeled into an inn-yard and put under a guard of soldiers. Resistance was out of the question. The foreign soldiers made the three travelers understand by signs that they were obeying orders, and that no one could be allowed to leave the carriage. For about two hours the Countess sat in tears, a prisoner surrounded by the guard, who smoked, laughed, and occasionally stared at her with insolent curiosity. At last, however, she saw her captors fall away from the carriage with a sort of respect, and heard at the same time the sound of horses entering the yard. Another moment, and a little group of foreign officers, with an Austrian general at their head, gathered about the door of the traveling carriage.

"Madame," said the General, "pray accept our apologies. A mistake has been made. You may continue your journey without fear; and here is a passport which will spare you all further annoyance of any kind."

Trembling the Countess took the paper, and faltered out some vague words of thanks. She saw Arthur, now wearing an English uniform, standing beside the General, and could not doubt that this prompt deliverance was due to him. The young Englishman himself looked half glad, half melancholy; his face was turned away, and he only dared to steal an occasional glance at Julie's face.

Thanks to the passport, Mme. d'Aiglemont reached Paris without further misadventure, and there she found her husband. Victor d'Aiglemont, released from his oath of allegiance to the Emperor, had met with a most flattering reception from the Comte d'Artois, recently appointed Lieutenant-General of the kingdom by his brother Louis XVIII. D'Aiglemont received a commission in the Life Guards, equivalent to the rank of general. But amid the rejoicings over the return of the Bourbons, fate dealt poor Julie a terrible blow. The death of the Marquise de Listomere-Landon was an irreparable loss. The old lady died of joy and of an accession of gout to the heart when the Duc d'Angouleme came back to Tours, and the one living being entitled by her age to enlighten Victor, the woman who, by discreet counsels, might have brought about perfect unanimity of husband and wife, was dead; and Julie felt the full extent of her loss. Henceforward she must stand alone between herself and her husband. But she was young and timid; there could be no doubt of the result, or that from the first she would elect to bear her lot in silence. The very perfections of her character forbade her to venture to swerve from her duties, or to attempt to inquire into the cause of her sufferings, for to put an end to them would have been to venture on delicate ground, and Julie's girlish modesty shrank from the thought.

A word as to M. d'Aiglemont's destinies under the Restoration.

How many men are there whose utter incapacity is a secret kept from most of their acquaintance. For such as these high rank, high office, illustrious birth, a certain veneer of politeness, and considerable reserve of manner, or the prestige of great fortunes, are but so many sentinels to turn back critics who would penetrate to the presence of the real man. Such men are like kings, in that their real figure, character, and life can never be known nor justly appreciated, because they are always seen from too near or too far. Factitious merit has a way of asking questions and saying little; and understands the art of putting others forward to save the necessity of posing before them; then, with a happy knack of its own, it draws and attaches others by the thread of the ruling passion of self-interest, keeping men of far greater abilities to play like puppets, and despising those whom it has brought down to its own level. The petty fixed idea naturally prevails; it has the advantage of persistence over the plasticity of great thoughts.

The observer who should seek to estimate and appraise the negative values of these empty heads needs subtlety rather than superior wit for the task; patience is a more necessary part of his judicial outfit than great mental grasp, cunning and tact rather than any elevation or greatness of ideas. Yet skilfully as such usurpers can cover and defend their weak points, it is difficult to delude wife and mother and children and the house-friend of the family; fortunately for them, however, these persons almost always keep a secret which in a manner touches the honor of all, and not unfrequently go so far as to help to foist the imposture upon the public. And if, thanks to such domestic conspiracy, many a noodle passes current for a man of ability, on the other hand many another who has real ability is taken for a noodle to redress the balance, and the total average of this kind of false coin in circulation in the state is a pretty constant quantity.

Bethink yourself now of the part to be played by a clever woman quick to think and feel, mated with a husband of this kind, and can you not see a vision of lives full of sorrow and self-sacrifice? Nothing upon earth can repay such hearts so full of love and tender tact. Put a strong-willed woman in this wretched situation, and she will force a way out of it for herself by a crime, like Catherine II., whom men nevertheless style "the Great." But these women are not all seated upon thrones, they are for the most part doomed to domestic unhappiness none the less terrible because obscure.

Those who seek consolation in this present world for their woes often effect nothing but a change of ills if they remain faithful to their duties; or they commit a sin if they break the laws for their pleasure. All these reflections are applicable to Julie's domestic life.

Before the fall of Napoleon nobody was jealous of d'Aiglemont. He was one colonel among many, an efficient orderly staff-officer, as good a man as you could find for a dangerous mission, as unfit as well could be for an important command. D'Aiglemont was looked upon as a dashing soldier such as the Emperor liked, the kind of man whom his mess usually calls "a good fellow." The Restoration gave him back his title of Marquis, and did not find him ungrateful; he followed the Bourbons into exile at Ghent, a piece of logical loyalty which falsified the horoscope drawn for him by his late father-in-law, who predicted that Victor would remain a colonel all his life. After the Hundred Days he received the appointment of Lieutenant-General, and for the second time became a marquis; but it was M. d'Aiglemont's ambition to be a peer of France. He adopted, therefore, the maxims and the politics of the Conservateur, cloaked himself in dissimulation which hid nothing (there being nothing to hide), cultivated gravity of countenance and the art of asking questions and saying little, and was taken for a man of profound wisdom. Nothing drew him from his intrenchments behind the forms of politeness; he laid in a provision of formulas, and made lavish use of his stock of the catch-words coined at need in Paris to give fools the small change for the ore of great ideas and events. Among men of the world he was reputed a man of taste and discernment; and as a bigoted upholder of aristocratic opinions he was held up for a noble character. If by chance he slipped now and again into his old light-heartedness or levity, others were ready to discover an undercurrent of diplomatic intention beneath his inanity and silliness. "Oh! he only says exactly as much as he means to say," thought these excellent people.

So d'Aiglemont's defects and good qualities stood him alike in good stead. He did nothing to forfeit a high military reputation gained by his dashing courage, for he had never been a commander-in-chief. Great thoughts surely were engraven upon that manly aristocratic countenance, which imposed upon every one but his own wife. And when everybody else believed in the Marquis d'Aiglemont's imaginary talents, the Marquis persuaded himself before he had done that he was one of the most remarkable men at Court, where, thanks to his purely external qualifications, he was in favor and taken at his own valuation.

At home, however, M. d'Aiglemont was modest. Instinctively he felt that his wife, young though she was, was his superior; and out of this involuntary respect there grew an occult power which the Marquise was obliged to wield in spite of all her efforts to shake off the burden. She became her husband's adviser, the director of his actions and his fortunes. It was an unnatural position; she felt it as something of a humiliation, a source of pain to be buried in the depths of her heart. From the first her delicately feminine instinct told her that it is a far better thing to obey a man of talent than to lead a fool; and that a young wife compelled to act and think like a man is neither man nor woman, but a being who lays aside all the charms of her womanhood along with its misfortunes, yet acquires none of the privileges which our laws give to the stronger sex. Beneath the surface her life was a bitter mockery. Was she not compelled to protect her protector, to worship a hollow idol, a poor creature who flung her the love of a selfish husband as the wages of her continual self-sacrifice; who saw nothing in her but the woman; and who either did not think it worth while, or (wrong quite as deep) did not think at all of troubling himself about her pleasures, of inquiring into the cause of her low spirits and dwindling health? And the Marquis, like most men who chafe under a wife's superiority, saved his self-love by arguing from Julie's physical feebleness a corresponding lack of mental power, for which he was pleased to pity her; and he would cry out upon fate which had given him a sickly girl for a wife. The executioner posed, in fact, as the victim.

All the burdens of this dreary lot fell upon the Marquise, who still must smile upon her foolish lord, and deck a house of mourning with flowers, and make a parade of happiness in a countenance wan with secret torture. And with this sense of responsibility for the honor of both, with the magnificent immolation of self, the young Marquise unconsciously acquired a wifely dignity, a consciousness of virtue which became her safeguard amid many dangers.

Perhaps, if her heart were sounded to the very depths, this intimate closely hidden wretchedness, following upon her unthinking, girlish first love, had roused in her an abhorrence of passion; possibly she had no conception of its rapture, nor of the forbidden but frenzied bliss for which some women will renounce all the laws of prudence and the principles of conduct upon which society is based. She put from her like a dream the thought of bliss and tender harmony of love promised by Mme. de Listomere-Landon's mature experience, and waited resignedly for the end of her troubles with a hope that she might die young.

Her health had declined daily since her return from Touraine; her life seemed to be measured to her in suffering; yet her ill-health was graceful, her malady seemed little more than languor, and might well be taken by careless eyes for a fine lady's whim of invalidism.

Her doctors had condemned her to keep to the sofa, and there among her flowers lay the Marquise, fading as they faded. She was not strong enough to walk, nor to bear the open air, and only went out in a closed carriage. Yet with all the marvels of modern luxury and invention about her, she looked more like an indolent queen than an invalid. A few of her friends, half in love perhaps with her sad plight and her fragile look, sure of finding her at home, and speculating no doubt upon her future restoration to health, would come to bring her the news of the day, and kept her informed of the thousand and one small events which fill life in Paris with variety. Her melancholy, deep and real though it was was still the melancholy of a woman rich in many ways. The Marquise d'Aiglemont was like a flower, with a dark insect gnawing at its root.

Occasionally she went into society, not to please herself, but in obedience to the exigencies of the position which her husband aspired to take. In society her beautiful voice and the perfection of her singing could always gain the social success so gratifying to a young woman; but what was social success to her, who drew nothing from it for her heart or her hopes? Her husband did not care for music. And, moreover, she seldom felt at her ease in salons, where her beauty attracted homage not wholly disinterested. Her position excited a sort of cruel compassion, a morbid curiosity. She was suffering from an inflammatory complaint not infrequently fatal, for which our nosology as yet has found no name, a complaint spoken of among women in confidential whispers. In spite of the silence in which her life was spent, the cause of her ill-health was no secret. She was still but a girl in spite of her marriage; the slightest glance threw her into confusion. In her endeavor not to blush, she was always laughing, always apparently in high spirits; she would never admit that she was not perfectly well, and anticipated questions as to her health by shame-stricken subterfuges.

In 1817, however, an event took place which did much to alleviate Julie's hitherto deplorable existence. A daughter was born to her, and she determined to nurse her child herself. For two years motherhood, its all-absorbing multiplicity of cares and anxious joys, made life less hard for her. She and her husband lived necessarily apart. Her physicians predicted improved health, but the Marquise herself put no faith in these auguries based on theory. Perhaps, like many a one for whom life has lost its sweetness, she looked forward to death as a happy termination of the drama.

But with the beginning of the year 1819 life grew harder than ever. Even while she congratulated herself upon the negative happiness which she had contrived to win, she caught a terrifying glimpse of yawning depths below it. She had passed by degrees out of her husband's life. Her fine tact and her prudence told her that misfortune must come, and that not singly, of this cooling of an affection already lukewarm and wholly selfish. Sure though she was of her ascendency over Victor, and certain as she felt of his unalterable esteem, she dreaded the influence of unbridled passions upon a head so empty, so full of rash self-conceit.

Julie's friends often found her absorbed in prolonged musings; the less clairvoyant among them would jestingly ask her what she was thinking about, as if a young wife would think of nothing but frivolity, as if there were not almost always a depth of seriousness in a mother's thoughts. Unhappiness, like great happiness, induces dreaming. Sometimes as Julie played with her little Helene, she would gaze darkly at her, giving no reply to the childish questions in which a mother delights, questioning the present and the future as to the destiny of this little one. Then some sudden recollection would bring back the scene of the review at the Tuileries and fill her eyes with tears. Her father's prophetic warnings rang in her ears, and conscience reproached her that she had not recognized its wisdom. Her troubles had all come of her own wayward folly, and often she knew not which among so many were the hardest to bear. The sweet treasures of her soul were unheeded, and not only so, she could never succeed in making her husband understand her, even in the commonest everyday things. Just as the power to love developed and grew strong and active, a legitimate channel for the affections of her nature was denied her, and wedded love was extinguished in grave physical and mental sufferings. Add to this that she now felt for her husband that pity closely bordering upon contempt, which withers all affection at last. Even if she had not learned from conversations with some of her friends, from examples in life, from sundry occurrences in the great world, that love can bring ineffable bliss, her own wounds would have taught her to divine the pure and deep happiness which binds two kindred souls each to each.

In the picture which her memory traced of the past, Arthur's frank face stood out daily nobler and purer; it was but a flash, for upon that recollection she dared not dwell. The young Englishman's shy, silent love for her was the one event since her marriage which had left a lingering sweetness in her darkened and lonely heart. It may be that all the blighted hopes, all the frustrated longings which gradually clouded Julie's mind, gathered, by a not unnatural trick of imagination, about this man—whose manners, sentiments, and character seemed to have so much in common with her own. This idea still presented itself to her mind fitfully and vaguely, like a dream; yet from that dream, which always ended in a sigh, Julie awoke to greater wretchedness, to keener consciousness of the latent anguish brooding beneath her imaginary bliss.

Occasionally her self-pity took wilder and more daring flights. She determined to have happiness at any cost; but still more often she lay a helpless victim of an indescribable numbing stupor, the words she heard had no meaning to her, or the thoughts which arose in her mind were so vague and indistinct that she could not find language to express them. Balked of the wishes of her heart, realities jarred harshly upon her girlish dreams of life, but she was obliged to devour her tears. To whom could she make complaint? Of whom be understood? She possessed, moreover, that highest degree of woman's sensitive pride, the exquisite delicacy of feeling which silences useless complainings and declines to use an advantage to gain a triumph which can only humiliate both victor and vanquished.

Julie tried to endow M. d'Aiglemont with her own abilities and virtues, flattering herself that thus she might enjoy the happiness lacking in her lot. All her woman's ingenuity and tact was employed in making the best of the situation; pure waste of pains unsuspected by him, whom she thus strengthened in his despotism. There were moments when misery became an intoxication, expelling all ideas, all self-control; but, fortunately, sincere piety always brought her back to one supreme hope; she found a refuge in the belief in a future life, a wonderful thought which enabled her to take up her painful task afresh. No elation of victory followed those terrible inward battles and throes of anguish; no one knew of those long hours of sadness; her haggard glances met no response from human eyes, and during the brief moments snatched by chance for weeping, her bitter tears fell unheeded and in solitude.

One evening in January 1820, the Marquise became aware of the full gravity of the crisis, gradually brought on by force of circumstances. When a husband and wife know each other thoroughly, and their relation has long been a matter of use and wont, when the wife has learned to interpret every slightest sign, when her quick insight discerns thoughts and facts which her husband keeps from her, a chance word, or a remark so carelessly let fall in the first instance, seems, upon subsequent reflection, like the swift breaking out of light. A wife not seldom suddenly awakes upon the brink of a precipice or in the depths of the abyss; and thus it was with the Marquise. She was feeling glad to have been left to herself for some days, when the real reason of her solitude flashed upon her. Her husband, whether fickle and tired of her, or generous and full of pity for her, was hers no longer.

In the moment of that discovery she forgot herself, her sacrifices, all that she had passed through, she remembered only that she was a mother. Looking forward, she thought of her daughter's fortune, of the future welfare of the one creature through whom some gleams of happiness came to her, of her Helene, the only possession which bound her to life.

Then Julie wished to live to save her child from a stepmother's terrible thraldom, which might crush her darling's life. Upon this new vision of threatened possibilities followed one of those paroxysms of thought at fever-heat which consume whole years of life.

Henceforward husband and wife were doomed to be separated by a whole world of thought, and all the weight of that world she must bear alone. Hitherto she had felt sure that Victor loved her, in so far as he could be said to love; she had been the slave of pleasures which she did not share; to-day the satisfaction of knowing that she purchased his contentment with her tears was hers no longer. She was alone in the world, nothing was left to her now but a choice of evils. In the calm stillness of the night her despondency drained her of all her strength. She rose from her sofa beside the dying fire, and stood in the lamplight gazing, dry-eyed, at her child, when M. d'Aiglemont came in. He was in high spirits. Julie called to him to admire Helene as she lay asleep, but he met his wife's enthusiasm with a commonplace:

"All children are nice at that age."

He closed the curtains about the cot after a careless kiss on the child's forehead. Then he turned his eyes on Julie, took her hand and drew her to sit beside him on the sofa, where she had been sitting with such dark thoughts surging up in her mind.

"You are looking very handsome to-night, Mme. d'Aiglemont," he exclaimed, with the gaiety intolerable to the Marquise, who knew its emptiness so well.

"Where have you spent the evening?" she asked, with a pretence of complete indifference.

"At Mme. de Serizy's."

He had taken up a fire-screen, and was looking intently at the gauze. He had not noticed the traces of tears on his wife's face. Julie shuddered. Words could not express the overflowing torrent of thoughts which must be forced down into inner depths.

"Mme. de Serizy is giving a concert on Monday, and is dying for you to go. You have not been anywhere for some time past, and that is enough to set her longing to see you at her house. She is a good-natured woman, and very fond of you. I should be glad if you would go; I all but promised that you should——"

"I will go."

There was something so penetrating, so significant in the tones of Julie's voice, in her accent, in the glance that went with the words, that Victor, startled out of his indifference, stared at his wife in astonishment.

That was all, Julie had guessed that it was Mme. de Serizy who had stolen her husband's heart from her. Her brooding despair benumbed her. She appeared to be deeply interested in the fire. Victor meanwhile still played with the fire-screen. He looked bored, like a man who has enjoyed himself elsewhere, and brought home the consequent lassitude. He yawned once or twice, then he took up a candle in one hand, and with the other languidly sought his wife's neck for the usual embrace; but Julie stooped and received the good-night kiss upon her forehead; the formal, loveless grimace seemed hateful to her at that moment.

As soon as the door closed upon Victor, his wife sank into a seat. Her limbs tottered beneath her, she burst into tears. None but those who have endured the torture of some such scene can fully understand the anguish that it means, or divine the horror of the long-drawn tragedy arising out of it.

Those simple, foolish words, the silence that followed between the husband and wife, the Marquis' gesture and expression, the way in which he sat before the fire, his attitude as he made that futile attempt to put a kiss on his wife's throat,—all these things made up a dark hour for Julie, and the catastrophe of the drama of her sad and lonely life. In her madness she knelt down before the sofa, burying her face in it to shut out everything from sight, and prayed to Heaven, putting a new significance into the words of the evening prayer, till it became a cry from the depths of her own soul, which would have gone to her husband's heart if he had heard it.

The following week she spent in deep thought for her future, utterly overwhelmed by this new trouble. She made a study of it, trying to discover a way to regain her ascendency over the Marquis, scheming how to live long enough to watch over her daughter's happiness, yet to live true to her own heart. Then she made up her mind. She would struggle with her rival. She would shine once more in society. She would feign the love which she could no longer feel, she would captivate her husband's fancy; and when she had lured him into her power, she would coquet with him like a capricious mistress who takes delight in tormenting a lover. This hateful strategy was the only possible way out of her troubles. In this way she would become mistress of the situation; she would prescribe her own sufferings at her good pleasure, and reduce them by enslaving her husband, and bringing him under a tyrannous yoke. She felt not the slightest remorse for the hard life which he should lead. At a bound she reached cold, calculating indifference—for her daughter's sake. She had gained a sudden insight into the treacherous, lying arts of degraded women; the wiles of coquetry, the revolting cunning which arouses such profound hatred in men at the mere suspicion of innate corruption in a woman.

Julie's feminine vanity, her interests, and a vague desire to inflict punishment, all wrought unconsciously with the mother's love within her to force her into a path where new sufferings awaited her. But her nature was too noble, her mind too fastidious, and, above all things, too open, to be the accomplice of these frauds for very long. Accustomed as she was to self-scrutiny, at the first step in vice—for vice it was—the cry of conscience must inevitably drown the clamor of the passions and of selfishness. Indeed, in a young wife whose heart is still pure, whose love has never been mated, the very sentiment of motherhood is overpowered by modesty. Modesty; is not all womanhood summed up in that? But just now Julie would not see any danger, anything wrong, in her life.

She went to Mme. de Serizy's concert. Her rival had expected to see a pallid, drooping woman. The Marquise wore rouge, and appeared in all the splendor of a toilet which enhanced her beauty.

Mme. de Serizy was one of those women who claim to exercise a sort of sway over fashions and society in Paris; she issued her decrees, saw them received in her own circle, and it seemed to her that all the world obeyed them. She aspired to epigram, she set up for an authority in matters of taste. Literature, politics, men and women, all alike were submitted to her censorship, and the lady herself appeared to defy the censorship of others. Her house was in every respect a model of good taste.

Julie triumphed over the Countess in her own salon, filled as it was with beautiful women and women of fashion. Julie's liveliness and sparkling wit gathered all the most distinguished men in the rooms about her. Her costume was faultless, for the despair of the women, who one and all envied her the fashion of her dress, and attributed the moulded outline of her bodice to the genius of some unknown dressmaker, for women would rather believe in miracles worked by the science of chiffons than in the grace and perfection of the form beneath.

When Julie went to the piano to sing Desdemona's song, the men in the rooms flocked about her to hear the celebrated voice so long mute, and there was a deep silence. The Marquise saw the heads clustered thickly in the doorways, saw all eyes turned upon her, and a sharp thrill of excitement quivered through her. She looked for her husband, gave him a coquettish side-glance, and it pleased her to see that his vanity was gratified to no small degree. In the joy of triumph she sang the first part of Al piu salice. Her audience was enraptured. Never had Malibran nor Pasta sung with expression and intonation so perfect. But at the beginning of the second part she glanced over the glistening groups and saw— Arthur. He never took his eyes from her face. A quick shudder thrilled through her, and her voice faltered. Up hurried Mme. de Serizy from her place.

"What is it, dear? Oh! poor little thing! she is in such weak health; I was so afraid when I saw her begin a piece so far beyond her strength."

The song was interrupted. Julie was vexed. She had not courage to sing any longer, and submitted to her rival's treacherous sympathy. There was a whisper among the women. The incident led to discussions; they guessed that the struggle had begun between the Marquise and Mme. de Serizy, and their tongues did not spare the latter.

Julie's strange, perturbing presentiments were suddenly realized. Through her preoccupation with Arthur she had loved to imagine that with that gentle, refined face he must remain faithful to his first love. There were times when she felt proud that this ideal, pure, and passionate young love should have been hers; the passion of the young lover whose thoughts are all for her to whom he dedicates every moment of his life, who blushes as a woman blushes, thinks as a woman might think, forgetting ambition, fame, and fortune in devotion to his love,—she need never fear a rival. All these things she had fondly and idly dreamed of Arthur; now all at once it seemed to her that her dream had come true. In the young Englishman's half-feminine face she read the same deep thoughts, the same pensive melancholy, the same passive acquiescence in a painful lot, and an endurance like her own. She saw herself in him. Trouble and sadness are the most eloquent of love's interpreters, and response is marvelously swift between two suffering creatures, for in them the powers of intuition and of assimilation of facts and ideas are well-nigh unerring and perfect. So with the violence of the shock the Marquise's eyes were opened to the whole extent of the future danger. She was only too glad to find a pretext for her nervousness in her chronic ill-health, and willingly submitted to be overwhelmed by Mme. de Serizy's insidious compassion.

That incident of the song caused talk and discussion which differed with the various groups. Some pitied Julie's fate, and regretted that such a remarkable woman was lost to society; others fell to wondering what the cause of her ill-health and seclusion could be.

"Well, now, my dear Ronquerolles," said the Marquis, addressing Mme. de Serizy's brother, "you used to envy me my good fortune, and you used to blame me for my infidelities. Pshaw, you would not find much to envy in my lot, if, like me, you had a pretty wife so fragile that for the past two years you might not so much as kiss her hand for fear of damaging her. Do not you encumber yourself with one of those fragile ornaments, only fit to put in a glass case, so brittle and so costly that you are always obliged to be careful of them. They tell me that you are afraid of snow or wet for that fine horse of yours; how often do you ride him? That is just my own case. It is true that my wife gives me no ground for jealousy, but my marriage is purely ornamental business; if you think that I am a married man, you are grossly mistaken. So there is some excuse for my unfaithfulness. I should dearly like to know what you gentlemen who laugh at me would do in my place. Not many men would be so considerate as I am. I am sure," (here he lowered his voice) "that Mme. d'Aiglemont suspects nothing. And then, of course, I have no right to complain at all; I am very well off. Only there is nothing more trying for a man who feels things than the sight of suffering in a poor creature to whom you are attached——"

"You must have a very sensitive nature, then," said M. de Ronquerolles, "for you are not often at home."

Laughter followed on the friendly epigram; but Arthur, who made one of the group, maintained a frigid imperturbability in his quality of an English gentleman who takes gravity for the very basis of his being. D'Aiglemont's eccentric confidence, no doubt, had kindled some kind of hope in Arthur, for he stood patiently awaiting an opportunity of a word with the Marquis. He had not to wait long.

"My Lord Marquis," he said, "I am unspeakably pained to see the state of Mme. d'Aiglemont's health. I do not think that you would talk jestingly about it if you knew that unless she adopts a certain course of treatment she must die miserably. If I use this language to you, it is because I am in a manner justified in using it, for I am quite certain that I can save Mme. d'Aiglemont's life and restore her to health and happiness. It is odd, no doubt, that a man of my rank should be a physician, yet nevertheless chance determined that I should study medicine. I find life dull enough here," he continued, affecting a cold selfishness to gain his ends, "it makes no difference to me whether I spend my time and travel for the benefit of a suffering fellow-creature, or waste it in Paris on some nonsense or other. It is very, very seldom that a cure is completed in these complaints, for they require constant care, time, and patience, and, above all things, money. Travel is needed, and a punctilious following out of prescriptions, by no means unpleasant, and varied daily. Two gentlemen" (laying a stress on the word in its English sense) "can understand each other. I give you warning that if you accept my proposal, you shall be a judge of my conduct at every moment. I will do nothing without consulting you, without your superintendence, and I will answer for the success of my method if you will consent to follow it. Yes, unless you wish to be Mme. d'Aiglemont's husband no longer, and that before long," he added in the Marquis' ear.

The Marquis laughed. "One thing is certain—that only an Englishman could make me such an extraordinary proposal," he said. "Permit me to leave it unaccepted and unrejected. I will think it over; and my wife must be consulted first in any case."

Julie had returned to the piano. This time she sang a song from Semiramide, Son regina, son guerriera, and the whole room applauded, a stifled outburst of wellbred acclamation which proved that the Faubourg Saint-Germain had been roused to enthusiasm by her singing.

The evening was over. D'Aiglemont brought his wife home, and

Julie saw with uneasy satisfaction that her first attempt had at once been successful. Her husband had been roused out of indifference by the part which she had played, and now he meant to honor her with such a passing fancy as he might bestow upon some opera nymph. It amused Julie that she, a virtuous married woman, should be treated thus. She tried to play with her power, but at the outset her kindness broke down once more, and she received the most terrible of all the lessons held in store for her by fate.

Between two and three o'clock in the morning Julie sat up, sombre and moody, beside her sleeping husband, in the room dimly lighted by the flickering lamp. Deep silence prevailed. Her agony of remorse had lasted near an hour; how bitter her tears had been none perhaps can realize save women who have known such an experience as hers. Only such natures as Julie's can feel her loathing for a calculated caress, the horror of a loveless kiss, of the heart's apostasy followed by dolorous prostitution. She despised herself; she cursed marriage. She could have longed for death; perhaps if it had not been for a cry from her child, she would have sprung from the window and dashed herself upon the pavement. M. d'Aiglemont slept on peacefully at her side; his wife's hot dropping tears did not waken him.

But next morning Julie could be gay. She made a great effort to look happy, to hide, not her melancholy, as heretofore, but an insuperable loathing. From that day she no longer regarded herself as a blameless wife. Had she not been false to herself? Why should she not play a double part in the future, and display astounding depths of cunning in deceiving her husband? In her there lay a hitherto undiscovered latent depravity, lacking only opportunity, and her marriage was the cause.

Even now she had asked herself why she should struggle with love, when, with her heart and her whole nature in revolt, she gave herself to the husband whom she loved no longer. Perhaps, who knows? some piece of fallacious reasoning, some bit of special pleading, lies at the root of all sins, of all crimes. How shall society exist unless every individual of which it is composed will make the necessary sacrifices of inclination demanded by its laws? If you accept the benefits of civilized society, do you not by implication engage to observe the conditions, the conditions of its very existence? And yet, starving wretches, compelled to respect the laws of property, are not less to be pitied than women whose natural instincts and sensitiveness are turned to so many avenues of pain.

A few days after that scene of which the secret lay buried in the midnight couch, d'Aiglemont introduced Lord Grenville. Julie gave the guest a stiffly polite reception, which did credit to her powers of dissimulation. Resolutely she silenced her heart, veiled her eyes, steadied her voice, and she kept her future in her own hands. Then, when by these devices, this innate woman-craft, as it may be called, she had discovered the full extent of the love which she inspired, Mme. d'Aiglemont welcomed the hope of a speedy cure, and no longer opposed her husband, who pressed her to accept the young doctor's offer. Yet she declined to trust herself with Lord Grenville until after some further study of his words and manner, she could feel certain that he had sufficient generosity to endure his pain in silence. She had absolute power over him, and she had begun to abuse that power already. Was she not a woman?

Montcontour is an old manor-house build upon the sandy cliffs above the Loire, not far from the bridge where Julie's journey was interrupted in 1814. It is a picturesque, white chateau, with turrets covered with fine stone carving like Mechlin lace; a chateau such as you often see in Touraine, spick and span, ivy clad, standing among its groves of mulberry trees and vineyards, with its hollow walks, its stone balustrades, and cellars mined in the rock escarpments mirrored in the Loire. The roofs of Montcontour gleam in the sun; the whole land glows in the burning heat. Traces of the romantic charm of Spain and the south hover about the enchanting spot. The breeze brings the scent of bell flowers and golden broom, the air is soft, all about you lies a sunny land, a land which casts its dreamy spell over your soul, a land of languor and of soft desire, a fair, sweet-scented country, where pain is lulled to sleep and passion wakes. No heart is cold for long beneath its clear sky, beside its sparkling waters. One ambition dies after another, and you sink into serene content and repose, as the sun sinks at the end of the day swathed about with purple and azure.

One warm August evening in 1821 two people were climbing the paths cut in the crags above the chateau, doubtless for the sake of the view from the heights above. The two were Julie and Lord Grenville, but this Julie seemed to be a new creature. The unmistakable color of health glowed in her face. Overflowing vitality had brought a light into her eyes, which sparkled through a moist film with that liquid brightness which gives such irresistible charm to the eyes of children. She was radiant with smiles; she felt the joy of living and all the possibilities of life. From the very way in which she lifted her little feet, it was easy to see that no suffering trammeled her lightest movements; there was no heaviness nor languor in her eyes, her voice, as heretofore. Under the white silk sunshade which screened her from the hot sunlight, she looked like some young bride beneath her veil, or a maiden waiting to yield to the magical enchantments of Love.

Arthur led her with a lover's care, helping her up the pathway as if she had been a child, finding the smoothest ways, avoiding the stones for her, bidding her see glimpses of distance, or some flower beside the path, always with the unfailing goodness, the same delicate design in all that he did; the intuitive sense of this woman's wellbeing seemed to be innate in him, and as much, nay, perhaps more, a part of his being as the pulse of his own life.

The patient and her doctor went step for step. There was nothing strange for them in a sympathy which seemed to have existed since the day when they first walked together. One will swayed them both; they stopped as their senses received the same impression; every word and every glance told of the same thought in either mind. They had climbed up through the vineyards, and now they turned to sit on one of the long white stones, quarried out of the caves in the hillside; but Julie stood awhile gazing out over the landscape.

"What a beautiful country!" she cried. "Let us put up a tent and live here. Victor, Victor, do come up here!"

M. d'Aiglemont answered by a halloo from below. He did not, however, hurry himself, merely giving his wife a glance from time to time when the windings of the path gave him a glimpse of her. Julie breathed the air with delight. She looked up at Arthur, giving him one of those subtle glances in which a clever woman can put the whole of her thought.

"Ah, I should like to live here always," she said. "Would it be possible to tire of this beautiful valley?—What is the picturesque river called, do you know?"

"That is the Cise."

"The Cise," she repeated. "And all this country below, before us?"

"Those are the low hills above the Cher."

"And away to the right? Ah, that is Tours. Only see how fine the cathedral towers look in the distance."

She was silent, and let fall the hand which she had stretched out towards the view upon Arthur's. Both admired the wide landscape made up of so much blended beauty. Neither of them spoke. The murmuring voice of the river, the pure air, and the cloudless heaven were all in tune with their thronging thoughts and their youth and the love in their hearts.

"Oh! mon Dieu, how I love this country!" Julie continued, with growing and ingenuous enthusiasm. "You lived here for a long while, did you not?" she added after a pause.

A thrill ran through Lord Grenville at her words.

"It was down there," he said, in a melancholy voice, indicating as he spoke a cluster of walnut trees by the roadside, "that I, a prisoner, saw you for the first time."

"Yes, but even at that time I felt very sad. This country looked wild to me then, but now——" She broke off, and Lord Grenville did not dare to look at her.

"All this pleasure I owe to you," Julie began at last, after a long silence. "Only the living can feel the joy of life, and until now have I not been dead to it all? You have given me more than health, you have made me feel all its worth—"

Women have an inimitable talent for giving utterance to strong feelings in colorless words; a woman's eloquence lies in tone and gesture, manner and glance. Lord Grenville hid his face in his hands, for his tears filled his eyes. This was Julie's first word of thanks since they left Paris a year ago.

For a whole year he had watched over the Marquise, putting his whole self into the task. D'Aiglemont seconding him, he had taken her first to Aix, then to la Rochelle, to be near the sea. From moment to moment he had watched the changes worked in Julie's shattered constitution by his wise and simple prescriptions. He had cultivated her health as an enthusiastic gardener might cultivate a rare flower. Yet, to all appearance, the Marquise had quietly accepted Arthur's skill and care with the egoism of a spoiled Parisienne, or like a courtesan who has no idea of the cost of things, nor of the worth of a man, and judges of both by their comparative usefulness to her.

The influence of places upon us is a fact worth remarking. If melancholy comes over us by the margin of a great water, another indelible law of our nature so orders it that the mountains exercise a purifying influence upon our feelings, and among the hills passion gains in depth by all that it apparently loses in vivacity. Perhaps it was the light of the wide country by the Loire, the height of the fair sloping hillside on which the lovers sat, that induced the calm bliss of the moment when the whole extent of the passion that lies beneath a few insignificant-sounding words is divined for the first time with a delicious sense of happiness.

Julie had scarcely spoken the words which had moved Lord Grenville so deeply, when a caressing breeze ruffled the treetops and filled the air with coolness from the river; a few clouds crossed the sky, and the soft cloud-shadows brought out all the beauty of the fair land below.

Julie turned away her head, lest Arthur should see the tears which she succeeded in repressing; his emotion had spread at once to her. She dried her eyes, but she dared not raise them lest he should read the excess of joy in a glance. Her woman's instinct told her that during this hour of danger she must hide her love in the depths of her heart. Yet silence might prove equally dangerous, and Julie saw that Lord Grenville was unable to utter a word. She went on, therefore, in a gentle voice:

"You are touched by what I have said. Perhaps such a quick outburst of feeling is the way in which a gracious and kind nature like yours reverses a mistaken judgment. You must have thought me ungrateful when I was cold and reserved, or cynical and hard, all through the journey which, fortunately, is very near its end. I should not have been worthy of your care if I had been unable to appreciate it. I have forgotten nothing. Alas! I shall forget nothing, not the anxious way in which you watched over me as a mother watches over her child, nor, and above all else, the noble confidence of our life as brother and sister, the delicacy of your conduct—winning charms, against which we women are defenceless. My lord, it is out of my power to make you a return——"

At these words Julie hastily moved further away, and Lord Grenville made no attempt to detain her. She went to a rock not far away, and there sat motionless. What either felt remained a secret known to each alone; doubtless they wept in silence. The singing of the birds about them, so blithe, so overflowing with tenderness at sunset time, could only increase the storm of passion which had driven them apart. Nature took up their story for them, and found a language for the love of which they did not dare to speak.

"And now, my lord," said Julie, and she came and stood before Arthur with a great dignity, which allowed her to take his hand in hers. "I am going to ask you to hallow and purify the life which you have given back to me. Here, we will part. I know," she added, as she saw how white his face grew, "I know that I am repaying you for your devotion by requiring of you a sacrifice even greater than any which you have hitherto made for me, sacrifices so great that they should receive some better recompense than this.... But it must be... You must not stay in France. By laying this command upon you, do I not give you rights which shall be held sacred?" she added, holding his hand against her beating heart.

"Yes," said Arthur, and he rose.

He looked in the direction of d'Aiglemont, who appeared on the opposite side of one of the hollow walks with the child in his arms. He had scrambled up on the balustrade by the chateau that little Helene might jump down.

"Julie, I will not say a word of my love; we understand each other too well. Deeply and carefully though I have hidden the pleasures of my heart, you have shared them all, I feel it, I know it, I see it. And now, at this moment, as I receive this delicious proof of the constant sympathy of our hearts, I must go.... Cunning schemes for getting rid of him have crossed my mind too often; the temptation might be irresistible if I stayed with you."

"I had the same thought," she said, a look of pained surprise in her troubled face.

Yet in her tone and involuntary shudder there was such virtue, such certainty of herself, won in many a hard-fought battle with a love that spoke in Julie's tones and involuntary gestures, that Lord Grenville stood thrilled with admiration of her. The mere shadow of a crime had been dispelled from that clear conscience. The religious sentiment enthroned on the fair forehead could not but drive away the evil thoughts that arise unbidden, engendered by our imperfect nature, thoughts which make us aware of the grandeur and the perils of human destiny.

"And then," she said, "I should have drawn down your scorn upon me, and—I should have been saved," she added, and her eyes fell. "To be lowered in your eyes, what is that but death?"

For a moment the two heroic lovers were silent, choking down their sorrow. Good or ill, it seemed that their thoughts were loyally one, and the joys in the depths of their heart were no more experiences apart than the pain which they strove most anxiously to hide.

"I have no right to complain," she said after a while, "my misery is of my own making," and she raised her tear-filled eyes to the sky.

"Perhaps you don't remember it, but that is the place where we met each other for the first time," shouted the General from below, and he waved his hand towards the distance. "There, down yonder, near those poplars!"

The Englishman nodded abruptly by way of answer.

"So I was bound to die young and to know no happiness," Julie continued. "Yes, do not think that I live. Sorrow is just as fatal as the dreadful disease which you have cured. I do not think that I am to blame. No. My love is stronger than I am, and eternal; but all unconsciously it grew in me; and I will not be guilty through my love. Nevertheless, though I shall be faithful to my conscience as a wife, to my duties as a mother, I will be no less faithful to the instincts of my heart. Hear me," she cried in an unsteady voice, "henceforth I belong to him no longer."

By a gesture, dreadful to see in its undisguised loathing she indicated her husband.

"The social code demands that I shall make his existence happy," she continued. "I will obey, I will be his servant, my devotion to him shall be boundless; but from to-day I am a widow. I will neither be a prostitute in my own eyes nor in those of the world.

If I do not belong to M. d'Aiglemont, I will never belong to another. You shall have nothing, nothing save this which you have wrung from me. This is the doom which I have passed upon myself," she said, looking proudly at him. "And now, know this—if you give way to a single criminal thought, M. d'Aiglemont's widow will enter a convent in Spain or Italy. By an evil chance we have spoken of our love; perhaps that confession was bound to come; but our hearts must never vibrate again like this. To-morrow you will receive a letter from England, and we shall part, and never see each other again."

The effort had exhausted all Julie's strength. She felt her knees trembling, and a feeling of deathly cold came over her. Obeying a woman's instinct, she sat down, lest she should sink into Arthur's arms.

"Julie!" cried Lord Grenville.

The sharp cry rang through the air like a crack of thunder. Till then he could not speak; now, all the words which the dumb lover could not utter gathered themselves in that heartrending appeal.

"Well, what is wrong with her?" asked the General, who had hurried up at that cry, and now suddenly confronted the two.

"Nothing serious," said Julie, with that wonderful self-possession which a woman's quick-wittedness usually brings to her aid when it is most called for. "The chill, damp air under the walnut tree made me feel quite faint just now, and that must have alarmed this doctor of mine. Does he not look on me as a very nearly finished work of art? He was startled, I suppose, by the idea of seeing it destroyed." With ostentatious coolness she took Lord Grenville's arm, smiled at her husband, took a last look at the landscape, and went down the pathway, drawing her traveling companion with her.

"This certainly is the grandest view that we have seen," she said; "I shall never forget it. Just look, Victor, what distance, what an expanse of country, and what variety in it! I have fallen in love with this landscape."

Her laughter was almost hysterical, but to her husband it sounded natural. She sprang gaily down into the hollow pathway and vanished.

"What?" she cried, when they had left M. d'Aiglemont far behind. "So soon? Is it so soon? Another moment, and we can neither of us be ourselves; we shall never be ourselves again, our life is over, in short—"

"Let us go slowly," said Lord Grenville, "the carriages are still some way off, and if we may put words into our glances, our hearts may live a little longer."

They went along the footpath by the river in the late evening light, almost in silence; such vague words as they uttered, low as the murmur of the Loire, stirred their souls to the depths. Just as the sun sank, a last red gleam from the sky fell over them; it was like a mournful symbol of their ill-starred love.

The General, much put out because the carriage was not at the spot where they had left it, followed and outstripped the pair without interrupting their converse. Lord Grenville's high minded and delicate behavior throughout the journey had completely dispelled the Marquis' suspicions. For some time past he had left his wife in freedom, reposing confidence in the noble amateur's Punic faith. Arthur and Julie walked on together in the close and painful communion of two hearts laid waste.

So short a while ago as they climbed the cliffs at Montcontour, there had been a vague hope in either mind, an uneasy joy for which they dared not account to themselves; but now as they came along the pathway by the river, they pulled down the frail structure of imaginings, the child's cardcastle, on which neither of them had dared to breathe. That hope was over.

That very evening Lord Grenville left them. His last look at Julie made it miserably plain that since the moment when sympathy revealed the full extent of a tyrannous passion, he did well to mistrust himself.

The next morning, M. d'Aiglemont and his wife took their places in the carriage without their traveling companion, and were whirled swiftly along the road to Blois. The Marquise was constantly put in mind of the journey made in 1814, when as yet she know nothing of love, and had been almost ready to curse it for its persistency. Countless forgotten impressions were revived. The heart has its own memory. A woman who cannot recollect the most important great events will recollect through a lifetime things which appealed to her feelings; and Julie d'Aiglemont found all the most trifling details of that journey laid up in her mind. It was pleasant to her to recall its little incidents as they occurred to her one by one; there were points in the road when she could even remember the thoughts that passed through her mind when she saw them first.

Victor had fallen violently in love with his wife since she had recovered the freshness of her youth and all her beauty, and now he pressed close to her side like a lover. Once he tried to put his arm round her, but she gently disengaged herself, finding some excuse or other for evading the harmless caress. In a little while she shrank from the close contact with Victor, the sensation of warmth communicated by their position. She tried to take the unoccupied place opposite, but Victor gallantly resigned the back seat to her. For this attention she thanked him with a sigh, whereupon he forgot

himself, and the Don Juan of the garrison construed his wife's
melancholy to his own advantage, so that at the end of the day she
was compelled to speak with a firmness which impressed him.

"You have all but killed me, dear, once already, as you know,"
said she. "If I were still an inexperienced girl, I might begin to
sacrifice myself afresh; but I am a mother, I have a daughter to
bring up, and I owe as much to her as to you. Let us resign ourselves
to a misfortune which affects us both alike. You are the less to be
pitied. Have you not, as it is, found consolations which duty and the
honor of both, and (stronger still) which Nature forbids to me?
Stay," she added, "you carelessly left three letters from Mme. de
Serizy in a drawer; here they are. My silence about this matter
should make it plain to you that in me you have a wife who has
plenty of indulgence and does not exact from you the sacrifices
prescribed by the law. But I have thought enough to see that the
roles of husband and wife are quite different, and that the wife alone
is predestined to misfortune. My virtue is based upon firmly fixed
and definite principles. I shall live blamelessly, but let me live."

The Marquis was taken aback by a logic which women grasp
with the clear insight of love, and overawed by a certain dignity
natural to them at such crises. Julie's instinctive repugnance for all
that jarred upon her love and the instincts of her heart is one of the
fairest qualities of woman, and springs perhaps from a natural
virtue which neither laws nor civilization can silence. And who shall
dare to blame women? If a woman can silence the exclusive
sentiment which bids her "forsake all other" for the man whom she
loves, what is she but a priest who has lost his faith? If a rigid mind
here and there condemns Julie for a sort of compromise between
love and wifely duty, impassioned souls will lay it to her charge as a
crime. To be thus blamed by both sides shows one of two things very
clearly—that misery necessarily follows in the train of broken laws,
or else that there are deplorable flaws in the institutions upon which
society in Europe is based.

Two years went by. M. and Mme. d'Aiglemont went their
separate ways, leading their life in the world, meeting each other
more frequently abroad than at home, a refinement upon divorce, in
which many a marriage in the great world is apt to end.

One evening, strange to say, found husband and wife in their
own drawing-room. Mme. d'Aiglemont had been dining at home
with a friend, and the General, who almost invariably dined in town,
had not gone out for once.

"There is a pleasant time in store for you, Madame la
Marquise," said M. d'Aiglemont, setting his coffee cup down upon

the table. He looked at the guest, Mme. de Wimphen, and half-pettishly, half-mischievously added, "I am starting off for several days' sport with the Master of the Hounds. For a whole week, at any rate, you will be a widow in good earnest; just what you wish for, I suppose.—Guillaume," he said to the servant who entered, "tell them to put the horses in."

Mme. de Wimphen was the friend to whom Julie had begun the letter upon her marriage. The glances exchanged by the two women said plainly that in her Julie had found an intimate friend, an indulgent and invaluable confidante. Mme. de Wimphen's marriage had been a very happy one. Perhaps it was her own happiness which secured her devotion to Julie's unhappy life, for under such circumstances, dissimilarity of destiny is nearly always a strong bond of union.

"Is the hunting season not over yet?" asked Julie, with an indifferent glance at her husband.

"The Master of the Hounds comes when and where he pleases, madame. We are going boar-hunting in the Royal Forest."

"Take care that no accident happens to you."

"Accidents are usually unforeseen," he said, smiling.

"The carriage is ready, my Lord Marquis," said the servant.

"Madame, if I should fall a victim to the boar—" he continued, with a suppliant air.

"What does this mean?" inquired Mme. de Wimphen.

"Come, come," said Mme. d'Aiglemont, turning to her husband; smiling at her friend as if to say, "You will soon see."

Julie held up her head; but as her husband came close to her, she swerved at the last, so that his kiss fell not on her throat, but on the broad frill about it.

"You will be my witness before heaven now that I need a firman to obtain this little grace of her," said the Marquis, addressing Mme. de Wimphen. "This is how this wife of mine understands love. She has brought me to this pass, by what trickery I am at a loss to know.... A pleasant time to you!" and he went.

"But your poor husband is really very good-natured," cried Louisa de Wimphen, when the two women were alone together. "He loves you."

"Oh! not another syllable after that last word. The name I bear makes me shudder——"

"Yes, but Victor obeys you implicitly," said Louisa.

"His obedience is founded in part upon the great esteem which I have inspired in him. As far as outward things go, I am a model wife. I make his house pleasant to him; I shut my eyes to his intrigues; I touch not a penny of his fortune. He is free to squander the interest exactly as he pleases; I only stipulate that he shall not touch the principal. At this price I have peace. He neither explains nor attempts to explain my life. But though my husband is guided by me, that does not say that I have nothing to fear from his character. I am a bear leader who daily trembles lest the muzzle should give way at last. If Victor once took it into his head that I had forfeited my right to his esteem, what would happen next I dare not think; for he is violent, full of personal pride, and vain above all things. While his wits are not keen enough to enable him to behave discreetly at a delicate crisis when his lowest passions are involved, his character is weak, and he would very likely kill me provisionally even if he died of remorse next day. But there is no fear of that fatal good fortune."

A brief pause followed. Both women were thinking of the real cause of this state of affairs. Julie gave Louisa a glance which revealed her thoughts.

"I have been cruelly obeyed," she cried. "Yet I never forbade him to write to me. Oh! he has forgotten me, and he is right. If his life had been spoiled, it would have been too tragical; one life is enough, is it not? Would you believe it, dear; I read English newspapers simply to see his name in print. But he has not yet taken his seat in the House of Lords."

"So you know English."

"Did I not tell you?—Yes, I learned."

"Poor little one!" cried Louisa, grasping Julie's hand in hers. "How can you still live?"

"That is the secret," said the Marquise, with an involuntary gesture almost childlike in its simplicity. "Listen, I take laudanum. That duchess in London suggested the idea; you know the story, Maturin made use of it in one of his novels. My drops are very weak, but I sleep; I am only awake for seven hours in the day, and those hours I spend with my child."

Louisa gazed into the fire. The full extent of her friend's misery was opening out before her for the first time, and she dared not look into her face.

"Keep my secret, Louisa," said Julie, after a moment's silence.

Just as she spoke the footman brought in a letter for the Marquise.

"Ah!" she cried, and her face grew white.

"I need not ask from whom it comes," said Mme. de Wimphen, but the Marquise was reading the letter, and heeded nothing else.

Mme. de Wimphen, watching her friend, saw strong feeling

wrought to the highest pitch, ecstasy of the most dangerous kind painted on Julie's face in swift changing white and red. At length Julie flung the sheet into the fire.

"It burns like fire," she said. "Oh! my heart beats till I cannot breathe."

She rose to her feet and walked up and down. Her eyes were blazing.

"He did not leave Paris!" she cried.

Mme. de Wimphen did not dare to interrupt the words that followed, jerked-out sentences, measured by dreadful pauses in between. After every break the deep notes of her voice sank lower and lower. There was something awful about the last words.

"He has seen me, constantly, and I have not known it.—A look, taken by stealth, every day, helps him to live.—Louisa, you do not know!—He is dying.—He wants to say good-bye to me. He knows that my husband has gone away for several days. He will be here in a moment. Oh! I shall die: I am lost.—Listen, Louisa, stay with me!—I am afraid!"

"But my husband knows that I have been dining with you; he is sure to come for me," said Mme. de Wimphen.

"Well, then, before you go I will send him away. I will play the executioner for us both. Oh me! he will think that I do not love him any more—And that letter of his! Dear, I can see those words in letters of fire."

A carriage rolled in under the archway.

"Ah!" cried the Marquise, with something like joy in her voice, "he is coming openly. He makes no mystery of it."

"Lord Grenville," announced the servant.

The Marquise stood up rigid and motionless; but at the sight of Arthur's white face, so thin and haggard, how was it possible to keep up the show of severity? Lord Grenville saw that Julie was not alone, but he controlled his fierce annoyance, and looked cool and unperturbed. Yet for the two women who knew his secret, his face, his tones, the look in his eyes had something of the power attributed to the torpedo. Their faculties were benumbed by the sharp shock of contact with his horrible pain. The sound of his voice set Julie's heart beating so cruelly that she could not trust herself to speak; she was afraid that he would see the full extent of his power over her. Lord Grenville did not dare to look at Julie, and Mme. de Wimphen was left to sustain a conversation to which no one listened. Julie glanced at her friend with touching gratefulness in her eyes to thank her for coming to her aid.

By this time the lovers had quelled emotion into silence, and could preserve the limits laid down by duty and convention. But M.

de Wimphen was announced, and as he came in the two friends exchanged glances. Both felt the difficulties of this fresh complication. It was impossible to enter into explanations with M. de Wimphen, and Louisa could not think of any sufficient pretext for asking to be left.

Julie went to her, ostensibly to wrap her up in her shawl. "I will be brave," she said, in a low voice. "He came here in the face of all the world, so what have I to fear? Yet but for you, in that first moment, when I saw how changed he looked, I should have fallen at his feet."

"Well, Arthur, you have broken your promise to me," she said, in a faltering voice, when she returned. Lord Grenville did not venture to take the seat upon the sofa by her side.

"I could not resist the pleasure of hearing your voice, of being near you. The thought of it came to be a sort of madness, a delirious frenzy. I am no longer master of myself. I have taken myself to task; it is no use, I am too weak, I ought to die. But to die without seeing you, without having heard the rustle of your dress, or felt your tears. What a death!"

He moved further away from her; but in his hasty uprising a pistol fell out of his pocket. The Marquise looked down blankly at the weapon; all passion, all expression had died out of her eyes. Lord Grenville stooped for the thing, raging inwardly over an accident which seemed like a piece of lovesick strategy.

"Arthur!"

"Madame," he said, looking down, "I came here in utter desperation; I meant——" he broke off.

"You meant to die by your own hand here in my house!"

"Not alone!" he said in a low voice.

"Not alone! My husband, perhaps——?"

"No, no," he cried in a choking voice. "Reassure yourself," he continued, "I have quite given up my deadly purpose. As soon as I came in, as soon as I saw you, I felt that I was strong enough to suffer in silence, and to die alone."

Julie sprang up, and flung herself into his arms. Through her sobbing he caught a few passionate words, "To know happiness, and then to die.—Yes, let it be so."

All Julie's story was summed up in that cry from the depths; it was the summons of nature and of love at which women without a religion surrender. With the fierce energy of unhoped-for joy, Arthur caught her up and carried her to the sofa; but in a moment she tore herself from her lover's arms, looked at him with a fixed despairing gaze, took his hand, snatched up a candle, and drew him into her room. When they stood by the cot where Helene lay sleeping, she put the curtains softly aside, shading the candle with her hand, lest the light should dazzle the half-closed eyes beneath the transparent lids. Helene lay smiling in her sleep, with her arms outstretched on the coverlet. Julie glanced from her child to Arthur's face. That look told him all.

"We may leave a husband, even though he loves us: a man is strong; he has consolations.—We may defy the world and its laws. But a motherless child!"—all these thoughts, and a thousand others more moving still, found language in that glance.

"We can take her with us," muttered he; "I will love her dearly."

"Mamma!" cried little Helene, now awake. Julie burst into tears. Lord Grenville sat down and folded his arms in gloomy silence.

"Mamma!" At the sweet childish name, so many nobler feelings, so many irresistible yearnings awoke, that for a moment love was effaced by the all-powerful instinct of motherhood; the mother triumphed over the woman in Julie, and Lord Grenville could not hold out, he was defeated by Julie's tears.

Just at that moment a door was flung noisily open. "Madame d'Aiglemont, are you hereabouts?" called a voice which rang like a crack of thunder through the hearts of the two lovers. The Marquis had come home.

Before Julie could recover her presence of mind, her husband was on the way to the door of her room which opened into his. Luckily, at a sign, Lord Grenville escaped into the dressing-closet, and she hastily shut the door upon him.

"Well, my lady, here am I," said Victor, "the hunting party did not come off. I am just going to bed."

"Good-night, so am I. So go and leave me to undress."

"You are very cross to-night, Madame la Marquise."

The General returned to his room, Julie went with him to the door and shut it. Then she sprang to the dressing-close to release Arthur. All her presence of mind returned; she bethought herself that it was quite natural that her sometime doctor should pay her a visit; she might have left him in the drawing-room while she put her little girl to bed. She was about to tell him, under her breath, to go back to the drawing-room, and had opened the door. Then she shrieked aloud. Lord Grenville's fingers had been caught and crushed in the door.

"Well, what is it?" demanded her husband.

"Oh! nothing, I have just pricked my finger with a pin."

The General's door opened at once. Julie imagined that the irruption was due to a sudden concern for her, and cursed a solicitude in which love had no part. She had barely time to close the dressing-closet, and Lord Grenville had not extricated his hand. The General did, in fact, appear, but his wife had mistaken his motives; his apprehensions were entirely on his own account.

"Can you lend me a bandana handkerchief? The stupid fool Charles leaves me without a single one. In the early days you used to bother me with looking after me so carefully. Ah, well, the honeymoon did not last very long for me, nor yet for my cravats. Nowadays I am given over to the secular arm, in the shape of servants who do not care one jack straw for what I say."

"There! There is a bandana for you. Did you go into the drawing-room?"

"No."

"Oh! you might perhaps have been in time to see Lord Grenville."

"Is he in Paris?"

"It seems so."

"Oh! I will go at once. The good doctor."

"But he will have gone by now!" exclaimed Julie.

The Marquis, standing in the middle of the room, was tying the handkerchief over his head. He looked complacently at himself in the glass.

"What has become of the servants is more than I know," he remarked. "I have rung the bell for Charles, and he has not answered it. And your maid is not here either. Ring for her. I should like another blanket on my bed to-night."

"Pauline is out," the Marquise said drily.

"What, at midnight!" exclaimed the General.

"I gave her leave to go to the Opera."

"That is funny!" returned her husband, continuing to undress. "I thought I saw her coming upstairs."

"She has come in then, of course," said Julie, with assumed impatience, and to allay any possible suspicion on her husband's part she pretended to ring the bell.

The whole history of that night has never been known, but no doubt it was as simple and as tragically commonplace as the domestic incidents that preceded it.

Next day the Marquise d'Aiglemont took to her bed, nor did she leave it for some days.

"What can have happened in your family so extraordinary that every one is talking about your wife?" asked M. de Ronquerolles of M. d'Aiglemont a short time after that night of catastrophes.

"Take my advice and remain a bachelor," said d'Aiglemont. "The curtains of Helene's cot caught fire, and gave my wife such a shock that it will be a twelvemonth before she gets over it; so the doctor says. You marry a pretty wife, and her looks fall off; you marry a girl in blooming health, and she turns into an invalid. You think she has a passionate temperament, and find her cold, or else under her apparent coldness there lurks a nature so passionate that she is the death of you, or she dishonors your name. Sometimes the meekest of them will turn out crotchety, though the crotchety ones never grow any sweeter. Sometimes the mere child, so simple and silly at first, will develop an iron will to thwart you and the ingenuity of a fiend. I am tired of marriage."

"Or of your wife?"

"That would be difficult. By-the-by, do you feel inclined to go to Saint-Thomas d'Aquin with me to attend Lord Grenville's funeral?"

"A singular way of spending time.—Is it really known how he came by his death?" added Ronquerolles.

"His man says that he spent a whole night sitting on somebody's window sill to save some woman's character, and it has been infernally cold lately."

"Such devotion would be highly creditable to one of us old stagers; but Lord Grenville was a youngster and—an Englishman. Englishmen never can do anything like anybody else."

"Pooh!" returned d'Aiglemont, "these heroic exploits all depend upon the woman in the case, and it certainly was not for one that I know, that poor Arthur came by his death."

II

A HIDDEN GRIEF

Between the Seine and the little river Loing lies a wide flat country, skirted on the one side by the Forest of Fontainebleau, and marked out as to its southern limits by the towns of Moret, Montereau, and Nemours. It is a dreary country; little knolls of hills appear only at rare intervals, and a coppice here and there among the fields affords for game; and beyond, upon every side, stretches the endless gray or yellowish horizon peculiar to Beauce, Sologne, and Berri.

In the very centre of the plain, at equal distances from Moret and Montereau, the traveler passes the old chateau of Saint-Lange, standing amid surroundings which lack neither dignity nor stateliness. There are magnificent avenues of elm-trees, great gardens encircled by the moat, and a circumference of walls about a huge manorial pile which represents the profits of the maltote, the gains of farmers-general, legalized malversation, or the vast fortunes of great houses now brought low beneath the hammer of the Civil Code.

Should any artist or dreamer of dreams chance to stray along the roads full of deep ruts, or over the heavy land which secures the place against intrusion, he will wonder how it happened that this romantic old place was set down in a savanna of corn-land, a desert of chalk, and sand, and marl, where gaiety dies away, and melancholy is a natural product of the soil. The voiceless solitude, the monotonous horizon line which weigh upon the spirits are negative beauties, which only suit with sorrow that refuses to be comforted.

Hither, at the close of the year 1820, came a woman, still young, well known in Paris for her charm, her fair face, and her wit; and to the immense astonishment of the little village a mile away, this woman of high rank and corresponding fortune took up her abode at Saint-Lange.

From time immemorial, farmers and laborers had seen no

gentry at the chateau. The estate, considerable though it was, had been left in charge of a land-steward and the house to the old servants. Wherefore the appearance of the lady of the manor caused a kind of sensation in the district.

A group had gathered in the yard of the wretched little wineshop at the end of the village (where the road forks to Nemours and Moret) to see the carriage pass. It went by slowly, for the Marquise had come from Paris with her own horses, and those on the lookout had ample opportunity of observing a waiting-maid, who sat with her back to the horses holding a little girl, with a somewhat dreamy look, upon her knee. The child's mother lay back in the carriage; she looked like a dying woman sent out into the country air by her doctors as a last resource. Village politicians were by no means pleased to see the young, delicate, downcast face; they had hoped that the new arrival at Saint-Lange would bring some life and stir into the neighborhood, and clearly any sort of stir or movement must be distasteful to the suffering invalid in the traveling carriage.

That evening, when the notables of Saint-Lange were drinking in the private room of the wineshop, the longest head among them declared that such depression could admit of but one construction— the Marquise was ruined. His lordship the Marquis was away in Spain with the Duc d'Angouleme (so they said in the papers), and beyond a doubt her ladyship had come to Saint-Lange to retrench after a run of ill-luck on the Bourse. The Marquis was one of the greatest gamblers on the face of the globe. Perhaps the estate would be cut up and sold in little lots. There would be some good strokes of business to be made in that case, and it behooved everybody to count up his cash, unearth his savings and to see how he stood, so as to secure his share of the spoil of Saint-Lange.

So fair did this future seem, that the village worthies, dying to know whether it was founded on fact, began to think of ways of getting at the truth through the servants at the chateau. None of these, however, could throw any light on the calamity which had brought their mistress into the country at the beginning of winter, and to the old chateau of Saint-Lange of all places, when she might have taken her choice of cheerful country-houses famous for their beautiful gardens.

His worship the mayor called to pay his respects; but he did not see the lady. Then the land-steward tried with no better success.

Madame la Marquise kept her room, only leaving it, while it was set in order, for the small adjoining drawing-room, where she dined; if, indeed, to sit down to a table, to look with disgust at the dishes, and take the precise amount of nourishment required to prevent death from sheer starvation, can be called dining. The meal over, she returned at once to the old-fashioned low chair, in which she had sat since the morning, in the embrasure of the one window that lighted her room.

Her little girl she only saw for a few minutes daily, during the dismal dinner, and even for a short time she seemed scarcely able to bear the child's presence. Surely nothing but the most unheard-of anguish could have extinguished a mother's love so early.

None of the servants were suffered to come near, her own woman was the one creature whom she liked to have about her; the chateau must be perfectly quiet, the child must play at the other end of the house. The slightest sound had grown so intolerable, that any human voice, even the voice of her own child, jarred upon her.

At first the whole countryside was deeply interested in these eccentricities; but time passed on, every possible hypothesis had been advanced to account for them and the peasants and dwellers in the little country towns thought no more of the invalid lady.

So the Marquise was left to herself. She might live on, perfectly silent, amid the silence which she herself had created; there was nothing to draw her forth from the tapestried chamber where her grandmother died, whither she herself had come that she might die, gently, without witnesses, without importunate solicitude, without suffering from the insincere demonstrations of egoism masquerading as affection, which double the agony of death in great cities.

She was twenty-six years old. At that age, with plenty of romantic illusions still left, the mind loves to dwell on the thought of death when death seems to come as a friend. But with youth, death is coy, coming up close only to go away, showing himself and hiding again, till youth has time to fall out of love with him during this dalliance. There is that uncertainty too that hangs over death's to-morrow. Youth plunges back into the world of living men, there to find the pain more pitiless than death, that does not wait to strike.

This woman who refused to live was to know the bitterness of these reprieves in the depths of her loneliness; in moral agony, which death would not come to end, she was to serve a terrible apprenticeship to the egoism which must take the bloom from her heart and break her in to the life of the world.

This harsh and sorry teaching is the usual outcome of our early sorrows. For the first, and perhaps for the last time in her life, the Marquise d'Aiglemont was in very truth suffering. And, indeed, would it not be an error to suppose that the same sentiment can be reproduced in us? Once develop the power to feel, is it not always there in the depths of our nature? The accidents of life may lull or awaken it, but there it is, of necessity modifying the self, its abiding place. Hence, every sensation should have its great day once and for all, its first day of storm, be it long or short. Hence, likewise, pain, the most abiding of our sensations, could be keenly felt only at its first irruption, its intensity diminishing with every subsequent paroxysm, either because we grow accustomed to these crises, or perhaps because a natural instinct of self-preservation asserts itself, and opposes to the destroying force of anguish an equal but passive force of inertia.

Yet of all kinds of suffering, to which does the name of anguish belong? For the loss of parents, Nature has in a manner prepared us; physical suffering, again, is an evil which passes over us and is gone; it lays no hold upon the soul; if it persists, it ceases to be an evil, it is death. The young mother loses her firstborn, but wedded love ere long gives her a successor. This grief, too, is transient. After all, these, and many other troubles like unto them, are in some sort wounds and bruises; they do not sap the springs of vitality, and only a succession of such blows can crush in us the instinct that seeks happiness. Great pain, therefore, pain that arises to anguish, should be suffering so deadly, that past, present, and future are alike included in its grip, and no part of life is left sound and whole. Never afterwards can we think the same thoughts as before. Anguish engraves itself in ineffaceable characters on mouth and brow; it passes through us, destroying or relaxing the springs that vibrate to enjoyment, leaving behind in the soul the seeds of a disgust for all things in this world.

Yet, again, to be measureless, to weigh like this upon body and soul, the trouble should befall when soul and body have just come to their full strength, and smite down a heart that beats high with life. Then it is that great scars are made. Terrible is the anguish. None, it may be, can issue from this soul-sickness without undergoing some dramatic change. Those who survive it, those who remain on earth, return to the world to wear an actor's countenance and to play an actor's part. They know the side-scenes where actors may retire to calculate chances, shed their tears, or pass their jests. Life holds no inscrutable dark places for those who have passed through this ordeal; their judgments are Rhadamanthine.

For young women of the Marquise d'Aiglemont's age, this first, this most poignant pain of all, is always referable to the same cause. A woman, especially if she is a young woman, greatly beautiful, and by nature great, never fails to stake her whole life as instinct and sentiment and society all unite to bid her. Suppose that that life fails her, suppose that she still lives on, she cannot but endure the most cruel pangs, inasmuch as a first love is the loveliest of all. How comes it that this catastrophe has found no painter, no poet? And yet, can it be painted? Can it be sung? No; for the anguish arising from it eludes analysis and defies the colors of art. And more than this, such pain is never confessed. To console the sufferer, you must be able to divine the past which she hugs in bitterness to her soul like a remorse; it is like an avalanche in a valley; it laid all waste before it found a permanent resting-place.

The Marquise was suffering from this anguish, which will for long remain unknown, because the whole world condemns it, while sentiment cherishes it, and the conscience of a true woman justifies her in it. It is with such pain as with children steadily disowned of life, and therefore bound more closely to the mother's heart than other children more bounteously endowed. Never, perhaps, was the awful catastrophe in which the whole world without dies for us, so deadly, so complete, so cruelly aggravated by circumstance as it had been for the Marquise. The man whom she had loved was young and generous; in obedience to the laws of the world, she had refused herself to his love, and he had died to save a woman's honor, as the world calls it. To whom could she speak of her misery? Her tears would be an offence against her husband, the origin of the tragedy. By all laws written and unwritten she was bound over to silence. A woman would have enjoyed the story; a man would have schemed for his own benefit. No; such grief as hers can only weep freely in solitude and in loneliness; she must consume her pain or be consumed by it; die or kill something within her—her conscience, it may be.

Day after day she sat gazing at the flat horizon. It lay out before her like her own life to come. There was nothing to discover, nothing to hope. The whole of it could be seen at a glance. It was the visible presentment in the outward world of the chill sense of desolation which was gnawing restlessly at her heart. The misty mornings, the pale, bright sky, the low clouds scudding under the gray dome of heaven, fitted with the moods of her soul-sickness. Her heart did not contract, was neither more nor less seared, rather it seemed as if her youth, in its full blossom, was slowly turned to stone by an anguish intolerable because it was barren. She suffered through herself and for herself. How could it end save in self-absorption? Ugly torturing thoughts probed her conscience. Candid self-examination pronounced that she was double, there were two selves within her; a woman who felt and a woman who thought; a self that suffered and a self that could fain suffer no longer. Her mind traveled back to the joys of childish days; they had gone by, and she had never known how happy they were. Scenes crowded up in her memory as in a bright mirror glass, to demonstrate the deception of a marriage which, all that it should be in the eyes of the world, was in reality wretched. What had the delicate pride of young womanhood done for her—the bliss foregone, the sacrifices made to the world? Everything in her expressed love, awaited love; her movements still were full of perfect grace; her smile, her charm, were hers as before; why? she asked herself. The sense of her own youth and physical loveliness no more affected her than some meaningless reiterated sound. Her very beauty had grown intolerable to her as a useless thing. She shrank aghast from the thought that through the rest of life she must remain an incomplete creature; had not the inner self lost its power of receiving impressions with that zest, that exquisite sense of freshness which is the spring of so much of life's gladness? The impressions of the future would for the most part be effaced as soon as received, and many of the thoughts which once would have moved her now would move her no more.

After the childhood of the creature dawns the childhood of the heart; but this second infancy was over, her lover had taken it down with him into the grave. The longings of youth remained; she was young yet; but the completeness of youth was gone, and with that lost completeness the whole value and savor of life had diminished somewhat. Should she not always bear within her the seeds of sadness and mistrust, ready to grow up and rob emotion of its springtide of fervor? Conscious she must always be that nothing could give her now the happiness so longed for, that seemed so fair in her dreams. The fire from heaven that sheds abroad its light in the heart, in the dawn of love, had been quenched in tears, the first real tears which she had shed; henceforth she must always suffer, because it was no longer in her power to be what once she might have been. This is a belief which turns us in aversion and bitterness of spirit from any proffered new delight.

Julie had come to look at life from the point of view of age about to die. Young though she felt, the heavy weight of joyless days had fallen upon her, and left her broken-spirited and old before her time. With a despairing cry, she asked the world what it could give her in exchange for the love now lost, by which she had lived. She asked herself whether in that vanished love, so chaste and pure, her will had not been more criminal than her deeds, and chose to believe herself guilty; partly to affront the world, partly for her own consolation, in that she had missed the close union of body and soul, which diminishes the pain of the one who is left behind by the knowledge that once it has known and given joy to the full, and retains within itself the impress of that which is no more.

Something of the mortification of the actress cheated of her part mingled with the pain which thrilled through every fibre of her heart and brain. Her nature had been thwarted, her vanity wounded, her woman's generosity cheated of self-sacrifice. Then, when she had raised all these questions, set vibrating all the springs in those different phases of being which we distinguish as social, moral, and physical, her energies were so far exhausted and relaxed that she was powerless to grasp a single thought amid the chase of conflicting ideas.

Sometimes as the mists fell, she would throw her window open, and would stay there, motionless, breathing in unheedingly the damp earthly scent in the air, her mind to all appearance an unintelligent blank, for the ceaseless burden of sorrow humming in her brain left her deaf to earth's harmonies and insensible to the delights of thought.

One day, towards noon, when the sun shone out for a little, her maid came in without a summons.

"This is the fourth time that M. le Cure has come to see Mme. la Marquise; to-day he is so determined about it, that we did not know what to tell him."

"He has come to ask for some money for the poor, no doubt; take him twenty-five louis from me."

The woman went only to return.

"M. le Cure will not take the money, my lady; he wants to speak to you."

"Then let him come!" said Mme. d'Aiglemont, with an involuntary shrug which augured ill for the priest's reception. Evidently the lady meant to put a stop to persecution by a short and sharp method.

Mme. d'Aiglemont had lost her mother in her early childhood; and as a natural consequence in her bringing-up, she had felt the influence of the relaxed notions which loosened the hold of religion upon France during the Revolution. Piety is a womanly virtue which women alone can really instil; and the Marquise, a child of the eighteenth century, had adopted her father's creed of philosophism, and practised no religious observances. A priest, to her way of thinking, was a civil servant of very doubtful utility. In her present position, the teaching of religion could only poison her wounds; she had, moreover, but scanty faith in the lights of country cures, and made up her mind to put this one gently but firmly in his place, and to rid herself of him, after the manner of the rich, by bestowing a benefit.

At first sight of the cure the Marquise felt no inclination to change her mind. She saw before her a stout, rotund little man, with a ruddy, wrinkled, elderly face, which awkwardly and unsuccessfully tried to smile. His bald, quadrant-shaped forehead, furrowed by intersecting lines, was too heavy for the rest of his face, which seemed to be dwarfed by it. A fringe of scanty white hair encircled the back of his head, and almost reached his ears. Yet the priest looked as if by nature he had a genial disposition; his thick lips, his slightly curved nose, his chin, which vanished in a double fold of wrinkles,—all marked him out as a man who took cheerful views of life.

At first the Marquise saw nothing but these salient characteristics, but at the first word she was struck by the sweetness of the speaker's voice. Looking at him more closely, she saw that the eyes under the grizzled eyebrows had shed tears, and his face, turned in profile, wore so sublime an impress of sorrow, that the Marquise recognized the man in the cure.

"Madame la Marquise, the rich only come within our province when they are in trouble. It is easy to see that the troubles of a young, beautiful, and wealthy woman, who has lost neither children nor relatives, are caused by wounds whose pangs religion alone can soothe. Your soul is in danger, madame. I am not speaking now of the hereafter which awaits us. No, I am not in the confessional. But it is my duty, is it not, to open your eyes to your future life here on earth? You will pardon an old man, will you not, for importunity which has your own happiness for its object?"

"There is no more happiness for me, monsieur. I shall soon be, as you say, in your province; but it will be for ever."

"Nay, madame. You will not die of this pain which lies heavy upon you, and can be read in your face. If you had been destined to die of it, you would not be here at Saint-Lange. A definite regret is not so deadly as hope deferred. I have known others pass through more intolerable and more awful anguish, and yet they live."

The Marquise looked incredulous.

"Madame, I know a man whose affliction was so sore that your trouble would seem to you to be light compared with his."

Perhaps the long solitary hours had begun to hang heavily; perhaps in the recesses of the Marquise's mind lay the thought that here was a friendly heart to whom she might be able to pour out her troubles. However, it was, she gave the cure a questioning glance which could not be mistaken.

"Madame," he continued, "the man of whom I tell you had but three children left of a once large family circle. He lost his parents, his daughter, and his wife, whom he dearly loved. He was left alone at last on the little farm where he had lived so happily for so long. His three sons were in the army, and each of the lads had risen in proportion to his time of service. During the Hundred Days, the oldest went into the Guard with a colonel's commission; the second was a major in the artillery; the youngest a major in a regiment of dragoons. Madame, those three boys loved their father as much as he loved them. If you but knew how careless young fellows grow of home ties when they are carried away by the current of their own lives, you would realize from this one little thing how warmly they loved the lonely old father, who only lived in and for them—never a week passed without a letter from one of the boys. But then he on his side had never been weakly indulgent, to lessen their respect for him; nor unjustly severe, to thwart their affection; or apt to grudge sacrifices, the thing that estranges children's hearts. He had been more than a father; he had been a brother to them, and their friend.

"At last he went to Paris to bid them good-bye before they set out for Belgium; he wished to see that they had good horses and all that they needed. And so they went, and the father returned to his home again. Then the war began. He had letters from Fleurus, and again from Ligny. All went well. Then came the battle of Waterloo, and you know the rest. France was plunged into mourning; every family waited in intense anxiety for news. You may imagine, madame, how the old man waited for tidings, in anxiety that knew no peace nor rest. He used to read the gazettes; he went to the coach office every day. One evening he was told that the colonel's servant had come. The man was riding his master's horse—what need was there to ask any questions?—the colonel was dead, cut in two by a shell. Before the evening was out the youngest son's servant arrived—the youngest had died on the eve of the battle. At midnight came a gunner with tidings of the death of the last; upon whom, in those few hours, the poor father had centered all his life. Madame, they all had fallen."

After a pause the good man controlled his feelings, and added gently:

"And their father is still living, madame. He realized that if God had left him on earth, he was bound to live on and suffer on earth; but he took refuge in the sanctuary. What could he be?"

The Marquise looked up and saw the cure's face, grown sublime in its sorrow and resignation, and waited for him to speak. When the words came, tears broke from her.

"A priest, madame; consecrated by his own tears previously shed at the foot of the altar."

Silence prevailed for a little. The Marquise and the cure looked out at the foggy landscape, as if they could see the figures of those who were no more.

"Not a priest in a city, but a simple country cure," added he.

"At Saint-Lange," she said, drying her eyes.

"Yes, madame."

Never had the majesty of grief seemed so great to Julie. The two words sank straight into her heart with the weight of infinite sorrow. The gentle, sonorous tones troubled her heart. Ah! that full, deep voice, charged with plangent vibration, was the voice of one who had suffered indeed.

"And if I do not die, monsieur, what will become of me?" The Marquise spoke almost reverently.

"Have you not a child, madame?"

"Yes," she said stiffly.

The cure gave her such a glance as a doctor gives a patient whose life is in danger. Then he determined to do all that in him lay to combat the evil spirit into whose clutches she had fallen.

"We must live on with our sorrows—you see it yourself, madame, and religion alone offers us real consolation. Will you permit me to come again?—to speak to you as a man who can sympathize with every trouble, a man about whom there is nothing very alarming, I think?"

"Yes, monsieur, come back again. Thank you for your thought of me."

"Very well, madame; then I shall return very shortly."

This visit relaxed the tension of soul, as it were; the heavy strain of grief and loneliness had been almost too much for the Marquise's strength. The priest's visit had left a soothing balm in her heart, his words thrilled through her with healing influence. She began to feel something of a prisoner's satisfaction, when, after he has had time to feel his utter loneliness and the weight of his chains, he hears a neighbor knocking on the wall, and welcomes the sound which brings a sense of human friendship. Here was an unhoped-for confidant. But this feeling did not last for long. Soon she sank back into the old bitterness of spirit, saying to herself, as the prisoner might say, that a companion in misfortune could neither lighten her own bondage nor her future.

In the first visit the cure had feared to alarm the susceptibilities of self-absorbed grief, in a second interview he hoped to make some progress towards religion. He came back again two days later, and from the Marquise's welcome it was plain that she had looked forward to the visit.

"Well, Mme. la Marquise, have you given a little thought to the great mass of human suffering? Have you raised your eyes above our earth and seen the immensity of the universe?—the worlds beyond worlds which crush our vanity into insignificance, and with our vanity reduce our sorrows?"

"No, monsieur," she said; "I cannot rise to such heights, our social laws lie too heavily upon me, and rend my heart with a too poignant anguish. And laws perhaps are less cruel than the usages of the world. Ah! the world!"

"Madame, we must obey both. Law is the doctrine, and custom the practice of society."

"Obey society?" cried the Marquise, with an involuntary shudder. "Eh! monsieur, it is the source of all our woes. God laid down no law to make us miserable; but mankind, uniting together in social life, have perverted God's work. Civilization deals harder measure to us women than nature does. Nature imposes upon us physical suffering which you have not alleviated; civilization has developed in us thoughts and feelings which you cheat continually. Nature exterminates the weak; you condemn them to live, and by so doing, consign them to a life of misery. The whole weight of the burden of marriage, an institution on which society is based, falls upon us; for the man liberty, duties for the woman. We must give up our whole lives to you, you are only bound to give us a few moments of yours. A man, in fact, makes a choice, while we blindly submit. Oh, monsieur, to you I can speak freely. Marriage, in these days, seems to me to be legalized prostitution. This is the cause of my wretchedness. But among so many miserable creatures so unhappily yoked, I alone am bound to be silent, I alone am to blame for my misery. My marriage was my own doing."

She stopped short, and bitter tears fell in the silence.

"In the depths of my wretchedness, in the midst of this sea of distress," she went on, "I found some sands on which to set foot and suffer at leisure. A great tempest swept everything away. And here am I, helpless and alone, too weak to cope with storms."

"We are never weak while God is with us," said the priest. "And if your cravings for affection cannot be satisfied here on earth, have you no duties to perform?"

"Duties continually!" she exclaimed, with something of impatience in her tone. "But where for me are the sentiments which give us strength to perform them? Nothing from nothing, nothing for nothing,—this, monsieur, is one of the most inexorable laws of nature, physical or spiritual. Would you have these trees break into leaf without the sap which swells the buds? It is the same with our human nature; and in me the sap is dried up at its source."

"I am not going to speak to you of religious sentiments of which resignation is born," said the cure, "but of motherhood, madame, surely—"

"Stop, monsieur!" said the Marquise, "with you I will be sincere. Alas! in future I can be sincere with no one; I am condemned to falsehood. The world requires continual grimaces, and we are bidden to obey its conventions if we would escape reproach. There are two kinds of motherhood, monsieur; once I knew nothing of such distinctions, but I know them now. Only half of me has become a mother; it were better for me if I had not been a mother at all. Helene is not his child! Oh! do not start. At Saint-Lange there are volcanic depths whence come lurid gleams of light and earthquake shocks to shake the fragile edifices of laws not based on nature. I have borne a child, that is enough, I am a mother in the eyes of the law. But you, monsieur, with your delicately compassionate soul, can perhaps understand this cry from an unhappy woman who has suffered no lying illusions to enter her heart. God will judge me, but surely I have only obeyed His laws by giving way to the affections which He Himself set in me, and this I have learned from my own soul.—What is a child, monsieur, but the image of two beings, the fruit of two sentiments spontaneously blended? Unless it is owned by every fibre of the body, as by every chord of tenderness in the heart; unless it recalls the bliss of love, the hours, the places where two creatures were happy, their words that overflowed with the music of humanity, and their sweet imaginings, that child is an incomplete creation. Yes, those two should find the poetic dreams of their intimate double life realized in their child as in an exquisite miniature; it should be for them a never-failing spring of emotion, implying their whole past and their whole future.

"My poor little Helene is her father's child, the offspring of duty and of chance. In me she finds nothing but the affection of instinct, the woman's natural compassion for the child of her womb. Socially speaking, I am above reproach. Have I not sacrificed my life and my happiness to my child? Her cries go to my heart; if she were to fall into the water, I should spring to save her, but she is not in my heart.

"Ah! love set me dreaming of a motherhood far greater and more complete. In a vanished dream I held in my arms a child conceived in desire before it was begotten, the exquisite flower of life that blossoms in the soul before it sees the light of day. I am Helene's mother only in the sense that I brought her forth. When she needs me no longer, there will be an end of my motherhood; with the extinction of the cause, the effects will cease. If it is a woman's adorable prerogative that her motherhood may last through her child's life, surely that divine persistence of sentiment is due to the far-reaching glory of the conception of the soul? Unless a child has lain wrapped about from life's first beginnings by the mother's soul, the instinct of motherhood dies in her as in the animals. This is true; I feel that it is true. As my poor little one grows older, my heart closes. My sacrifices have driven us apart. And yet I know, monsieur, that to another child my heart would have gone out in inexhaustible love; for that other I should not have known what sacrifice meant, all had been delight. In this, monsieur, my instincts are stronger than reason, stronger than religion or all else in me. Does the woman who is neither wife nor mother sin in wishing to die when, for her misfortune, she has caught a glimpse of the infinite beauty of love, the limitless joy of motherhood? What can become of her? I can tell you what she feels. I cannot put that memory from me so resolutely but that a hundred times, night and day, visions of a happiness, greater it may be than the reality, rise before me, followed by a shudder which shakes brain and heart and body. Before these cruel visions, my feelings and thoughts grow colorless, and I ask myself, 'What would my life have been if——?'"

She hid her face in her hands and burst into tears.

"There you see the depths of my heart!" she continued. "For his child I could have acquiesced in any lot however dreadful. He who died, bearing the burden of the sins of the world will forgive this thought of which I am dying; but the world, I know, is merciless. In its ears my words are blasphemies; I am outraging all its codes. Oh! that I could wage war against this world and break down and refashion its laws and traditions! Has it not turned all my thoughts, and feelings, and longings, and hopes, and every fibre in me into so many sources of pain? Spoiled my future, present, and past? For me the daylight is full of gloom, my thoughts pierce me like a sword, my child is and is not.

"Oh, when Helene speaks to me, I wish that her voice were different, when she looks into my face I wish that she had other eyes. She constantly keeps me in mind of all that should have been and is not. I cannot bear to have her near me. I smile at her, I try to make up to her for the real affection of which she is defrauded. I am wretched, monsieur, too wretched to live. And I am supposed to be a pattern wife. And I have committed no sins. And I am respected! I have fought down forbidden love which sprang up at unawares within me; but if I have kept the letter of the law, have I kept it in my heart? There has never been but one here," she said, laying her right hand on her breast, "one and no other; and my child feels it. Certain looks and tones and gestures mould a child's nature, and my poor little one feels no thrill in the arm I put about her, no tremor comes into my voice, no softness into my eyes when I speak to her or take her up. She looks at me, and I cannot endure the reproach in her eyes. There are times when I shudder to think that some day she may be my judge and condemn her mother unheard. Heaven grant that hate may not grow up between us! Ah! God in heaven, rather let the tomb open for me, rather let me end my days here at Saint-Lange!—I want to go back to the world where I shall find my other soul and become wholly a mother. Ah! forgive me, sir, I am mad. Those words were choking me; now they are spoken. Ah! you are weeping too! You will not despise me—"

She heard the child come in from a walk. "Helene, my child, come here!" she called. The words sounded like a cry of despair.

The little girl ran in, laughing and calling to her mother to see a butterfly which she had caught; but at the sight of that mother's tears she grew quiet of a sudden, and went up close, and received a kiss on her forehead.

"She will be very beautiful some day," said the priest.

"She is her father's child," said the Marquise, kissing the little one with eager warmth, as if she meant to pay a debt of affection or to extinguish some feeling of remorse.

"How hot you are, mamma!"

"There, go away, my angel," said the Marquise.

The child went. She did not seem at all sorry to go; she did not look back; glad perhaps to escape from a sad face, and instinctively comprehending already an antagonism of feeling in its expression. A mother's love finds language in smiles, they are a part of the divine right of motherhood. The Marquise could not smile. She flushed red as she felt the cure's eyes. She had hoped to act a mother's part before him, but neither she nor her child could deceive him. And, indeed, when a woman loves sincerely, in the kiss she gives there is a divine honey; it is as if a soul were breathed forth in the caress, a subtle flame of fire which brings warmth to the heart; the kiss that lacks this delicious unction is meagre and formal. The priest had felt the difference. He could fathom the depths that lie between the motherhood of the flesh and the motherhood of the heart. He gave the Marquise a keen, scrutinizing glance, then he said:

"You are right, madame; it would be better for you if you were dead——"

"Ah!" she cried, "then you know all my misery; I see you do if, Christian priest as you are, you can guess my determination to die and sanction it. Yes, I meant to die, but I have lacked the courage. The spirit was strong, but the flesh was weak, and when my hand did not tremble, the spirit within me wavered.

"I do not know the reason of these inner struggles, and alternations. I am very pitiably a woman no doubt, weak in my will, strong only to love. Oh, I despise myself. At night, when all my household was asleep, I would go out bravely as far as the lake; but when I stood on the brink, my cowardice shrank from self-destruction. To you I will confess my weakness. When I lay in my bed, again, shame would come over me, and courage would come back. Once I took a dose of laudanum; I was ill, but I did not die. I thought I had emptied the phial, but I had only taken half the dose."

"You are lost, madame," the cure said gravely, with tears in his voice. "You will go back into the world, and you will deceive the world. You will seek and find a compensation (as you imagine it to be) for your woes; then will come a day of reckoning for your pleasures—"

"Do you think," she cried, "that I shall bestow the last, the most precious treasures of my heart upon the first base impostor who can play the comedy of passion? That I would pollute my life for a moment of doubtful pleasure? No; the flame which shall consume my soul shall be love, and nothing but love. All men, monsieur, have the senses of their sex, but not all have the man's soul which satisfies all the requirements of our nature, drawing out the melodious harmony which never breaks forth save in response to the pressure of feeling. Such a soul is not found twice in our lifetime. The future that lies before me is hideous; I know it. A woman is nothing without love; beauty is nothing without pleasure. And even if happiness were offered to me a second time, would not the world frown upon it? I owe my daughter an honored mother. Oh! I am condemned to live in an iron circle, from which there is but one shameful way of escape. The round of family duties, a thankless and irksome task, is in store for me. I shall curse life; but my child shall have at least a fair semblance of a mother. I will give her treasures of virtue for the treasures of love of which I defraud her.

"I have not even the mother's desire to live to enjoy her child's happiness. I have no belief in happiness. What will Helene's fate be? My own, beyond doubt. How can a mother ensure that the man to whom she gives her daughter will be the husband of her heart? You pour scorn on the miserable creatures who sell themselves for a few coins to any passer-by, though want and hunger absolve the brief union; while another union, horrible for quite other reasons, is tolerated, nay encouraged, by society, and a young and innocent girl is married to a man whom she has only met occasionally during the previous three months. She is sold for her whole lifetime. It is true that the price is high! If you allow her no compensation for her sorrows, you might at least respect her; but no, the most virtuous of women cannot escape calumny. This is our fate in its double aspect. Open prostitution and shame; secret prostitution and unhappiness. As for the poor, portionless girls, they may die or go mad, without a soul to pity them. Beauty and virtue are not marketable in the bazaar where souls and bodies are bought and sold—in the den of selfishness which you call society. Why not disinherit daughters? Then, at least, you might fulfil one of the laws of nature, and guided by your own inclinations, choose your companions."

"Madame, from your talk it is clear to me that neither the spirit of family nor the sense of religion appeals to you. Why should you hesitate between the claims of the social selfishness which irritates you, and the purely personal selfishness which craves satisfactions-"

"The family, monsieur—does such a thing exist? I decline to recognize as a family a knot of individuals bidden by society to divide the property after the death of father and mother, and to go their separate ways. A family means a temporary association of persons brought together by no will of their own, dissolved at once by death. Our laws have broken up homes and estates, and the old family tradition handed down from generation to generation. I see nothing but wreck and ruin about me."

"Madame, you will only return to God when His hand has been heavy upon you, and I pray that you have time enough given to you in which to make your peace with Him. Instead of looking to heaven for comfort, you are fixing your eyes on earth. Philosophism and personal interest have invaded your heart; like the children of the sceptical eighteenth century, you are deaf to the voice of religion. The pleasures of this life bring nothing but misery. You are about to make an exchange of sorrows, that is all."

She smiled bitterly.

"I will falsify your predictions," she said. "I shall be faithful to him who died for me."

"Sorrow," he answered, "is not likely to live long save in souls disciplined by religion," and he lowered his eyes respectfully lest the Marquise should read his doubts in them. The energy of her outburst had grieved him. He had seen the self that lurked beneath so many forms, and despaired of softening a heart which affliction seemed to sear. The divine Sower's seed could not take root in such a soil, and His gentle voice was drowned by the clamorous outcry of self-pity. Yet the good man returned again and again with an apostle's earnest persistence, brought back by a hope of leading so noble and proud a soul to God; until the day when he made the discovery that the Marquise only cared to talk with him because it was sweet to speak of him who was no more. He would not lower his ministry by condoning her passion, and confined the conversation more and more to generalities and commonplaces.

Spring came, and with the spring the Marquise found distraction from her deep melancholy. She busied herself for lack of other occupation with her estate, making improvements for amusement.

In October she left the old chateau. In the life of leisure at Saint-Lange she had recovered from her grief and grown fair and fresh. Her grief had been violent at first in its course, as the quoit hurled forth with all the player's strength, and like the quoit after many oscillations, each feebler than the last, it had slackened into melancholy. Melancholy is made up of a succession of such oscillations, the first touching upon despair, the last on the border between pain and pleasure; in youth, it is the twilight of dawn; in age, the dusk of night.

As the Marquise drove through the village in her traveling carriage, she met the cure on his way back from the church. She bowed in response to his farewell greeting, but it was with lowered eyes and averted face. She did not wish to see him again. The village cure had judged this poor Diana of Ephesus only too well.

III

AT THIRTY YEARS

Madame Firmiani was giving a ball. M. Charles de Vandenesse, a young man of great promise, the bearer of one of those historic names which, in spite of the efforts of legislation, are always associated with the glory of France, had received letters of introduction to some of the great lady's friends in Naples, and had come to thank the hostess and to take his leave.

Vandenesse had already acquitted himself creditably on several diplomatic missions; and now that he had received an appointment as attache to a plenipotentiary at the Congress of Laybach, he wished to take advantage of the opportunity to make some study of Italy on the way. This ball was a sort of farewell to Paris and its amusements and its rapid whirl of life, to the great eddying intellectual centre and maelstrom of pleasure; and a pleasant thing it is to be borne along by the current of this sufficiently slandered great city of Paris. Yet Charles de Vandenesse had little to regret, accustomed as he had been for the past three years to salute European capitals and turn his back upon them at the capricious bidding of a diplomatist's destiny. Women no longer made any impression upon him; perhaps he thought that a real passion would play too large a part in a diplomatist's life; or perhaps that the paltry amusements of frivolity were too empty for a man of strong character. We all of us have huge claims to strength of character. There is no man in France, be he ever so ordinary a member of the rank and file of humanity, that will waive pretensions to something beyond mere cleverness.

Charles, young though he was—he was scarcely turned thirty—looked at life with a philosophic mind, concerning himself with theories and means and ends, while other men of his age were thinking of pleasure, sentiments, and the like illusions. He forced back into some inner depth the generosity and enthusiasms of youth, and by nature he was generous. He tried hard to be cool and calculating, to coin the fund of wealth which chanced to be in his nature into gracious manners, and courtesy, and attractive arts; 'tis the proper task of an ambitious man, to play a sorry part to gain "a good position," as we call it in modern days.

He had been dancing, and now he gave a farewell glance over the rooms, to carry away a distinct impression of the ball, moved, doubtless, to some extent by the feeling which prompts a theatre-goer to stay in his box to see the final tableau before the curtain falls. But M. de Vandenesse had another reason for his survey. He gazed curiously at the scene before him, so French in character and in movement, seeking to carry away a picture of the light and laughter and the faces at this Parisian fete, to compare with the novel faces and picturesque surroundings awaiting him at Naples, where he meant to spend a few days before presenting himself at his post. He seemed to be drawing the comparison now between this France so variable, changing even as you study her, with the manners and aspects of that other land known to him as yet only by contradictory hearsay tales or books of travel, for the most part unsatisfactory. Thoughts of a somewhat poetical cast, albeit hackneyed and trite to our modern ideas, crossed his brain, in response to some longing of which, perhaps, he himself was hardly conscious, a desire in the depths of a heart fastidious rather than jaded, vacant rather than seared.

"These are the wealthiest and most fashionable women and the greatest ladies in Paris," he said to himself. "These are the great men of the day, great orators and men of letters, great names and titles; artists and men in power; and yet in it all it seems to me as if there were nothing but petty intrigues and still-born loves, meaningless smiles and causeless scorn, eyes lighted by no flame within, brain-power in abundance running aimlessly to waste. All those pink-and-white faces are here not so much for enjoyment, as to escape from dulness. None of the emotion is genuine. If you ask for nothing but court feathers properly adjusted, fresh gauzes and pretty toilettes and fragile, fair women, if you desire simply to skim the surface of life, here is your world for you. Be content with meaningless phrases and fascinating simpers, and do not ask for real feeling. For my own part, I abhor the stale intrigues which end in sub-prefectures and receiver-generals' places and marriages; or, if love comes into the question, in stealthy compromises, so ashamed are we of the mere semblance of passion. Not a single one of all these eloquent faces tells you of a soul, a soul wholly absorbed by one idea as by remorse. Regrets and misfortune go about shame-facedly clad in jests. There is not one woman here whose resistance I should care to overcome, not one who could drag you down to the pit. Where will you find energy in Paris? A poniard here is a curious toy to hang from a gilt nail, in a picturesque sheath to match. The women, the brains, and hearts of Paris are all on a par. There is no passion left, because we have no individuality. High birth and intellect and fortune are all reduced to one level; we all have taken to the uniform black coat by way of mourning for a dead France. There is no love between equals. Between two lovers there should be differences to efface, wide gulfs to fill. The charm of love fled from us in 1789. Our dulness and our humdrum lives are the outcome of the political system. Italy at any rate is the land of sharp contrasts. Woman there is a malevolent animal, a dangerous unreasoning siren, guided only by her tastes and appetites, a creature no more to be trusted than a tiger—"

Mme. Firmiani here came up to interrupt this soliloquy made up of vague, conflicting, and fragmentary thoughts which cannot be reproduced in words. The whole charm of such musing lies in its vagueness—what is it but a sort of mental haze?

"I want to introduce you to some one who has the greatest wish to make your acquaintance, after all that she has heard of you," said the lady, taking his arm.

She brought him into the next room, and with such a smile and glance as a Parisienne alone can give, she indicated a woman sitting by the hearth.

"Who is she?" the Comte de Vandenesse asked quickly.

"You have heard her name more than once coupled with praise or blame. She is a woman who lives in seclusion—a perfect mystery."

"Oh! if ever you have been merciful in your life, for pity's sake tell me her name."

"She is the Marquise d'Aiglemont."

"I will take lessons from her; she had managed to make a peer of France of that eminently ordinary person her husband, and a dullard into a power in the land. But, pray tell me this, did Lord Grenville die for her sake, do you think, as some women say?"

"Possibly. Since that adventure, real or imaginary, she is very much changed, poor thing! She has not gone into society since. Four years of constancy—that is something in Paris. If she is here to-night——" Here Mme. Firmiani broke off, adding with a mysterious expression, "I am forgetting that I must say nothing. Go and talk with her."

For a moment Charles stood motionless, leaning lightly against the frame of the doorway, wholly absorbed in his scrutiny of a woman who had become famous, no one exactly knew how or why. Such curious anomalies are frequent enough in the world. Mme. d'Aiglemont's reputation was certainly no more extraordinary than plenty of other great reputations. There are men who are always in travail of some great work which never sees the light, statisticians held to be profound on the score of calculations which they take very good care not to publish, politicians who live on a newspaper article, men of letters and artists whose performances are never given to the world, men of science, much as Sganarelle is a Latinist for those who know no Latin; there are the men who are allowed by general consent to possess a peculiar capacity for some one thing, be it for the direction of arts, or for the conduct of an important mission. The admirable phrase, "A man with a special subject," might have been invented on purpose for these acephalous species in the domain of literature and politics.

Charles gazed longer than he intended. He was vexed with himself for feeling so strongly interested; it is true, however, that the lady's appearance was a refutation of the young man's ballroom generalizations.

The Marquise had reached her thirtieth year. She was beautiful in spite of her fragile form and extremely delicate look. Her greatest charm lay in her still face, revealing unfathomed depths of soul. Some haunting, ever-present thought veiled, as it were, the full brilliance of eyes which told of a fevered life and boundless resignation. So seldom did she raise the eyelids soberly downcast, and so listless were her glances, that it almost seemed as if the fire in her eyes were reserved for some occult contemplation. Any man of genius and feeling must have felt strangely attracted by her gentleness and silence. If the mind sought to explain the mysterious problem of a constant inward turning from the present to the past, the soul was no less interested in initiating itself into the secrets of a heart proud in some sort of its anguish. Everything about her, moreover, was in keeping with these thoughts which she inspired. Like almost all women who have very long hair, she was very pale and perfectly white. The marvelous fineness of her skin (that almost unerring sign) indicated a quick sensibility which could be seen yet more unmistakably in her features; there was the same minute and wonderful delicacy of finish in them that the Chinese artist gives to his fantastic figures. Perhaps her neck was rather too long, but such necks belong to the most graceful type, and suggest vague affinities between a woman's head and the magnetic curves of the serpent. Leave not a single one of the thousand signs and tokens by which the most inscrutable character betrays itself to an observer of human nature, he has but to watch carefully the little movements of a woman's head, the ever-varying expressive turns and curves of her neck and throat, to read her nature.

Mme. d'Aiglemont's dress harmonized with the haunting

thought that informed the whole woman. Her hair was gathered up into a tall coronet of broad plaits, without ornament of any kind; she seemed to have bidden farewell for ever to elaborate toilettes. Nor were any of the small arts of coquetry which spoil so many women to be detected in her. Perhaps her bodice, modest though it was, did not altogether conceal the dainty grace of her figure, perhaps, too, her gown looked rich from the extreme distinction of its fashion, and if it is permissible to look for expression in the arrangement of stuffs, surely those numerous straight folds invested her with a great dignity. There may have been some lingering trace of the indelible feminine foible in the minute care bestowed upon her hand and foot; yet, if she allowed them to be seen with some pleasure, it would have tasked the utmost malice of a rival to discover any affectation in her gestures, so natural did they seem, so much a part of old childish habit, that her careless grace absolved this vestige of vanity.

All these little characteristics, the nameless trifles which combine to make up the sum of a woman's prettiness or ugliness, her charm or lack of charm, can only be indicated, when, as with Mme. d'Aiglemont, a personality dominates and gives coherence to the details, informing them, blending them all in an exquisite whole. Her manner was perfectly in accord with her style of beauty and her dress. Only to certain women at a certain age is it given to put language into their attitude. Is it joy or is it sorrow that teaches a woman of thirty the secret of that eloquence of carriage, so that she must always remain an enigma which each interprets by the aid of his hopes, desires, or theories?

The way in which the Marquise leaned both elbows on the arm of her chair, the toying of her interclasped fingers, the curve of her throat, the indolent lines of her languid but lissome body as she lay back in graceful exhaustion, as it were; her indolent limbs, her unstudied pose, the utter lassitude of her movements,—all suggested that this was a woman for whom life had lost its interest, a woman who had known the joys of love only in dreams, a woman bowed down by the burden of memories of the past, a woman who had long since despaired of the future and despaired of herself, an unoccupied woman who took the emptiness of her own life for the nothingness of life.

Charles de Vandenesse saw and admired the beautiful picture before him, as a kind of artistic success beyond an ordinary woman's powers of attainment. He was acquainted with d'Aiglemont; and now, at the first sight of d'Aiglemont's wife, the young diplomatist saw at a glance a disproportionate marriage, an incompatibility (to use the legal jargon) so great that it was impossible that the Marquise should love her husband. And yet—the Marquise d'Aiglemont's life was above reproach, and for any observer the mystery about her was the more interesting on this account. The first impulse of surprise over, Vandenesse cast about for the best way of approaching Mme. d'Aiglemont. He would try a commonplace piece of diplomacy, he thought; he would disconcert her by a piece of clumsiness and see how she would receive it.

"Madame," he said, seating himself near her, "through a fortunate indiscretion I have learned that, for some reason unknown to me, I have had the good fortune to attract your notice. I owe you the more thanks because I have never been so honored before. At the same time, you are responsible for one of my faults, for I mean never to be modest again—"

"You will make a mistake, monsieur," she laughed; "vanity should be left to those who have nothing else to recommend them."

The conversation thus opened ranged at large, in the usual way, over a multitude of topics—art and literature, politics, men and things—till insensibly they fell to talking of the eternal theme in France and all the world over—love, sentiment, and women.

"We are bond-slaves."

"You are queens."

This was the gist and substance of all the more or less ingenious discourse between Charles and the Marquise, as of all such discourses—past, present, and to come. Allow a certain space of time, and the two formulas shall begin to mean "Love me," and "I will love you."

"Madame," Charles de Vandenesse exclaimed under his breath, "you have made me bitterly regret that I am leaving Paris. In Italy I certainly shall not pass hours in intellectual enjoyment such as this has been."

"Perhaps, monsieur, you will find happiness, and happiness is worth more than all the brilliant things, true and false, that are said every evening in Paris."

Before Charles took leave, he asked permission to pay a farewell call on the Marquise d'Aiglemont, and very lucky did he feel himself when the form of words in which he expressed himself for once was used in all sincerity; and that night, and all day long on the morrow, he could not put the thought of the Marquise out of his mind.

At times he wondered why she had singled him out, what she had meant when she asked him to come to see her, and thought supplied an inexhaustible commentary. Again it seemed to him that he had discovered the motives of her curiosity, and he grew intoxicated with hope or frigidly sober with each new construction put upon that piece of commonplace civility. Sometimes it meant everything, sometimes nothing. He made up his mind at last that he would not yield to this inclination, and—went to call on Mme. d'Aiglemont.

There are thoughts which determine our conduct, while we do not so much as suspect their existence. If at first sight this assertion appears to be less a truth than a paradox, let any candid inquirer look into his own life and he shall find abundant confirmation therein. Charles went to Mme. d'Aiglemont, and so obeyed one of these latent, pre-existent germs of thought, of which our experience and our intellectual gains and achievements are but later and tangible developments.

For a young man a woman of thirty has irresistible attractions. There is nothing more natural, nothing better established, no human tie of stouter tissue than the heart-deep attachment between such a woman as the Marquise d'Aiglemont and such a man as Charles de Vandenesse. You can see examples of it every day in the world. A girl, as a matter of fact, has too many young illusions, she is too inexperienced, the instinct of sex counts for too much in her love for a young man to feel flattered by it. A woman of thirty knows all that is involved in the self-surrender to be made. Among the impulses of the first, put curiosity and other motives than love; the second acts with integrity of sentiment. The first yields; the second makes deliberate choice. Is not that choice in itself an immense flattery? A woman armed with experience, forewarned by knowledge, almost always dearly bought, seems to give more than herself; while the inexperienced and credulous girl, unable to draw comparisons for lack of knowledge, can appreciate nothing at its just worth. She accepts love and ponders it. A woman is a counselor and a guide at an age when we love to be guided and obedience is delight; while a girl would fain learn all things, meeting us with a girl's naivete instead of a woman's tenderness. She affords a single triumph; with a woman there is resistance upon resistance to overcome; she has but joy and tears, a woman has rapture and remorse.

A girl cannot play the part of a mistress unless she is so corrupt that we turn from her with loathing; a woman has a thousand ways of preserving her power and her dignity; she has risked so much for love, that she must bid him pass through his myriad transformations, while her too submissive rival gives a sense of too serene security which palls. If the one sacrifices her maidenly pride, the other immolates the honor of a whole family. A girl's coquetry is of the simplest, she thinks that all is said when the veil is laid aside; a woman's coquetry is endless, she shrouds herself in veil after veil, she satisfies every demand of man's vanity, the novice responds but to one.

And there are terrors, fears, and hesitations—trouble and storm in the love of a woman of thirty years, never to be found in a young girl's love. At thirty years a woman asks her lover to give her back the esteem she has forfeited for his sake; she lives only for him, her thoughts are full of his future, he must have a great career, she bids him make it glorious; she can obey, entreat, command, humble herself, or rise in pride; times without number she brings comfort when a young girl can only make moan. And with all the advantages of her position, the woman of thirty can be a girl again, for she can play all parts, assume a girl's bashfulness, and grow the fairer even for a mischance.

Between these two feminine types lies the immeasurable difference which separates the foreseen from the unforeseen, strength from weakness. The woman of thirty satisfies every requirement; the young girl must satisfy none, under penalty of ceasing to be a young girl. Such ideas as these, developing in a young man's mind, help to strengthen the strongest of all passions, a passion in which all spontaneous and natural feeling is blended with the artificial sentiment created by conventional manners.

The most important and decisive step in a woman's life is the very one that she invariably regards as the most insignificant. After her marriage she is no longer her own mistress, she is the queen and the bond-slave of the domestic hearth. The sanctity of womanhood is incompatible with social liberty and social claims; and for a woman emancipation means corruption. If you give a stranger the right of entry into the sanctuary of home, do you not put yourself at his mercy? How then if she herself bids him enter it? Is not this an offence, or, to speak more accurately, a first step towards an offence? You must either accept this theory with all its consequences, or absolve illicit passion. French society hitherto has chosen the third and middle course of looking on and laughing when offences come, apparently upon the Spartan principle of condoning the theft and punishing clumsiness. And this system, it may be, is a very wise one. 'Tis a most appalling punishment to have all your neighbors pointing the finger of scorn at you, a punishment that a woman feels in her very heart. Women are tenacious, and all of them should be tenacious of respect; without esteem they cannot exist, esteem is the first demand that they make of love. The most corrupt among them feels that she must, in the first place, pledge the future to buy absolution for the past, and strives to make her lover understand that only for irresistible bliss can she barter the respect which the world henceforth will refuse to her.

Some such reflections cross the mind of any woman who for the first time and alone receives a visit from a young man; and this especially when, like Charles de Vandenesse, the visitor is handsome or clever. And similarly there are not many young men who would fail to base some secret wish on one of the thousand and one ideas which justify the instinct that attracts them to a beautiful, witty, and unhappy woman like the Marquise d'Aiglemont.

Mme. d'Aiglemont, therefore, felt troubled when M. de Vandenesse was announced; and as for him, he was almost confused in spite of the assurance which is like a matter of costume for a diplomatist. But not for long. The Marquise took refuge at once in the friendliness of manner which women use as a defence against the misinterpretations of fatuity, a manner which admits of no afterthought, while it paves the way to sentiment (to make use of a figure of speech), tempering the transition through the ordinary forms of politeness. In this ambiguous position, where the four roads leading respectively to Indifference, Respect, Wonder, and Passion meet, a woman may stay as long as she pleases, but only at thirty years does she understand all the possibilities of the situation. Laughter, tenderness, and jest are all permitted to her at the crossing of the ways; she has acquired the tact by which she finds all the responsive chords in a man's nature, and skill in judging the sounds which she draws forth. Her silence is as dangerous as her speech. You will never read her at that age, nor discover if she is frank or false, nor how far she is serious in her admissions or merely laughing at you. She gives you the right to engage in a game of fence with her, and suddenly by a glance, a gesture of proved potency, she closes the combat and turns from you with your secret in her keeping, free to offer you up in a jest, free to interest herself in you, safe alike in her weakness and your strength.

Although the Marquise d'Aiglemont took up her position upon this neutral ground during the first interview, she knew how to preserve a high womanly dignity. The sorrows of which she never spoke seemed to hang over her assumed gaiety like a light cloud obscuring the sun. When Vandenesse went out, after a conversation which he had enjoyed more than he had thought possible, he carried with him the conviction that this was like to be too costly a conquest for his aspirations.

"It would mean sentiment from here to yonder," he thought, "and correspondence enough to wear out a deputy second-clerk on his promotion. And yet if I really cared——"

Luckless phrase that has been the ruin of many an infatuated mortal. In France the way to love lies through self-love. Charles went back to Mme. d'Aiglemont, and imagined that she showed symptoms of pleasure in his conversion. And then, instead of giving himself up like a boy to the joy of falling in love, he tried to play a double role. He did his best to act passion and to keep cool enough to analyze the progress of this flirtation, to be lover and diplomatist at once; but youth and hot blood and analysis could only end in one way, over head and ears in love; for, natural or artificial, the Marquise was more than his match. Each time he went out from Mme. d'Aiglemont, he strenuously held himself to his distrust, and submitted the progressive situations of his case to a rigorous scrutiny fatal to his own emotions.

"To-day she gave me to understand that she has been very unhappy and lonely," said he to himself, after the third visit, "and that but for her little girl she would have longed for death. She was perfectly resigned. Now as I am neither her brother nor her spiritual director, why should she confide her troubles to me? She loves me."

Two days later he came away apostrophizing modern manners.

"Love takes on the hue of every age. In 1822 love is a doctrinaire. Instead of proving love by deeds, as in times past, we have taken to argument and rhetoric and debate. Women's tactics are reduced to three shifts. In the first place, they declare that we cannot love as they love. (Coquetry! the Marquise simply threw it at me, like a challenge, this evening!) Next they grow pathetic, to appeal to our natural generosity or self-love; for does it not flatter a young man's vanity to console a woman for a great calamity? And lastly, they have a craze for virginity. She must have thought that I thought her very innocent. My good faith is like to become an excellent speculation."

But a day came when every suspicious idea was exhausted. He asked himself whether the Marquise was not sincere; whether so much suffering could be feigned, and why she should act the part of resignation? She lived in complete seclusion; she drank in silence of a cup of sorrow scarcely to be guessed unless from the accent of some chance exclamation in a voice always well under control. From that moment Charles felt a keen interest in Mme. d'Aiglemont. And yet, though his visits had come to be a recognized thing, and in some sort a necessity to them both, and though the hour was kept free by tacit agreement, Vandenesse still thought that this woman with whom he was in love was more clever than sincere. "Decidedly, she is an uncommonly clever woman," he used to say to himself as he went away.

When he came into the room, there was the Marquise in her favorite attitude, melancholy expressed in her whole form. She made no movement when he entered, only raised her eyes and looked full at him, but the glance that she gave him was like a smile.

Mme. d'Aiglemont's manner meant confidence and sincere friendship, but of love there was no trace. Charles sat down and found nothing to say. A sensation for which no language exists troubled him.

"What is the matter with you?" she asked in a softened voice.

"Nothing.... Yes; I am thinking of something of which, as yet, you have not thought at all."

"What is it?"

"Why—the Congress is over."

"Well," she said, "and ought you to have been at the Congress?"

A direct answer would have been the most eloquent and delicate declaration of love; but Charles did not make it. Before the candid friendship in Mme. d'Aiglemont's face all the calculations of vanity, the hopes of love, and the diplomatist's doubts died away. She did not suspect, or she seemed not to suspect, his love for her; and Charles, in utter confusion turning upon himself, was forced to admit that he had said and done nothing which could warrant such a belief on her part. For M. de Vandenesse that evening, the Marquise was, as she had always been, simple and friendly, sincere in her sorrow, glad to have a friend, proud to find a nature responsive to her own—nothing more. It had not entered her mind that a woman could yield twice; she had known love—love lay bleeding still in the depths of her heart, but she did not imagine that bliss could bring her its rapture twice, for she believed not merely in the intellect, but in the soul; and for her love was no simple attraction; it drew her with all noble attractions.

In a moment Charles became a young man again, enthralled by the splendor of a nature so lofty. He wished for a fuller initiation into the secret history of a life blighted rather by fate than by her own fault. Mme. d'Aiglemont heard him ask the cause of the overwhelming sorrow which had blended all the harmonies of sadness with her beauty; she gave him one glance, but that searching look was like a seal set upon some solemn compact.

"Ask no more such questions of me," she said. "Four years ago, on this very day, the man who loved me, for whom I would have given up everything, even my own self-respect, died, and died to save my name. That love was still young and pure and full of illusions when it came to an end. Before I gave way to passion—and never was a woman so urged by fate—I had been drawn into the mistake that ruins many a girl's life, a marriage with a man whose agreeable manners concealed his emptiness. Marriage plucked my hopes away one by one. And now, to-day, I have forfeited happiness through marriage, as well as the happiness styled criminal, and I have known no happiness. Nothing is left to me. If I could not die, at least I ought to be faithful to my memories."

No tears came with the words. Her eyes fell, and there was a slight twisting of the fingers interclasped, according to her wont. It was simply said, but in her voice there was a note of despair, deep as her love seemed to have been, which left Charles without a hope. The dreadful story of a life told in three sentences, with that twisting of the fingers for all comment, the might of anguish in a fragile woman, the dark depths masked by a fair face, the tears of four years of mourning fascinated Vandenesse; he sat silent and diminished in the presence of her woman's greatness and nobleness, seeing not the physical beauty so exquisite, so perfectly complete, but the soul so great in its power to feel. He had found, at last, the ideal of his fantastic imaginings, the ideal so vigorously invoked by all who look on life as the raw material of a passion for which many a one seeks ardently, and dies before he has grasped the whole of the dreamed-of treasure.

With those words of hers in his ears, in the presence of her sublime beauty, his own thoughts seemed poor and narrow. Powerless as he felt himself to find words of his own, simple enough and lofty enough to scale the heights of this exaltation, he took refuge in platitudes as to the destiny of women.

"Madame, we must either forget our pain, or hollow out a tomb for ourselves."

But reason always cuts a poor figure beside sentiment; the one being essentially restricted, like everything that is positive, while the other is infinite. To set to work to reason where you are required to feel, is the mark of a limited nature. Vandenesse therefore held his peace, sat awhile with his eyes fixed upon her, then came away. A prey to novel thoughts which exalted woman for him, he was in something the same position as a painter who has taken the vulgar studio model for a type of womanhood, and suddenly confronts the Mnemosyne of the Musee—that noblest and least appreciated of antique statues.

Charles de Vandenesse was deeply in love. He loved Mme. d'Aiglemont with the loyalty of youth, with the fervor that communicates such ineffable charm to a first passion, with a simplicity of heart of which a man only recovers some fragments when he loves again at a later day. Delicious first passion of youth, almost always deliciously savored by the woman who calls it forth; for at the golden prime of thirty, from the poetic summit of a woman's life, she can look out over the whole course of love—backwards into the past, forwards into the future—and, knowing all the price to be paid for love, enjoys her bliss with the dread of losing it ever present with her. Her soul is still fair with her waning youth, and passion daily gathers strength from the dismaying prospect of the coming days.

"This is love," Vandenesse said to himself this time as he left the Marquise, "and for my misfortune I love a woman wedded to her memories. It is hard work to struggle against a dead rival, never present to make blunders and fall out of favor, nothing of him left but his better qualities. What is it but a sort of high treason against the Ideal to attempt to break the charm of memory, to destroy the hopes that survive a lost lover, precisely because he only awakened longings, and all that is loveliest and most enchanting in love?"

These sober reflections, due to the discouragement and dread of failure with which love begins in earnest, were the last expiring effort of diplomatic reasoning. Thenceforward he knew no afterthoughts, he was the plaything of his love, and lost himself in the nothings of that strange inexplicable happiness which is full fed by a chance word, by silence, or a vague hope. He tried to love Platonically, came daily to breathe the air that she breathed, became almost a part of her house, and went everywhere with her, slave as he was of a tyrannous passion compounded of egoism and devotion of the completest. Love has its own instinct, finding the way to the heart, as the feeblest insect finds the way to its flower, with a will which nothing can dismay or turn aside. If feeling is sincere, its destiny is not doubtful. Let a woman begin to think that her life depends on the sincerity or fervor or earnestness which her lover shall put into his longings, and is there not sufficient in the thought to put her through all the tortures of dread? It is impossible for a woman, be she wife or mother, to be secure from a young man's love. One thing it is within her power to do—to refuse to see him as soon as she learns a secret which she never fails to guess. But this is too decided a step to take at an age when marriage has become a prosaic and tiresome yoke, and conjugal affection is something less than tepid (if indeed her husband has not already begun to neglect her). Is a woman plain? she is flattered by a love which gives her fairness. Is she young and charming? She is only to be won by a fascination as great as her own power to charm, that is to say, a fascination well-nigh irresistible. Is she virtuous? There is a love sublime in its earthliness which leads her to find something like absolution in the very greatness of the surrender and glory in a hard struggle. Everything is a snare. No lesson, therefore, is too severe where the temptation is so strong. The seclusion in which the Greeks and Orientals kept and keep their women, an example more and more followed in modern England, is the only safeguard of domestic morality; but under this system there is an end of all the charm of social intercourse; and society, and good breeding, and refinement of manners become impossible. The nations must take their choice.

So a few months went by, and Mme. d'Aiglemont discovered that her life was closely bound with this young man's life, without overmuch confusion in her surprise, and felt with something almost like pleasure that she shared his tastes and his thoughts. Had she adopted Vandenesse's ideas? Or was it Vandenesse who had made her lightest whims his own? She was not careful to inquire. She had been swept out already into the current of passion, and yet this adorable woman told herself with the confident reiteration of misgiving;

"Ah! no. I will be faithful to him who died for me."

Pascal said that "the doubt of God implies belief in God." And similarly it may be said that a woman only parleys when she has surrendered. A day came when the Marquise admitted to herself that she was loved, and with that admission came a time of wavering among countless conflicting thoughts and feelings. The superstitions of experience spoke their language. Should she be happy? Was it possible that she should find happiness outside the limits of the laws which society rightly or wrongly has set up for humanity to live by? Hitherto her cup of life had been full of bitterness. Was there any happy issue possible for the ties which united two human beings held apart by social conventions? And might not happiness be bought too dear? Still, this so ardently desired happiness, for which it is so natural to seek, might perhaps be found after all. Curiosity is always retained on the lover's side in the suit. The secret tribunal was still sitting when Vandenesse appeared, and his presence put the metaphysical spectre, reason, to flight.

If such are the successive transformations through which a sentiment, transient though it be, passes in a young man and a woman of thirty, there comes a moment of time when the shades of difference blend into each other, when all reasonings end in a single and final reflection which is lost and absorbed in the desire which it confirms. Then the longer the resistance, the mightier the voice of love. And here endeth this lesson, or rather this study made from the ecorche, to borrow a most graphic term from the studio, for in this history it is not so much intended to portray love as to lay bare its mechanism and its dangers. From this moment every day adds color to these dry bones, clothes them again with living flesh and blood and the charm of youth, and puts vitality into their movements; till they glow once more with the beauty, the persuasive grace of sentiment, the loveliness of life.

Charles found Mme. d'Aiglemont absorbed in thought, and to his "What is it?" spoken in thrilling tones grown persuasive with the heart's soft magic, she was careful not to reply. The delicious question bore witness to the perfect unity of their spirits; and the Marquise felt, with a woman's wonderful intuition, that to give any expression to the sorrow in her heart would be to make an advance. If, even now, each one of those words was fraught with significance for them both, in what fathomless depths might she not plunge at the first step? She read herself with a clear and lucid glance. She was silent, and Vandenesse followed her example.

"I am not feeling well," she said at last, taking alarm at the pause fraught with such great moment for them both, when the language of the eyes completely filled the blank left by the helplessness of speech.

"Madame," said Charles, and his voice was tender but unsteady with strong feeling, "soul and body are both dependent on each other. If you were happy, you would be young and fresh. Why do you refuse to ask of love all that love has taken from you? You think that your life is over when it is only just beginning. Trust yourself to a friend's care. It is so sweet to be loved."

"I am old already," she said; "there is no reason why I should not continue to suffer as in the past. And 'one must love,' do you say? Well, I must not, and I cannot. Your friendship has put some sweetness into my life, but beside you I care for no one, no one could efface my memories. A friend I accept; I should fly from a lover. Besides, would it be a very generous thing to do, to exchange a withered heart for a young heart; to smile upon illusions which now I cannot share, to cause happiness in which I should either have no belief, or tremble to lose? I should perhaps respond to his devotion with egoism, should weigh and deliberate while he felt; my memory would resent the poignancy of his happiness. No, if you love once, that love is never replaced, you see. Indeed, who would have my heart at this price?"

There was a tinge of heartless coquetry in the words, the last effort of discretion.

"If he loses courage, well and good, I shall live alone and faithful." The thought came from the very depths of the woman, for her it was the too slender willow twig caught in vain by a swimmer swept out by the current.

Vandenesse's involuntary shudder at her dictum plead more eloquently for him than all his past assiduity. Nothing moves a woman so much as the discovery of a gracious delicacy in us, such a refinement of sentiment as her own, for a woman the grace and delicacy are sure tokens of truth. Charles' start revealed the sincerity of his love. Mme. d'Aiglemont learned the strength of his affection from the intensity of his pain.

"Perhaps you are right," he said coldly. "New love, new vexation of spirit."

Then he changed the subject, and spoke of indifferent matters; but he was visibly moved, and he concentrated his gaze on Mme. d'Aiglemont as if he were seeing her for the last time.

"Adieu, madame," he said, with emotion in his voice.

"Au revoir," said she, with that subtle coquetry, the secret of a very few among women.

He made no answer and went.

When Charles was no longer there, when his empty chair spoke for him, regrets flocked in upon her, and she found fault with herself. Passion makes an immense advance as soon as a woman persuades herself that she has failed somewhat in generosity or hurt a noble nature. In love there is never any need to be on our guard against the worst in us; that is a safeguard; a woman only surrenders at the summons of a virtue. "The floor of hell is paved with good intentions,"—it is no preacher's paradox.

Vandenesse stopped away for several days. Every evening at the accustomed hour the Marquise sat expectant in remorseful impatience. She could not write—that would be a declaration, and, moreover, her instinct told her that he would come back. On the sixth day he was announced, and never had she heard the name with such delight. Her joy frightened her.

"You have punished me well," she said, addressing him.

Vandenesse gazed at her in astonishment.

"Punished?" he echoed. "And for what?" He understood her quite well, but he meant to be avenged for all that he had suffered as soon as she suspected it.

"Why have you not come to see me?" she demanded with a smile.

"Then you have seen no visitors?" asked he, parrying the question.

"Yes. M. de Ronquerolles and M. de Marsay and young d'Escrignon came and stayed for nearly two hours, the first two yesterday, the last this morning. And besides, I have had a call, I believe, from Mme. Firmiani and from your sister, Mme. de Listomere."

Here was a new infliction, torture which none can comprehend unless they know love as a fierce and all-invading tyrant whose mildest symptom is a monstrous jealousy, a perpetual desire to snatch away the beloved from every other influence.

"What!" thought he to himself, "she has seen visitors, she has been with happy creatures, and talking to them, while I was unhappy and all alone."

He buried his annoyance forthwith, and consigned love to the depths of his heart, like a coffin to the sea. His thoughts were of the kind that never find expression in words; they pass through the mind swiftly as a deadly acid, that poisons as it evaporates and vanishes. His brow, however, was over-clouded; and Mme. d'Aiglemont, guided by her woman's instinct, shared his sadness without understanding it. She had hurt him, unwittingly, as Vandenesse knew. He talked over his position with her, as if his jealousy were one of those hypothetical cases which lovers love to discuss. Then the Marquise understood it all. She was so deeply moved, that she could not keep back the tears—and so these lovers entered the heaven of love.

Heaven and Hell are two great imaginative conceptions formulating our ideas of Joy and Sorrow—those two poles about which human existence revolves. Is not heaven a figure of speech covering now and for evermore an infinite of human feeling impossible to express save in its accidents—since that Joy is one? And what is Hell but the symbol of our infinite power to suffer tortures so diverse that of our pain it is possible to fashion works of art, for no two human sorrows are alike?

One evening the two lovers sat alone and side by side, silently watching one of the fairest transformations of the sky, a cloudless heaven taking hues of pale gold and purple from the last rays of the sunset. With the slow fading of the daylight, sweet thoughts seem to awaken, and soft stirrings of passion, and a mysterious sense of trouble in the midst of calm. Nature sets before us vague images of bliss, bidding us enjoy the happiness within our reach, or lament it when it has fled. In those moments fraught with enchantment, when the tender light in the canopy of the sky blends in harmony with the spells working within, it is difficult to resist the heart's desires grown so magically potent. Cares are blunted, joy becomes ecstasy; pain, intolerable anguish. The pomp of sunset gives the signal for confessions and draws them forth. Silence grows more dangerous than speech for it gives to eyes all the power of the infinite of the heavens reflected in them. And for speech, the least word has irresistible might. Is not the light infused into the voice and purple into the glances? Is not heaven within us, or do we feel that we are in the heavens?

Vandenesse and Julie—for so she had allowed herself to be called for the past few days by him whom she loved to speak of as Charles—Vandenesse and Julie were talking together, but they had drifted very far from their original subject; and if their spoken words had grown meaningless they listened in delight to the unspoken thoughts that lurked in the sounds. Her hand lay in his. She had abandoned it to him without a thought that she had granted a proof of love.

Together they leaned forward to look out upon a majestic cloud country, full of snows and glaciers and fantastic mountain peaks with gray stains of shadow on their sides, a picture composed of sharp contrasts between fiery red and the shadows of darkness, filling the skies with a fleeting vision of glory which cannot be reproduced—magnificent swaddling-bands of sunrise, bright shrouds of the dying sun. As they leaned Julie's hair brushed lightly against Vandenesse's cheek. She felt that light contact, and shuddered violently, and he even more, for imperceptibly they both had reached one of those inexplicable crises when quiet has wrought upon the senses until every faculty of perception is so keen that the slightest shock fills the heart lost in melancholy with sadness that overflows in tears; or raises joy to ecstasy in a heart that is lost in the vertigo of love. Almost involuntarily Julie pressed her lover's hand. That wooing pressure gave courage to his timidity. All the joy of the present, all the hopes of the future were blended in the emotion of a first caress, the bashful trembling kiss that Mme. d'Aiglemont received upon her cheek. The slighter the concession, the more dangerous and insinuating it was. For their double misfortune it was only too sincere a revelation. Two noble natures had met and blended, drawn each to each by every law of natural attraction, held apart by every ordinance.

General d'Aiglemont came in at that very moment.

"The Ministry has gone out," he said. "Your uncle will be in the new cabinet. So you stand an uncommonly good chance of an embassy, Vandenesse."

Charles and Julie looked at each other and flushed red. That blush was one more tie to unite them; there was one thought and one remorse in either mind; between two lovers guilty of a kiss there is a bond quite as strong and terrible as the bond between two robbers who have murdered a man. Something had to be said by way of reply.

"I do not care to leave Paris now," Charles said.

"We know why," said the General, with the knowing air of a man who discovers a secret. "You do not like to leave your uncle, because you do not wish to lose your chance of succeeding to the title."

The Marquise took refuge in her room, and in her mind passed a pitiless verdict upon her husband.

"His stupidity is really beyond anything!"

IV

THE FINGER OF GOD

Between the Barriere d'Italie and the Barriere de la Sante, along the boulevard which leads to the Jardin des Plantes, you have a view of Paris fit to send an artist or the tourist, the most blase in matters of landscape, into ecstasies. Reach the slightly higher ground where the line of boulevard, shaded by tall, thick-spreading trees, curves with the grace of some green and silent forest avenue, and you see spread out at your feet a deep valley populous with factories looking almost countrified among green trees and the brown streams of the Bievre or the Gobelins.

On the opposite slope, beneath some thousands of roofs packed close together like heads in a crowd, lurks the squalor of the Faubourg Saint-Marceau. The imposing cupola of the Pantheon, and the grim melancholy dome of the Val-du-Grace, tower proudly up above a whole town in itself, built amphitheatre-wise; every tier being grotesquely represented by a crooked line of street, so that the two public monuments look like a huge pair of giants dwarfing into insignificance the poor little houses and the tallest poplars in the valley. To your left behold the observatory, the daylight, pouring athwart its windows and galleries, producing such fantastical strange effects that the building looks like a black spectral skeleton. Further yet in the distance rises the elegant lantern tower of the Invalides, soaring up between the bluish pile of the Luxembourg and the gray tours of Saint-Sulpice. From this standpoint the lines of the architecture are blended with green leaves and gray shadows, and change every moment with every aspect of the heavens, every alteration of light or color in the sky. Afar, the skyey spaces themselves seem to be full of buildings; near, wind the serpentine curves of waving trees and green footpaths.

Away to your right, through a great gap in this singular landscape, you see the canal Saint-Martin, a long pale stripe with its edging of reddish stone quays and fringes of lime avenue. The long rows of buildings beside it, in genuine Roman style, are the public granaries.

Beyond, again, on the very last plane of all, see the smoke-dimmed slopes of Belleville covered with houses and windmills, which blend their freaks of outline with the chance effects of cloud. And still, between that horizon, vague as some childish recollection, and the serried range of roofs in the valley, a whole city lies out of sight: a huge city, engulfed, as it were, in a vast hollow between the pinnacles of the Hopital de la Pitie and the ridge line of the Cimetiere de l'Est, between suffering on the one hand and death on the other; a city sending up a smothered roar like Ocean grumbling at the foot of a cliff, as if to let you know that "I am here!"

When the sunlight pours like a flood over this strip of Paris, purifying and etherealizing the outlines, kindling answering lights here and there in the window panes, brightening the red tiles, flaming about the golden crosses, whitening walls and transforming the atmosphere into a gauzy veil, calling up rich contrasts of light and fantastic shadow; when the sky is blue and earth quivers in the heat, and the bells are pealing, then you shall see one of the eloquent fairy scenes which stamp themselves for ever on the imagination, a scene that shall find as fanatical worshipers as the wondrous views of Naples and Byzantium or the isles of Florida. Nothing is wanting to complete the harmony, the murmur of the world of men and the idyllic quiet of solitude, the voices of a million human creatures and the voice of God. There lies a whole capital beneath the peaceful cypresses of Pere-Lachaise.

The landscape lay in all its beauty, sparkling in the spring sunlight, as I stood looking out over it one morning, my back against a huge elm-tree that flung its yellow flowers to the wind. At the sight of the rich and glorious view before me, I thought bitterly of the scorn with which even in our literature we affect to hold this land of ours, and poured maledictions on the pitiable plutocrats who fall out of love with fair France, and spend their gold to acquire the right of sneering at their own country, by going through Italy at a gallop and inspecting that desecrated land through an opera-glass. I cast loving eyes on modern Paris. I was beginning to dream dreams, when the sound of a kiss disturbed the solitude and put philosophy to flight. Down the sidewalk, along the steep bank, above the rippling water, I saw beyond the Ponte des Gobelins the figure of a woman, dressed with the daintiest simplicity; she was still young, as it seemed to me, and the blithe gladness of the landscape was reflected in her sweet face. Her companion, a handsome young man, had just set down a little boy. A prettier child has never been seen, and to this day I do not know whether it was the little one or his mother who received the kiss. In their young faces, in their eyes, their smile, their every movement, you could read the same deep and tender thought. Their arms were interlaced with such glad swiftness; they drew close together with such marvelous unanimity of impulse that, conscious of nothing but themselves, they did not so much as see me. A second child, however—a little girl, who had turned her back upon them in sullen discontent—threw me a glance, and the expression in her eyes startled me. She was as pretty and engaging as the little brother whom she left to run about by himself, sometimes before, sometimes after their mother and her companion; but her charm was less childish, and now, as she stood mute and motionless, her attitude and demeanor suggested a torpid snake. There was something indescribably mechanical in the way in which the pretty woman and her companion paced up and down. In absence of mind, probably, they were content to walk to and fro between the little bridge and a carriage that stood waiting nearby at a corner in the boulevard, turning, stopping short now and again, looking into each other's eyes, or breaking into laughter as their casual talk grew lively or languid, grave or gay.

I watched this delicious picture a while from my hiding-place by the great elm-tree, and should have turned away no doubt and respected their privacy, if it had not been for a chance discovery. In the face of the brooding, silent, elder child I saw traces of thought overdeep for her age. When her mother and the young man at her side turned and came near, her head was frequently lowered; the furtive sidelong glances of intelligence that she gave the pair and the child her brother were nothing less than extraordinary. Sometimes the pretty woman or her friend would stroke the little boy's fair curls, or lay a caressing finger against the baby throat or the white collar as he played at keeping step with them; and no words can describe the shrewd subtlety, the ingenuous malice, the fierce intensity which lighted up that pallid little face with the faint circles already round the eyes. Truly there was a man's power of passion in the strange-looking, delicate little girl. Here were traces of suffering or of thought in her; and which is the more certain token of death when life is in blossom—physical suffering, or the malady of too early thought preying upon a soul as yet in bud? Perhaps a mother knows. For my own part, I know of nothing more dreadful to see than an old man's thoughts on a child's forehead; even blasphemy from girlish lips is less monstrous.

The almost stupid stolidity of this child who had begun to think already, her rare gestures, everything about her, interested me. I scrutinized her curiously. Then the common whim of the observer drew me to compare her with her brother, and to note their likeness and unlikeness.

Her brown hair and dark eyes and look of precocious power made a rich contrast with the little one's fair curled head and sea-green eyes and winning helplessness. She, perhaps, was seven or eight years of age; the boy was full four years younger. Both children were dressed alike; but here again, looking closely, I noticed a difference. It was very slight, a little thing enough; but in the light of after events I saw that it meant a whole romance in the past, a whole tragedy to come. The little brown-haired maid wore a linen collar with a plain hem, her brother's was edged with dainty embroidery, that was all; but therein lay the confession of a heart's secret, a tacit preference which a child can read in the mother's inmost soul as clearly as if the spirit of God revealed it. The fair-haired child, careless and glad, looked almost like a girl, his skin was so fair and fresh, his movements so graceful, his look so sweet; while his older sister, in spite of her energy, in spite of the beauty of her features and her dazzling complexion, looked like a sickly little boy. In her bright eyes there was none of the humid softness which lends such charm to children's faces; they seemed, like courtiers' eyes, to be dried by some inner fire; and in her pallor there was a certain swarthy olive tint, the sign of vigorous character. Twice her little brother came to her, holding out a tiny hunting-horn with a touching charm, a winning look, and wistful expression, which would have sent Charlet into ecstasies, but she only scowled in answer to his "Here, Helene, will you take it?" so persuasively spoken. The little girl, so sombre and vehement beneath her apparent indifference, shuddered, and even flushed red when her brother came near her; but the little one seemed not to notice his sister's dark mood, and his unconsciousness, blended with earnestness, marked a final difference in character between the child and the little girl, whose brow was overclouded already by the gloom of a man's knowledge and cares.

"Mamma, Helene will not play," cried the little one, seizing an opportunity to complain while the two stood silent on the Ponte des Gobelins.

"Let her alone, Charles; you know very well that she is always cross."

Tears sprang to Helene's eyes at the words so thoughtlessly uttered by her mother as she turned abruptly to the young man by her side. The child devoured the speech in silence, but she gave her brother one of those sagacious looks that seemed inexplicable to me, glancing with a sinister expression from the bank where he stood to the Bievre, then at the bridge and the view, and then at me.

I was afraid lest my presence should disturb the happy couple; I slipped away and took refuge behind a thicket of elder trees, which completely screened me from all eyes. Sitting quietly on the summit of the bank, I watched the ever-changing landscape and the fierce-looking little girl, for with my head almost on a level with the boulevard I could still see her through the leaves. Helene seemed uneasy over my disappearance, her dark eyes looked for me down the alley and behind the trees with indefinable curiosity. What was I to her? Then Charles' baby laughter rang out like a bird's song in the silence. The tall, young man, with the same fair hair, was dancing him in his arms, showering kisses upon him, and the meaningless baby words of that "little language" which rises to our lips when we play with children. The mother looked on smiling, now and then, doubtless, putting in some low word that came up from the heart, for her companion would stop short in his full happiness, and the blue eyes that turned towards her were full of glowing light and love and worship. Their voices, blending with the child's voice, reached me with a vague sense of a caress. The three figures, charming in themselves, composed a lovely scene in a glorious landscape, filling it with a pervasive unimaginable grace. A delicately fair woman, radiant with smiles, a child of love, a young man with the irresistible charm of youth, a cloudless sky; nothing was wanting in nature to complete a perfect harmony for the delight of the soul. I found myself smiling as if their happiness had been my own.

The clocks struck nine. The young man gave a tender embrace to his companion, and went towards the tilbury which an old servant drove slowly to meet him. The lady had grown grave and almost sad. The child's prattle sounded unchecked through the last farewell kisses. Then the tilbury rolled away, and the lady stood motionless, listening to the sound of the wheels, watching the little cloud of dust raised by its passage along the road. Charles ran down the green pathway back to the bridge to join his sister. I heard his silver voice calling to her.

"Why did you not come to say good-bye to my good friend?" cried he.

Helene looked up. Never surely did such hatred gleam from a child's eyes as from hers at that moment when she turned them on the brother who stood beside her on the bank side. She gave him an angry push. Charles lost his footing on the steep slope, stumbled over the roots of a tree, and fell headlong forwards, dashing his forehead on the sharp-edged stones of the embankment, and, covered with blood, disappeared over the edge into the muddy river. The turbid water closed over a fair, bright head with a shower of splashes; one sharp shriek after another rang in my ears; then the sounds were stifled by the thick stream, and the poor child sank with a dull sound as if a stone had been thrown into the water. The accident had happened with more than lightning swiftness. I sprang down the footpath, and Helene, stupefied with horror, shrieked again and again:

"Mamma! mamma!"

The mother was there at my side. She had flown to the spot like a bird. But neither a mother's eyes nor mine could find the exact place where the little one had gone under. There was a wide space of black hurrying water, and below in the bed of the Bievre ten feet of mud. There was not the smallest possibility of saving the child. No one was stirring at that hour on a Sunday morning, and there are neither barges nor anglers on the Bievre. There was not a creature in sight, not a pole to plumb the filthy stream. What need was there for me to explain how the ugly-looking accident had happened—accident or misfortune, whichever it might be? Had Helene avenged her father? Her jealousy surely was the sword of God. And yet when I looked at the mother I shivered. What fearful ordeal awaited her when she should return to her husband, the judge before whom she must stand all her days? And here with her was an inseparable, incorruptible witness. A child's forehead is transparent, a child's face hides no thoughts, and a lie, like a red flame set within glows out red that colors even the eyes. But the unhappy woman had not thought as yet of the punishment awaiting her at home; she was staring into the Bievre.

Such an event must inevitably send ghastly echoes through a woman's life, and here is one of the most terrible of the reverberations that troubled Julie's love from time to time.

Several years had gone by. The Marquis de Vandenesse wore mourning for his father, and succeeded to his estates. One evening, therefore, after dinner it happened that a notary was present in his house. This was no pettifogging lawyer after Sterne's pattern, but a very solid, substantial notary of Paris, one of your estimable men who do a stupid thing pompously, set down a foot heavily upon your private corn, and then ask what in the world there is to cry out about? If, by accident, they come to know the full extent of the enormity, "Upon my word," cry they, "I hadn't a notion!" This was a well-intentioned ass, in short, who could see nothing in life but deeds and documents.

Mme. de Aiglemont had been dining with M. de Vandenesse; her husband had excused himself before dinner was over, for he was taking his two children to the play. They were to go to some Boulevard theatre or other, to the Ambigu-Comique or the Gaiete, sensational melodrama being judged harmless here in Paris, and suitable pabulum for childhood, because innocence is always triumphant in the fifth act. The boy and girl had teased their father to be there before the curtain rose, so he had left the table before dessert was served.

But the notary, the imperturbable notary, utterly incapable of asking himself why Mme. d'Aiglemont should have allowed her husband and children to go without her to the play, sat on as if he were screwed to his chair. Dinner was over, dessert had been prolonged by discussion, and coffee delayed. All these things consumed time, doubtless precious, and drew impatient movements from that charming woman; she looked not unlike a thoroughbred pawing the ground before a race; but the man of law, to whom horses and women were equally unknown quantities, simply thought the Marquise a very lively and sparkling personage. So enchanted was he to be in the company of a woman of fashion and a political celebrity, that he was exerting himself to shine in conversation, and taking the lady's forced smile for approbation, talked on with unflagging spirit, till the Marquise was almost out of patience.

The master of the house, in concert with the lady, had more than once maintained an eloquent silence when the lawyer expected a civil reply; but these significant pauses were employed by the talkative nuisance in looking for anecdotes in the fire. M. de Vandenesse had recourse to his watch; the charming Marquise tried the experiment of fastening her bonnet strings, and made as if she would go. But she did not go, and the notary, blind and deaf, and delighted with himself, was quite convinced that his interesting conversational powers were sufficient to keep the lady on the spot.

"I shall certainly have that woman for a client," said he to himself.

Meanwhile the Marquise stood, putting on her gloves, twisting her fingers, looking from the equally impatient Marquis de Vandenesse to the lawyer, still pounding away. At every pause in the worthy man's fire of witticisms the charming pair heaved a sigh of relief, and their looks said plainly, "At last! He is really going!"

Nothing of the kind. It was a nightmare which could only end in exasperating the two impassioned creatures, on whom the lawyer had something of the fascinating effect of a snake on a pair of birds; before long they would be driven to cut him short.

The clever notary was giving them the history of the discreditable ways in which one du Tillet (a stockbroker then much in favor) had laid the foundations of his fortune; all the ins and outs of the whole disgraceful business were accurately put before them; and the narrator was in the very middle of his tale when M. de

Vandenesse heard the clock strike nine. Then it became clear to him that his legal adviser was very emphatically an idiot who must be sent forthwith about his business. He stopped him resolutely with a gesture.

"The tongs, my lord Marquis?" queried the notary, handing the object in question to his client.

"No, monsieur, I am compelled to send you away. Mme. d'Aiglemont wishes to join her children, and I shall have the honor of escorting her."

"Nine o'clock already! Time goes like a shadow in pleasant company," said the man of law, who had talked on end for the past hour.

He looked for his hat, planted himself before the fire, with a suppressed hiccough; and, without heeding the Marquise's withering glances, spoke once more to his impatient client:

"To sum up, my lord Marquis. Business before all things. To-morrow, then, we must subpoena your brother; we will proceed to make out the inventory, and faith, after that——"

So ill had the lawyer understood his instructions, that his impression was the exact opposite to the one intended. It was a delicate matter, and Vandenesse, in spite of himself, began to put the thick-headed notary right. The discussion which followed took up a certain amount of time.

"Listen," the diplomatist said at last at a sign from the lady, "You are puzzling my brains; come back to-morrow, and if the writ is not issued by noon to-morrow, the days of grace will expire, and then—"

As he spoke, a carriage entered the courtyard. The poor woman turned sharply away at the sound to hide the tears in her eyes. The Marquis rang to give the servant orders to say that he was not at home; but before the footman could answer the bell, the lady's husband reappeared. He had returned unexpectedly from the Gaiete, and held both children by the hand. The little girl's eyes were red; the boy was fretful and very cross.

"What can have happened?" asked the Marquise.

"I will tell you by and by," said the General, and catching a glimpse through an open door of newspapers on the table in the adjoining sitting-room, he went off. The Marquise, at the end of her patience, flung herself down on the sofa in desperation. The notary, thinking it incumbent upon him to be amiable with the children, spoke to the little boy in an insinuating tone:

"Well, my little man, and what is there on at the theatre?"

"The Valley of the Torrent," said Gustave sulkily.

"Upon my word and honor," declared the notary, "authors

nowadays are half crazy. The Valley of the Torrent! Why not the Torrent of the Valley? It is conceivable that a valley might be without a torrent in it; now if they had said the Torrent of the Valley, that would have been something clear, something precise, something definite and comprehensible. But never mind that. Now, how is the drama to take place in a torrent and in a valley? You will tell me that in these days the principal attraction lies in the scenic effect, and the title is a capital advertisement.—And did you enjoy it, my little friend?" he continued, sitting down before the child.

When the notary pursued his inquiries as to the possibilities of a drama in the bed of a torrent, the little girl turned slowly away and began to cry. Her mother did not notice this in her intense annoyance.

"Oh! yes, monsieur, I enjoyed it very much," said the child. "There is a dear little boy in the play, and he was all alone in the world, because his papa could not have been his real papa. And when he came to the top of the bridge over the torrent, a big, naughty man with a beard, dressed all in black, came and threw him into the water. And then Helene began to sob and cry, and everybody scolded us, and father brought us away quick, quick——"

M. de Vandenesse and the Marquise looked on in dull amazement, as if all power to think or move had been suddenly paralyzed.

"Do be quiet, Gustave!" cried the General. "I told you that you were not to talk about anything that happened at the play, and you have forgotten what I said already."

"Oh, my lord Marquis, your lordship must excuse him," cried the notary. "I ought not to have asked questions, but I had no idea-"

"He ought not to have answered them," said the General, looking sternly at the child.

It seemed that the Marquise and the master of the house both perfectly understood why the children had come back so suddenly. Mme. d'Aiglemont looked at her daughter, and rose as if to go to her, but a terrible convulsion passed over her face, and all that could be read in it was relentless severity.

"That will do, Helene," she said. "Go into the other room, and leave off crying."

"What can she have done, poor child!" asked the notary, thinking to appease the mother's anger and to stop Helene's tears at one stroke. "So pretty as she is, she must be as good as can be; never anything but a joy to her mother, I will be bound. Isn't that so, my little girl?"

Helene cowered, looked at her mother, dried her eyes, struggled for composure, and took refuge in the next room.

"And you, madame, are too good a mother not to love all your children alike. You are too good a woman, besides, to have any of those lamentable preferences which have such fatal effects, as we lawyers have only too much reason to know. Society goes through our hands; we see its passions in that most revolting form, greed. Here it is the mother of a family trying to disinherit her husband's children to enrich the others whom she loves better; or it is the husband who tries to leave all his property to the child who has done his best to earn his mother's hatred. And then begin quarrels, and fears, and deeds, and defeasances, and sham sales, and trusts, and all the rest of it; a pretty mess, in fact, it is pitiable, upon my honor, pitiable! There are fathers that will spend their whole lives in cheating their children and robbing their wives. Yes, robbing is the only word for it. We were talking of tragedy; oh! I can assure you of this that if we were at liberty to tell the real reasons of some donations that I know of, our modern dramatists would have the material for some sensational bourgeois dramas. How the wife manages to get her way, as she invariably does, I cannot think; for in spite of appearances, and in spite of their weakness, it is always the women who carry the day. Ah! by the way, they don't take me in. I always know the reason at the bottom of those predilections which the world politely styles 'unaccountable.' But in justice to the husbands, I must say that they never discover anything. You will tell me that this is a merciful dispens—"

Helene had come back to the drawing-room with her father, and was listening attentively. So well did she understand all that was said, that she gave her mother a frightened glance, feeling, with a child's quick instinct, that these remarks would aggravate the punishment hanging over her. The Marquise turned her white face to Vandenesse; and, with terror in her eyes, indicated her husband, who stood with his eyes fixed absently on the flower pattern of the carpet. The diplomatist, accomplished man of the world though he was, could no longer contain his wrath, he gave the man of law a withering glance.

"Step this way, sir," he said, and he went hurriedly to the door of the ante-chamber; the notary left his sentence half finished, and followed, quaking, and the husband and wife were left together.

"Now, sir" said the Marquise de Vandenesse—he banged the drawing-room door, and spoke with concentrated rage—"ever since dinner you have done nothing but make blunders and talk folly. For heaven's sake, go. You will make the most frightful mischief before you have done. If you are a clever man in your profession, keep to your profession; and if by any chance you should go into society, endeavor to be more circumspect."

With that he went back to the drawing-room, and did not even wish the notary good-evening. For a moment that worthy stood dumfounded, bewildered, utterly at a loss. Then, when the buzzing in his ears subsided, he thought he heard someone moaning in the next room. Footsteps came and went, and bells were violently rung. He was by no means anxious to meet the Marquis again, and found the use of his legs to make good his escape, only to run against a hurrying crowd of servants at the door.

"Just the way of all these grand folk," said he to himself outside in the street as he looked about for a cab. "They lead you on to talk with compliments, and you think you are amusing them. Not a bit of it. They treat you insolently; put you at a distance; even put you out at the door without scruple. After all, I talked very cleverly, I said nothing but what was sensible, well turned, and discreet; and, upon my word, he advises me to be more circumspect in future. I will take good care of that! Eh! the mischief take it! I am a notary and a member of my chamber!—Pshaw! it was an ambassador's fit of temper, nothing is sacred for people of that kind. To-morrow he shall explain what he meant by saying that I had done nothing but blunder and talk nonsense in his house. I will ask him for an explanation—that is, I will ask him to explain my mistake. After all is done and said, I am in the wrong perhaps—— Upon my word, it is very good of me to cudgel my brains like this. What business is it of mine?"

So the notary went home and laid the enigma before his spouse, with a complete account of the evening's events related in sequence.

And she replied, "My dear Crottat, His Excellency was perfectly right when he said that you had done nothing but blunder and talk folly."

"Why?"

"My dear, if I told you why, it would not prevent you from doing the same thing somewhere else to-morrow. I tell you again—talk of nothing but business when you go out; that is my advice to you."

"If you will not tell me, I shall ask him to-morrow—"

"Why, dear me! the veriest noodle is careful to hide a thing of that kind, and do you suppose that an ambassador will tell you about it? Really, Crottat, I have never known you so utterly devoid of common-sense."

"Thank you, my dear."

V

TWO MEETINGS

One of Napoleon's orderly staff-officers, who shall be known in this history only as the General or the Marquis, had come to spend the spring at Versailles. He made a large fortune under the Restoration; and as his place at Court would not allow him to go very far from Paris, he had taken a country house between the church and the barrier of Montreuil, on the road that leads to the Avenue de Saint-Cloud.

The house had been built originally as a retreat for the short-lived loves of some grand seigneur. The grounds were very large; the gardens on either side extending from the first houses of Montreuil to the thatched cottages near the barrier, so that the owner could enjoy all the pleasures of solitude with the city almost at his gates. By an odd piece of contradiction, the whole front of the house itself, with the principal entrance, gave directly upon the street. Perhaps in time past it was a tolerably lonely road, and indeed this theory looks all the more probable when one comes to think of it; for not so very far away, on this same road, Louis Quinze built a delicious summer villa for Mlle. de Romans, and the curious in such things will discover that the wayside casinos are adorned in a style that recalls traditions of the ingenious taste displayed in debauchery by our ancestors who, with all the license paid to their charge, sought to invest it with secrecy and mystery.

One winter evening the family were by themselves in the lonely house. The servants had received permission to go to Versailles to celebrate the wedding of one of their number. It was Christmas time, and the holiday makers, presuming upon the double festival, did not scruple to outstay their leave of absence; yet, as the General was well known to be a man of his word, the culprits felt some twinges of conscience as they danced on after the hour of return. The clocks struck eleven, and still there was no sign of the servants.

A deep silence prevailed over the country-side, broken only by the sound of the northeast wind whistling through the black branches, wailing about the house, dying in gusts along the corridors. The hard frost had purified the air, and held the earth in its grip; the roads gave back every sound with the hard metallic ring which always strikes us with a new surprise; the heavy footsteps of some belated reveler, or a cab returning to Paris, could be heard for a long distance with unwonted distinctness. Out in the courtyard a few dead leaves set a-dancing by some eddying gust found a voice for the night which fain had been silent. It was, in fact, one of those sharp, frosty evenings that wring barren expressions of pity from our selfish ease for wayfarers and the poor, and fills us with a luxurious sense of the comfort of the fireside.

But the family party in the salon at that hour gave not a thought to absent servants nor houseless folk, nor to the gracious charm with which a winter evening sparkles. No one played the philosopher out of season. Secure in the protection of an old soldier, women and children gave themselves up to the joys of home life, so delicious when there is no restraint upon feeling; and talk and play and glances are bright with frankness and affection.

The General sat, or more properly speaking, lay buried, in the depths of a huge, high-back armchair by the hearth. The heaped-up fire burned scorching clear with the excessive cold of the night. The good father leaned his head slightly to one side against the back of the chair, in the indolence of perfect serenity and a glow of happiness. The languid, half-sleepy droop of his outstretched arms seemed to complete his expression of placid content. He was watching his youngest, a boy of five or thereabouts, who, half clad as he was, declined to allow his mother to undress him. The little one fled from the night-gown and cap with which he was threatened now and again, and stoutly declined to part with his embroidered collar, laughing when his mother called to him, for he saw that she too was laughing at this declaration of infant independence. The next step was to go back to a game of romps with his sister. She was as much a child as he, but more mischievous; and she was older by two years, and could speak distinctly already, whereas his inarticulate words and confused ideas were a puzzle even to his parents. Little Moina's playfulness, somewhat coquettish already, provoked inextinguishable laughter, explosions of merriment which went off like fireworks for no apparent cause. As they tumbled about before the fire, unconcernedly displaying little plump bodies and delicate white contours, as the dark and golden curls mingled in a collision of rosy cheeks dimpled with childish glee, a father surely, a mother most certainly, must have understood those little souls, and seen the character and power of passion already developed for their eyes. As the cherubs frolicked about, struggling, rolling, and tumbling without fear of hurt on the soft carpet, its flowers looked pale beside the glowing white and red of their cheeks and the brilliant color of their shining eyes.

On the sofa by the fire, opposite the great armchair, the children's mother sat among a heap of scattered garments, with a little scarlet shoe in her hand. She seemed to have given herself up completely to the enjoyment of the moment; wavering discipline had relaxed into a sweet smile engraved upon her lips. At the age of six-and-thirty, or thereabouts, she was a beautiful woman still, by reason of the rare perfection of the outlines of her face, and at this moment light and warmth and happiness filled it with preternatural brightness.

Again and again her eyes wandered from her children, and their tender gaze was turned upon her husband's grave face; and now and again the eyes of husband and wife met with a silent exchange of happiness and thoughts from some inner depth.

The General's face was deeply bronzed, a stray lock of gray hair scored shadows on his forehead. The reckless courage of the battlefield could be read in the lines carved in his hollow cheeks, and gleams of rugged strength in the blue eyes; clearly the bit of red ribbon flaunting at his button-hole had been paid for by hardship and toil. An inexpressible kindliness and frankness shone out of the strong, resolute face which reflected his children's merriment; the gray-haired captain found it not so very hard to become a child again. Is there not always a little love of children in the heart of a soldier who has seen enough of the seamy side of life to know something of the piteous limitations of strength and the privileges of weakness?

At a round table rather further away, in a circle of bright lamplight that dimmed the feebler illumination of the wax candles on the chimney-piece, sat a boy of thirteen, rapidly turning the pages of a thick volume which he was reading, undisturbed by the shouts of the children. There was a boy's curiosity in his face. From his lyceens uniform he was evidently a schoolboy, and the book he was reading was the Arabian Nights. Small wonder that he was deeply absorbed. He sat perfectly still in a meditative attitude, with his elbow on the table, and his hand propping his head—the white fingers contrasting strongly with the brown hair into which they were thrust. As he sat, with the light turned full upon his face, and the rest of his body in shadow, he looked like one of Raphael's dark portraits of himself—a bent head and intent eyes filled with visions of the future.

Between the table and the Marquise a tall, beautiful girl sat at her tapestry frame; sometimes she drew back from her work, sometimes she bent over it, and her hair, picturesque in its ebony smoothness and darkness, caught the light of the lamp. Helene was a picture in herself. In her beauty there was a rare distinctive character of power and refinement. Though her hair was gathered up and drawn back from her face, so as to trace a clearly marked line about her head, so thick and abundant was it, so recalcitrant to the comb, that it sprang back in curl-tendrils to the nape of her neck. The bountiful line of eyebrows was evenly marked out in dark contrasting outline upon her pure forehead. On her upper lip, beneath the Grecian nose with its sensitively perfect curve of nostril, there lay a faint, swarthy shadow, the sign-manual of courage; but the enchanting roundness of contour, the frankly innocent expression of her other features, the transparence of the delicate carnations, the voluptuous softness of the lips, the flawless oval of the outline of the face, and with these, and more than all these, the saintlike expression in the girlish eyes, gave to her vigorous loveliness the distinctive touch of feminine grace, that enchanting modesty which we look for in these angels of peace and love. Yet there was no suggestion of fragility about her; and, surely, with so grand a woman's frame, so attractive a face, she must possess a corresponding warmth of heart and strength of soul.

She was as silent as her schoolboy brother. Seemingly a prey to the fateful maiden meditations which baffle a father's penetration and even a mother's sagacity, it was impossible to be certain whether it was the lamplight that cast those shadows that flitted over her face like thin clouds over a bright sky, or whether they were passing shades of secret and painful thoughts.

Husband and wife had quite forgotten the two older children at that moment, though now and again the General's questioning glance traveled to that second mute picture; a larger growth, a gracious realization, as it were, of the hopes embodied in the baby forms rioting in the foreground. Their faces made up a kind of living poem, illustrating life's various phases. The luxurious background of the salon, the different attitudes, the strong contrasts of coloring in the faces, differing with the character of differing ages, the modeling of the forms brought into high relief by the light—altogether it was a page of human life, richly illuminated beyond the art of painter, sculptor, or poet. Silence, solitude, night and winter lent a final touch of majesty to complete the simplicity and sublimity of this exquisite effect of nature's contriving. Married life is full of these sacred hours, which perhaps owe their indefinable charm to some vague memory of a better world. A divine radiance surely shines upon them, the destined compensation for some portion of earth's sorrows, the solace which enables man to accept life. We seem to behold a vision of an enchanted universe, the great conception of its system widens out before our eyes, and social life pleads for its laws by bidding us look to the future.

Yet in spite of the tender glances that Helene gave Abel and Moina after a fresh outburst of merriment; in spite of the look of gladness in her transparent face whenever she stole a glance at her father, a deep melancholy pervaded her gestures, her attitude, and more than all, her eyes veiled by their long lashes. Those white, strong hands, through which the light passed, tinting them with a diaphanous, almost fluid red—those hands were trembling. Once only did the eyes of the mother and daughter clash without shrinking, and the two women read each other's thoughts in a look, cold, wan, and respectful on Helene's part, sombre and threatening on her mother's. At once Helene's eyes were lowered to her work, she plied her needle swiftly, and it was long before she raised her head, bowed as it seemed by a weight of thought too heavy to bear. Was the Marquise over harsh with this one of her children? Did she think this harshness needful? Was she jealous of Helene's beauty?— She might still hope to rival Helene, but only by the magic arts of the toilette. Or again, had her daughter, like many a girl who reaches the clairvoyant age, read the secrets which this wife (to all appearance so religiously faithful in the fulfilment of her duties) believed to be buried in her own heart as deeply as in a grave?

Helene had reached an age when purity of soul inclines to pass over-rigid judgments. A certain order of mind is apt to exaggerate transgression into crime; imagination reacts upon conscience, and a young girl is a hard judge because she magnifies the seriousness of the offence. Helene seemed to think herself worthy of no one. Perhaps there was a secret in her past life, perhaps something had happened, unintelligible to her at the time, but with gradually developing significance for a mind grown susceptible to religious influences; something which lately seemed to have degraded her, as it were, in her own eyes, and according to her own romantic standard. This change in her demeanor dated from the day of reading Schiller's noble tragedy of Wilhelm Tell in a new series of translations. Her mother scolded her for letting the book fall, and then remarked to herself that the passage which had so worked on Helene's feelings was the scene in which Wilhelm Tell, who spilt the blood of a tyrant to save a nation, fraternizes in some sort with John the Parricide. Helene had grown humble, dutiful, and self-contained; she no longer cared for gaiety. Never had she made so much of her father, especially when the Marquise was not by to watch her girlish caresses. And yet, if Helene's affection for her mother had cooled at all, the change in her manner was so slight as to be almost imperceptible; so slight that the General could not have noticed it, jealous though he might be of the harmony of home. No masculine insight could have sounded the depths of those two feminine natures; the one was young and generous, the other sensitive and proud; the first had a wealth of indulgence in her nature, the second was full of craft and love. If the Marquise made her daughter's life a burden to her by a woman's subtle tyranny, it was a tyranny invisible to all but the victim; and for the rest, these conjectures only called forth after the event must remain conjectures. Until this night no accusing flash of light had escaped either of them, but an ominous mystery was too surely growing up between them, a mystery known only to themselves and God.

"Come, Abel," called the Marquise, seizing on her opportunity when the children were tired of play and still for a moment. "Come, come, child; you must be put to bed—"

And with a glance that must be obeyed, she caught him up and took him on her knee.

"What!" exclaimed the General. "Half-past ten o'clock, and not one of the servants has come back! The rascals!—Gustave," he added, turning to his son, "I allowed you to read that book only on the condition that you should put it away at ten o'clock. You ought to have shut up the book at the proper time and gone to bed, as you promised. If you mean to make your mark in the world, you must keep your word; let it be a second religion to you, and a point of honor. Fox, one of the greatest English orators, was remarkable, above all things, for the beauty of his character, and the very first of his qualities was the scrupulous faithfulness with which he kept his engagements. When he was a child, his father (an Englishman of the old school) gave him a pretty strong lesson which he never forgot. Like most rich Englishmen, Fox's father had a country house and a considerable park about it. Now, in the park there was an old summer-house, and orders had been given that this summer-house was to be pulled down and put up somewhere else where there was a finer view. Fox was just about your age, and had come home for the holidays. Boys are fond of seeing things pulled to pieces, so young Fox asked to stay on at home for a few days longer to see the old summer-house taken down; but his father said that he must go back to school on the proper day, so there was anger between father and son. Fox's mother (like all mammas) took the boy's part. Then the father solemnly promised that the summer-house should stay where it was till the next holidays.

"So Fox went back to school; and his father, thinking that lessons would soon drive the whole thing out of the boy's mind, had the summer-house pulled down and put up in the new position. But as it happened, the persistent youngster thought of nothing but that summer-house; and as soon as he came home again, his first care was to go out to look at the old building, and he came in to breakfast looking quite doleful, and said to his father, 'You have broken your promise.' The old English gentleman said with confusion full of dignity, 'That is true, my boy; but I will make amends. A man ought to think of keeping his word before he thinks of his fortune; for by keeping his word he will gain fortune, while all the fortunes in the world will not efface the stain left on your conscience by a breach of faith.' Then he gave orders that the summer-house should be put up again in the old place, and when it had been rebuilt he had it taken down again for his son to see. Let this be a lesson to you, Gustave."

Gustave had been listening with interest, and now he closed the book at once. There was a moment's silence, while the General took possession of Moina, who could scarcely keep her eyes open. The little one's languid head fell back on her father's breast, and in a moment she was fast asleep, wrapped round about in her golden curls.

Just then a sound of hurrying footsteps rang on the pavement out in the street, immediately followed by three knocks on the street door, waking the echoes of the house. The reverberating blows told, as plainly as a cry for help that here was a man flying for his life. The house dog barked furiously. A thrill of excitement ran through Helene and Gustave and the General and his wife; but neither Abel, with the night-cap strings just tied under his chin, nor Moina awoke.

"The fellow is in a hurry!" exclaimed the General. He put the little girl down on the chair, and hastened out of the room, heedless of his wife's entreating cry, "Dear, do not go down—"

He stepped into his own room for a pair of pistols, lighted a dark lantern, sprang at lightning speed down the staircase, and in another minute reached the house door, his oldest boy fearlessly following.

"Who is there?" demanded he.

"Let me in," panted a breathless voice.

"Are you a friend?"

"Yes, friend."

"Are you alone?"

"Yes! But let me in; they are after me!"

The General had scarcely set the door ajar before a man slipped into the porch with the uncanny swiftness of a shadow. Before the master of the house could prevent him, the intruder had closed the door with a well-directed kick, and set his back against it resolutely, as if he were determined that it should not be opened again. In a moment the General had his lantern and pistol at a level with the stranger's breast, and beheld a man of medium height in a fur-lined pelisse. It was an old man's garment, both too large and too long for its present wearer. Chance or caution had slouched the man's hat over his eyes.

"You can lower your pistol, sir," said this person. "I do not claim to stay in your house against your will; but if I leave it, death is waiting for me at the barrier. And what a death! You would be answerable to God for it! I ask for your hospitality for two hours. And bear this in mind, sir, that, suppliant as I am, I have a right to command with the despotism of necessity. I want the Arab's hospitality. Either I and my secret must be inviolable, or open the door and I will go to my death. I want secrecy, a safe hiding-place, and water. Oh! water!" he cried again, with a rattle in his throat.

"Who are you?" demanded the General, taken aback by the stranger's feverish volubility.

"Ah! who am I? Good, open the door, and I will put a distance between us," retorted the other, and there was a diabolical irony in his tone.

Dexterously as the Marquis passed the light of the lantern over the man's face, he could only see the lower half of it, and that in nowise prepossessed him in favor of this singular claimant of hospitality. The cheeks were livid and quivering, the features dreadfully contorted. Under the shadow of the hat-brim a pair of eyes gleamed out like flames; the feeble candle-light looked almost dim in comparison. Some sort of answer must be made however.

"Your language, sir, is so extraordinary that in my place you yourself—"

"My life is in your hands!" the intruder broke in. The sound of his voice was dreadful to hear.

"Two hours?" said the Marquis, wavering.

"Two hours," echoed the other.

Then quite suddenly, with a desperate gesture, he pushed back his hat and left his forehead bare, and, as if he meant to try a final expedient, he gave the General a glance that seemed to plunge like a vivid flash into his very soul. That electrical discharge of intelligence and will was swift as lightning and crushing as a thunderbolt; for there are moments when a human being is invested for a brief space with inexplicable power.

"Come, whoever you may be, you shall be in safety under my roof," the master of the house said gravely at last, acting, as he imagined, upon one of those intuitions which a man cannot always explain to himself.

"God will repay you!" said the stranger, with a deep, involuntary sigh.

"Have you weapons?" asked the General.

For all answer the stranger flung open his fur pelisse, and scarcely gave the other time for a glance before he wrapped it about him again. To all appearance he was unarmed and in evening dress. Swift as the soldier's scrutiny had been, he saw something, however, which made him exclaim:

"Where the devil have you been to get yourself in such a mess in such dry weather?"

"More questions!" said the stranger haughtily.

At the words the Marquis caught sight of his son, and his own late homily on the strict fulfilment of a given word came up to his mind. In lively vexation, he exclaimed, not without a touch of anger:

"What! little rogue, you here when you ought to be in bed?"

"Because I thought I might be of some good in danger," answered Gustave.

"There, go up to your room," said his father, mollified by the reply.—"And you" (addressing the stranger), "come with me."

The two men grew as silent as a pair of gamblers who watch each other's play with mutual suspicions. The General himself began to be troubled with ugly presentiments. The strange visit weighed upon his mind already like a nightmare; but he had passed his word, there was no help for it now, and he led the way along the passages and stairways till they reached a large room on the second floor immediately above the salon. This was an empty room where linen was dried in the winter. It had but the one door, and for all decoration boasted one solitary shabby looking-glass above the chimney-piece, left by the previous owner, and a great pier glass, placed provisionally opposite the fireplace until such time as a use should be found for it in the rooms below. The four yellowish walls were bare. The floor had never been swept. The huge attic was icy-cold, and the furniture consisted of a couple of rickety straw-bottomed chairs, or rather frames of chairs. The General set the lantern down upon the chimney-piece. Then he spoke:

"It is necessary for your own safety to hide you in this comfortless attic. And, as you have my promise to keep your secret, you will permit me to lock you in."

The other bent his head in acquiescence.

"I asked for nothing but a hiding-place, secrecy, and water," returned he.

"I will bring you some directly," said the Marquis, shutting the door cautiously. He groped his way down into the salon for a lamp before going to the kitchen to look for a carafe.

"Well, what is it?" the Marquise asked quickly.

"Nothing, dear," he returned coolly.

"But we listened, and we certainly heard you go upstairs with somebody."

"Helene," said the General, and he looked at his daughter, who raised her face, "bear in mind that your father's honor depends upon your discretion. You must have heard nothing."

The girl bent her head in answer. The Marquise was confused and smarting inwardly at the way in which her husband had thought fit to silence her.

Meanwhile the General went for the bottle and a tumbler, and returned to the room above. His prisoner was leaning against the chimney-piece, his head was bare, he had flung down his hat on one of the two chairs. Evidently he had not expected to have so bright a light turned upon him, and he frowned and looked anxious as he met the General's keen eyes; but his face softened and wore a gracious expression as he thanked his protector. When the latter placed the bottle and glass on the mantel-shelf, the stranger's eyes flashed out on him again; and when he spoke, it was in musical tones with no sign of the previous guttural convulsion, though his voice was still unsteady with repressed emotion.

"I shall seem to you to be a strange being, sir, but you must pardon the caprices of necessity. If you propose to remain in the room, I beg that you will not look at me while I am drinking."

Vexed at this continual obedience to a man whom he disliked, the General sharply turned his back upon him. The stranger thereupon drew a white handkerchief from his pocket and wound it about his right hand. Then he seized the carafe and emptied it at a draught. The Marquis, staring vacantly into the tall mirror across the room, without a thought of breaking his implicit promise, saw the stranger's figure distinctly reflected by the opposite looking-glass, and saw, too, a red stain suddenly appear through the folds of the white bandage. The man's hands were steeped in blood.

"Ah! you saw me!" cried the other. He had drunk off the water and wrapped himself again in his cloak, and now scrutinized the General suspiciously. "It is all over with me! Here they come!"

"I don't hear anything," said the Marquis.

"You have not the same interest that I have in listening for sounds in the air."

"You have been fighting a duel, I suppose, to be in such a state?" queried the General, not a little disturbed by the color of those broad, dark patches staining his visitor's cloak.

"Yes, a duel; you have it," said the other, and a bitter smile flitted over his lips.

As he spoke a sound rang along the distant road, a sound of galloping horses; but so faint as yet, that it was the merest dawn of a sound. The General's trained ear recognized the advance of a troop of regulars.

"That is the gendarmerie," said he.

He glanced at his prisoner to reassure him after his own involuntary indiscretion, took the lamp, and went down to the salon. He had scarcely laid the key of the room above upon the chimney-piece when the hoof beats sounded louder and came swiftly nearer and nearer the house. The General felt a shiver of excitement, and indeed the horses stopped at the house door; a few words were exchanged among the men, and one of them dismounted and knocked loudly. There was no help for it; the General went to open the door. He could scarcely conceal his inward perturbation at the sight of half a dozen gendarmes outside, the metal rims of their caps gleaming like silver in the moonlight.

"My lord," said the corporal, "have you heard a man run past towards the barrier within the last few minutes?"

"Towards the barrier? No."

"Have you opened the door to any one?"

"Now, am I in the habit of answering the door myself—"

"I ask your pardon, General, but just now it seems to me that—"

"Really!" cried the Marquis wrathfully. "Have you a mind to try joking with me? What right have you—?"

"None at all, none at all, my lord," cried the corporal, hastily putting in a soft answer. "You will excuse our zeal. We know, of course, that a peer of France is not likely to harbor a murderer at this time of night; but as we want any information we can get—"

"A murderer!" cried the General. "Who can have been—"

"M. le Baron de Mauny has just been murdered. It was a blow from an axe, and we are in hot pursuit of the criminal. We know for certain that he is somewhere in this neighborhood, and we shall hunt him down. By your leave, General," and the man swung himself into the saddle as he spoke. It was well that he did so, for a corporal of gendarmerie trained to alert observation and quick surmise would have had his suspicions at once if he had caught sight of the General's face. Everything that passed through the soldier's mind was faithfully revealed in his frank countenance.

"Is it known who the murderer is?" asked he.

"No," said the other, now in the saddle. "He left the bureau full of banknotes and gold untouched."

"It was revenge, then," said the Marquis.

"On an old man? pshaw! No, no, the fellow hadn't time to take it, that was all," and the corporal galloped after his comrades, who were almost out of sight by this time.

For a few minutes the General stood, a victim to perplexities which need no explanation; but in a moment he heard the servants returning home, their voices were raised in some sort of dispute at the cross-roads of Montreuil. When they came in, he gave vent to his feelings in an explosion of rage, his wrath fell upon them like a thunderbolt, and all the echoes of the house trembled at the sound of his voice. In the midst of the storm his own man, the boldest and cleverest of the party, brought out an excuse; they had been stopped, he said, by the gendarmerie at the gate of Montreuil, a murder had been committed, and the police were in pursuit. In a moment the General's anger vanished, he said not another word; then, bethinking himself of his own singular position, drily ordered them all off to bed at once, and left them amazed at his readiness to accept their fellow servant's lying excuse.

While these incidents took place in the yard, an apparently trifling occurrence had changed the relative positions of three characters in this story. The Marquis had scarcely left the room before his wife looked first towards the key on the mantel-shelf, and then at Helene; and, after some wavering, bent towards her daughter and said in a low voice, "Helene your father has left the key on the chimney-piece."

The girl looked up in surprise and glanced timidly at her mother. The Marquise's eyes sparkled with curiosity.

"Well, mamma?" she said, and her voice had a troubled ring.

"I should like to know what is going on upstairs. If there is anybody up there, he has not stirred yet. Just go up—"

"I?" cried the girl, with something like horror in her tones.

"Are you afraid?"

"No, mamma, but I thought I heard a man's footsteps."

"If I could go myself, I should not have asked you to go, Helene," said her mother with cold dignity. "If your father were to come back and did not see me, he would go to look for me perhaps, but he would not notice your absence."

"Madame, if you bid me go, I will go," said Helene, "but I shall lose my father's good opinion—"

"What is this!" cried the Marquise in a sarcastic tone. "But since you take a thing that was said in joke in earnest, I now order you to go upstairs and see who is in the room above. Here is the key, child. When your father told you to say nothing about this thing that happened, he did not forbid you to go up to the room. Go at once—and learn that a daughter ought never to judge her mother."

The last words were spoken with all the severity of a justly offended mother. The Marquise took the key and handed it to Helene, who rose without a word and left the room.

"My mother can always easily obtain her pardon," thought the girl; "but as for me, my father will never think the same of me again. Does she mean to rob me of his tenderness? Does she want to turn me out of his house?"

These were the thoughts that set her imagination in a sudden ferment, as she went down the dark passage to the mysterious door at the end. When she stood before it, her mental confusion grew to a fateful pitch. Feelings hitherto forced down into inner depths crowded up at the summons of these confused thoughts. Perhaps hitherto she had never believed that a happy life lay before her, but now, in this awful moment, her despair was complete. She shook convulsively as she set the key in the lock; so great indeed was her agitation, that she stopped for a moment and laid her hand on her heart, as if to still the heavy throbs that sounded in her ears. Then she opened the door.

The creaking of the hinges sounded doubtless in vain on the murderer's ears. Acute as were his powers of hearing, he stood as if lost in thought, and so motionless that he might have been glued to the wall against which he leaned. In the circle of semi-opaque darkness, dimly lit by the bull's-eye lantern, he looked like the shadowy figure of some dead knight, standing for ever in his shadowy mortuary niche in the gloom of some Gothic chapel. Drops of cold sweat trickled over the broad, sallow forehead. An incredible fearlessness looked out from every tense feature. His eyes of fire were fixed and tearless; he seemed to be watching some struggle in the darkness beyond him. Stormy thoughts passed swiftly across a face whose firm decision spoke of a character of no common order. His whole person, bearing, and frame bore out the impression of a tameless spirit. The man looked power and strength personified; he stood facing the darkness as if it were the visible image of his own future.

These physical characteristics had made no impression upon the General, familiar as he was with the powerful faces of the group of giants gathered about Napoleon; speculative curiosity, moreover, as to the why and wherefore of the apparition had completely filled his mind; but Helene, with feminine sensitiveness to surface impressions, was struck by the blended chaos of light and darkness, grandeur and passion, suggesting a likeness between this stranger and Lucifer recovering from his fall. Suddenly the storm apparent in his face was stilled as if by magic; and the indefinable power to sway which the stranger exercised upon others, and perhaps unconsciously and as by reflex action upon himself, spread its influence about him with the progressive swiftness of a flood. A torrent of thought rolled away from his brow as his face resumed its ordinary expression. Perhaps it was the strangeness of this meeting, or perhaps it was the mystery into which she had penetrated, that held the young girl spellbound in the doorway, so that she could look at a face pleasant to behold and full of interest. For some moments she stood in the magical silence; a trouble had come upon her never known before in her young life. Perhaps some exclamation broke from Helene, perhaps she moved unconsciously; or it may be that the hunted criminal returned of his own accord from the world of ideas to the material world, and heard some one breathing in the room; however it was, he turned his head towards his host's daughter, and saw dimly in the shadow a noble face and queenly form, which he must have taken for an angel's, so motionless she stood, so vague and like a spirit.

"Monsieur…" a trembling voice cried.

The murderer trembled.

"A woman!" he cried under his breath. "Is it possible? Go," he cried, "I deny that any one has a right to pity, to absolve, or condemn me. I must live alone. Go, my child," he added, with an imperious gesture, "I should ill requite the service done me by the master of the house if I were to allow a single creature under his roof to breathe the same air with me. I must submit to be judged by the laws of the world."

The last words were uttered in a lower voice. Even as he realized with a profound intuition all the manifold misery awakened by that melancholy thought, the glance that he gave Helene had something of the power of the serpent, stirring a whole dormant world in the mind of the strange girl before him. To her that glance was like a light revealing unknown lands. She was stricken with strange trouble, helpless, quelled by a magnetic power exerted unconsciously. Trembling and ashamed, she went out and returned to the salon. She had scarcely entered the room before her father came back, so that she had not time to say a word to her mother.

The General was wholly absorbed in thought. He folded his arms, and paced silently to and fro between the windows which looked out upon the street and the second row which gave upon the garden. His wife lay the sleeping Abel on her knee, and little Moina lay in untroubled slumber in the low chair, like a bird in its nest. Her older sister stared into the fire, a skein of silk in one hand, a needle in the other.

Deep silence prevailed, broken only by lagging footsteps on the stairs, as one by one the servants crept away to bed; there was an occasional burst of stifled laughter, a last echo of the wedding festivity, or doors were opened as they still talked among themselves, then shut. A smothered sound came now and again from the bedrooms, a chair fell, the old coachman coughed feebly, then all was silent.

In a little while the dark majesty with which sleeping earth is invested at midnight brought all things under its sway. No lights shone but the light of the stars. The frost gripped the ground. There was not a sound of a voice, nor a living creature stirring. The crackling of the fire only seemed to make the depth of the silence more fully felt.

The church clock of Montreuil had just struck one, when an almost inaudible sound of a light footstep came from the second flight of stairs. The Marquis and his daughter, both believing that M. de Mauny's murderer was a prisoner above, thought that one of the maids had come down, and no one was at all surprised to hear the door open in the ante-chamber. Quite suddenly the murderer appeared in their midst. The Marquis himself was sunk in deep musings, the mother and daughter were silent, the one from keen curiosity, the other from sheer astonishment, so that the visitor was almost half-way across the room when he spoke to the General.

"Sir, the two hours are almost over," he said, in a voice that was strangely calm and musical.

"You here!" cried the General. "By what means——?" and he gave wife and daughter a formidable questioning glance. Helene grew red as fire.

"You!" he went on, in a tone filled with horror. "You among us! A murderer covered with blood! You are a blot on this picture! Go, go out!" he added in a burst of rage.

At that word "murderer," the Marquise cried out; as for Helene, it seemed to mark an epoch in her life, there was not a trace of surprise in her face. She looked as if she had been waiting for this—for him. Those so vast thoughts of hers had found a meaning. The punishment reserved by Heaven for her sins flamed out before her. In her own eyes she was as great a criminal as this murderer; she confronted him with her quiet gaze; she was his fellow, his sister. It seemed to her that in this accident the command of God had been made manifest. If she had been a few years older, reason would have disposed of her remorse, but at this moment she was like one distraught.

The stranger stood impassive and self-possessed; a scornful smile overspread his features and his thick, red lips.

"You appreciate the magnanimity of my behavior very badly," he said slowly. "I would not touch with my fingers the glass of water you brought me to allay my thirst; I did not so much as think of washing my blood-stained hands under your roof; I am going away, leaving nothing of my crime" (here his lips were compressed) "but the memory; I have tried to leave no trace of my presence in this house. Indeed, I would not even allow your daughter to—"

"My daughter!" cried the General, with a horror-stricken glance at Helene. "Vile wretch, go, or I will kill you—"

"The two hours are not yet over," said the other; "if you kill me or give me up, you must lower yourself in your own eyes—and in mine."

At these last words, the General turned to stare at the criminal in dumb amazement; but he could not endure the intolerable light in those eyes which for the second time disorganized his being. He was afraid of showing weakness once more, conscious as he was that his will was weaker already.

"An old man! You can never have seen a family," he said, with a father's glance at his wife and children.

"Yes, an old man," echoed the stranger, frowning slightly.

"Fly!" cried the General, but he did not dare to look at his guest. "Our compact is broken. I shall not kill you. No! I will never be purveyor to the scaffold. But go out. You make us shudder."

"I know that," said the other patiently. "There is not a spot on French soil where I can set foot and be safe; but if man's justice, like God's, took all into account, if man's justice deigned to inquire which was the monster—the murderer or his victim—then I might hold up my head among my fellows. Can you not guess that other crimes preceded that blow from an axe? I constituted myself his judge and executioner; I stepped in where man's justice failed. That was my crime. Farewell, sir. Bitter though you have made your hospitality, I shall not forget it. I shall always bear in my heart a feeling of gratitude towards one man in the world, and you are that man.... But I could wish that you had showed yourself more generous!"

He turned towards the door, but in the same instant Helene leaned to whisper something in her mother's ear.

"Ah!..."

At the cry that broke from his wife, the General trembled as if he had seen Moina lying dead. There stood Helene and the murderer had turned instinctively, with something like anxiety about these folk in his face.

"What is it, dear?" asked the General.

"Helene wants to go with him."

The murderer's face flushed.

"If that is how my mother understands an almost involuntary exclamation," Helene said in a low voice, "I will fulfil her wishes.

She glanced about her with something like fierce pride; then the girl's eyes fell, and she stood, admirable in her modesty.

"Helene, did you go up to the room where——?"

"Yes, father."

"Helene" (and his voice shook with a convulsive tremor), "is this the first time that you have seen this man?"

"Yes, father."

"Then it is not natural that you should intend to—"

"If it is not natural, father, at any rate it is true."

"Oh! child," said the Marquise, lowering her voice, but not so much but that her husband could hear her, "you are false to all the principles of honor, modesty, and right which I have tried to cultivate in your heart. If until this fatal hour you life has only been one lie, there is nothing to regret in your loss. It can hardly be the moral perfection of this stranger that attracts you to him? Can it be the kind of power that commits crime? I have too good an opinion of you to suppose that—"

"Oh, suppose everything, madame," Helene said coldly.

But though her force of character sustained this ordeal, her flashing eyes could scarcely hold the tears that filled them. The stranger, watching her, guessed the mother's language from the girl's tears, and turned his eagle glance upon the Marquise. An irresistible power constrained her to look at this terrible seducer; but as her eyes met his bright, glittering gaze, she felt a shiver run through her frame, such a shock as we feel at the sight of a reptile or the contact of a Leyden jar.

"Dear!" she cried, turning to her husband, "this is the Fiend himself. He can divine everything!"

The General rose to his feet and went to the bell.

"He means ruin for you," Helene said to the murderer.

The stranger smiled, took one forward stride, grasped the General's arm, and compelled him to endure a steady gaze which benumbed the soldier's brain and left him powerless.

"I will repay you now for your hospitality," he said, "and then we shall be quits. I will spare you the shame by giving myself up. After all, what should I do now with my life?"

"You could repent," answered Helene, and her glance conveyed such hope as only glows in a young girl's eyes.

"I shall never repent," said the murderer in a sonorous voice, as he raised his head proudly.

"His hands are stained with blood," the father said.

"I will wipe it away," she answered.

"But do you so much as know whether he cares for you?" said her father, not daring now to look at the stranger.

The murderer came up a little nearer. Some light within seemed to glow through Helene's beauty, grave and maidenly though it was, coloring and bringing into relief, as it were, the least details, the most delicate lines in her face. The stranger, with that terrible face still blazing in his eyes, gave one tender glance to her enchanting loveliness, then he spoke, his tones revealing how deeply he had been moved.

"And if I refuse to allow this sacrifice of yourself, and so discharge my debt of two hours of existence to your father; is not this love, love for yourself alone?"

"Then do you too reject me?" Helene's cry rang painfully through the hearts of all who heard her. "Farewell, then, to you all; I will die."

"What does this mean?" asked the father and mother.

Helene gave her mother an eloquent glance and lowered her eyes.

Since the first attempt made by the General and his wife to contest by word or action the intruder's strange presumption to the right of staying in their midst, from their first experience of the power of those glittering eyes, a mysterious torpor had crept over them, and their benumbed faculties struggled in vain with the preternatural influence. The air seemed to have suddenly grown so heavy, that they could scarcely breathe; yet, while they could not find the reason of this feeling of oppression, a voice within told them that this magnetic presence was the real cause of their helplessness. In this moral agony, it flashed across the General that he must make every effort to overcome this influence on his daughter's reeling brain; he caught her by the waist and drew her into the embrasure of a window, as far as possible from the murderer.

"Darling," he murmured, "if some wild love has been suddenly born in your heart, I cannot believe that you have not the strength of soul to quell the mad impulse; your innocent life, your pure and dutiful soul, has given me too many proofs of your character. There must be something behind all this. Well, this heart of mine is full of indulgence, you can tell everything to me; even if it breaks, dear child, I can be silent about my grief, and keep your confession a secret. What is it? Are you jealous of our love for your brothers or your little sister? Is it some love trouble? Are you unhappy here at home? Tell me about it, tell me the reasons that urge you to leave your home, to rob it of its greatest charm, to leave your mother and brothers and your little sister?"

"I am in love with no one, father, and jealous of no one, not even of your friend the diplomatist, M. de Vandenesse."

The Marquise turned pale; her daughter saw this, and stopped short.

"Sooner or later I must live under some man's protection, must I not?"

"That is true."

"Do we ever know," she went on, "the human being to whom we link our destinies? Now, I believe in this man."

"Oh, child," said the General, raising his voice, "you have no idea of all the misery that lies in store for you."

"I am thinking of his."

"What a life!" groaned the father.

"A woman's life," the girl murmured.

"You have a great knowledge of life!" exclaimed the Marquise, finding speech at last.

"Madame, my answers are shaped by the questions; but if you desire it, I will speak more clearly."

"Speak out, my child... I am a mother."

Mother and daughter looked each other in the face, and the Marquise said no more. At last she said:

"Helene, if you have any reproaches to make, I would rather bear them than see you go away with a man from whom the whole world shrinks in horror."

"Then you see yourself, madame, that but for me he would be quite alone."

"That will do, madame," the General cried; "we have but one daughter left to us now," and he looked at Moina, who slept on. "As for you," he added, turning to Helene, "I will put you in a convent."

"So be it, father," she said, in calm despair, "I shall die there. You are answerable to God alone for my life and for his soul."

A deep sullen silence fell after these words. The on-lookers during this strange scene, so utterly at variance with all the sentiments of ordinary life, shunned each other's eyes.

Suddenly the Marquis happened to glance at his pistols. He caught up one of them, cocked the weapon, and pointed it at the intruder. At the click of firearms the other turned his piercing gaze full upon the General; the soldier's arm slackened indescribably and fell heavily to his side. The pistol dropped to the floor.

"Girl, you are free," said he, exhausted by this ghastly struggle. "Kiss your mother, if she will let you kiss her. For my own part, I wish never to see nor to hear of you again."

"Helene," the mother began, "only think of the wretched life before you."

A sort of rattling sound came from the intruder's deep chest, all eyes were turned to him. Disdain was plainly visible in his face.

The General rose to his feet. "My hospitality has cost me dear," he cried. "Before you came you had taken an old man's life; now your are dealing a deadly blow at a whole family. Whatever happens, there must be unhappiness in this house."

"And if your daughter is happy?" asked the other, gazing steadily at the General.

The father made a superhuman effort for self-control. "If she is happy with you," he said, "she is not worth regretting."

Helene knelt timidly before her father.

"Father, I love and revere you," she said, "whether you lavish all the treasures of your kindness upon me, or make me feel to the full the rigor of disgrace.... But I entreat that your last words of farewell shall not be words of anger."

The General could not trust himself to look at her. The stranger came nearer; there was something half-diabolical, half-divine in the smile that he gave Helene.

"Angel of pity, you that do not shrink in horror from a murderer, come, since you persist in your resolution of intrusting your life to me."

"Inconceivable!" cried her father.

The Marquise then looked strangely at her daughter, opened her arms, and Helene fled to her in tears.

"Farewell," she said, "farewell, mother!" The stranger trembled as Helene, undaunted, made sign to him that she was ready. She kissed her father's hand; and, as if performing a duty, gave a hasty kiss to Moina and little Abel, then she vanished with the murderer.

"Which way are they going?" exclaimed the General, listening to the footsteps of the two fugitives.—"Madame," he turned to his wife, "I think I must be dreaming; there is some mystery behind all this, I do not understand it; you must know what it means."

The Marquise shivered.

"For some time past your daughter has grown extraordinarily romantic and strangely high-flown in her ideas. In spite of the pains I have taken to combat these tendencies in her character—"

"This will not do——" began the General, but fancying that he heard footsteps in the garden, he broke off to fling open the window.

"Helene!" he shouted.

His voice was lost in the darkness like a vain prophecy. The utterance of that name, to which there should never be answer any more, acted like a counterspell; it broke the charm and set him free from the evil enchantment which lay upon him. It was as if some spirit passed over his face. He now saw clearly what had taken place, and cursed his incomprehensible weakness. A shiver of heat rushed from his heart to his head and feet; he became himself once more, terrible, thirsting for revenge. He raised a dreadful cry.

"Help!" he thundered, "help!"

He rushed to the bell-pull, pulled till the bells rang with a strange clamor of din, pulled till the cord gave way. The whole house was roused with a start. Still shouting, he flung open the windows that looked upon the street, called for the police, caught up his pistols, and fired them off to hurry the mounted patrols, the newly-aroused servants, and the neighbors. The dogs barked at the sound of their master's voice; the horses neighed and stamped in their stalls. The quiet night was suddenly filled with hideous uproar. The General on the staircase, in pursuit of his daughter, saw the scared faces of the servants flocking from all parts of the house.

"My daughter!" he shouted. "Helene has been carried off. Search the garden. Keep a lookout on the road! Open the gates for the gendarmerie!—Murder! Help!"

With the strength of fury he snapped the chain and let loose the great house-dog.

"Helene!" he cried, "Helene!"

The dog sprang out like a lion, barking furiously, and dashed into the garden, leaving the General far behind. A troop of horses came along the road at a gallop, and he flew to open the gates himself.

"Corporal!" he shouted, "cut off the retreat of M. de Mauny's murderer. They have gone through my garden. Quick! Put a cordon of men to watch the ways by the Butte de Picardie.—I will beat up the grounds, parks, and houses.—The rest of you keep a lookout along the road," he ordered the servants, "form a chain between the barrier and Versailles. Forward, every man of you!"

He caught up the rifle which his man had brought out, and dashed into the garden.

"Find them!" he called to the dog.

An ominous baying came in answer from the distance, and he plunged in the direction from which the growl seemed to come.

It was seven o'clock in the morning; all the search made by gendarmes, servants, and neighbors had been fruitless, and the dog had not come back. The General entered the salon, empty now for him though the other three children were there; he was worn out with fatigue, and looked old already with that night's work.

"You have been very cold to your daughter," he said, turning his eyes on his wife.—"And now this is all that is left to us of her," he added, indicating the embroidery frame, and the flower just begun. "Only just now she was there, and now she is lost... lost!"

Tears followed; he hid his face in his hands, and for a few

minutes he said no more; he could not bear the sight of the room, which so short a time ago had made a setting to a picture of the sweetest family happiness. The winter dawn was struggling with the dying lamplight; the tapers burned down to their paper-wreaths and flared out; everything was all in keeping with the father's despair.

"This must be destroyed," he said after a pause, pointing to the tambour-frame. "I shall never bear to see anything again that reminds us of her!"

The terrible Christmas night when the Marquis and his wife lost their oldest daughter, powerless to oppose the mysterious influence exercised by the man who involuntarily, as it were, stole Helene from them, was like a warning sent by Fate. The Marquis was ruined by the failure of his stock-broker; he borrowed money on his wife's property, and lost it in the endeavor to retrieve his fortunes. Driven to desperate expedients, he left France. Six years went by. His family seldom had news of him; but a few days before Spain recognized the independence of the American Republics, he wrote that he was coming home.

So, one fine morning, it happened that several French merchants were on board a Spanish brig that lay a few leagues out from Bordeaux, impatient to reach their native land again, with wealth acquired by long years of toil and perilous adventures in Venezuela and Mexico.

One of the passengers, a man who looked aged by trouble rather than by years, was leaning against the bulwark netting, apparently quite unaffected by the sight to be seen from the upper deck. The bright day, the sense that the voyage was safely over, had brought all the passengers above to greet their land. The larger number of them insisted that they could see, far off in the distance, the houses and lighthouses on the coast of Gascony and the Tower of Cardouan, melting into the fantastic erections of white cloud along the horizon. But for the silver fringe that played about their bows, and the long furrow swiftly effaced in their wake, they might have been perfectly still in mid-ocean, so calm was the sea. The sky was magically clear, the dark blue of the vault above paled by imperceptible gradations, until it blended with the bluish water, a gleaming line that sparkled like stars marking the dividing line of sea. The sunlight caught myriads of facets over the wide surface of the ocean, in such a sort that the vast plains of salt water looked perhaps more full of light than the fields of sky.

The brig had set all her canvas. The snowy sails, swelled by the strangely soft wind, the labyrinth of cordage, and the yellow flags flying at the masthead, all stood out sharp and uncompromisingly clear against the vivid background of space, sky, and sea; there was nothing to alter the color but the shadow cast by the great cloudlike sails.

A glorious day, a fair wind, and the fatherland in sight, a sea like a mill-pond, the melancholy sound of the ripples, a fair, solitary vessel, gliding across the surface of the water like a woman stealing out to a tryst—it was a picture full of harmony. That mere speck full of movement was a starting-point whence the soul of man could descry the immutable vast of space. Solitude and bustling life, silence and sound, were all brought together in strange abrupt contrast; you could not tell where life, or sound, or silence, and nothingness lay, and no human voice broke the divine spell.

The Spanish captain, the crew, and the French passengers sat or stood, in a mood of devout ecstasy, in which many memories blended. There was idleness in the air. The beaming faces told of complete forgetfulness of past hardships, the men were rocked on the fair vessel as in a golden dream. Yet, from time to time the elderly passenger, leaning over the bulwark nettings, looked with something like uneasiness at the horizon. Distrust of the ways of Fate could be read in his whole face; he seemed to fear that he should not reach the coast of France in time. This was the Marquis. Fortune had not been deaf to his despairing cry and struggles. After five years of endeavor and painful toil, he was a wealthy man once more. In his impatience to reach his home again and to bring the good news to his family, he had followed the example set by some French merchants in Havana, and embarked with them on a Spanish vessel with a cargo for Bordeaux. And now, grown tired of evil forebodings, his fancy was tracing out for him the most delicious pictures of past happiness. In that far-off brown line of land he seemed to see his wife and children. He sat in his place by the fireside; they were crowding about him; he felt their caresses. Moina had grown to be a young girl; she was beautiful, and tall, and striking. The fancied picture had grown almost real, when the tears filled his eyes, and, to hide his emotion, he turned his face towards the sea-line, opposite the hazy streak that meant land.

"There she is again.... She is following us!" he said.

"What?" cried the Spanish captain.

"There is a vessel," muttered the General.

"I saw her yesterday," answered Captain Gomez. He looked at his interlocutor as if to ask what he thought; then he added in the General's ear, "She has been chasing us all along."

"Then why she has not come up with us, I do not know," said the General, "for she is a faster sailor than your damned Saint-Ferdinand."

"She will have damaged herself, sprung a leak—"

"She is gaining on us!" the General broke in.

"She is a Columbian privateer," the captain said in his ear, "and we are still six leagues from land, and the wind is dropping."

"She is not going ahead, she is flying, as if she knew that in two hours' time her prey would escape her. What audacity!"

"Audacity!" cried the captain. "Oh! she is not called the Othello for nothing. Not so long back she sank a Spanish frigate that carried thirty guns! This is the one thing I was afraid of, for I had a notion that she was cruising about somewhere off the Antilles.—Aha!" he added after a pause, as he watched the sails of his own vessel, "the wind is rising; we are making way. Get through we must, for 'the Parisian' will show us no mercy."

"She is making way too!" returned the General.

The Othello was scarce three leagues away by this time; and although the conversation between the Marquis and Captain Gomez had taken place apart, passengers and crew, attracted by the sudden appearance of a sail, came to that side of the vessel. With scarcely an exception, however, they took the privateer for a merchantman, and watched her course with interest, till all at once a sailor shouted with some energy of language:

"By Saint-James, it is all up with us! Yonder is the Parisian captain!"

At that terrible name dismay, and a panic impossible to describe, spread through the brig. The Spanish captain's orders put energy into the crew for a while; and in his resolute determination to make land at all costs, he set all the studding sails, and crowded on every stitch of canvas on board. But all this was not the work of a moment; and naturally the men did not work together with that wonderful unanimity so fascinating to watch on board a man-of-war. The Othello meanwhile, thanks to the trimming of her sails, flew over the water like a swallow; but she was making, to all appearance, so little headway, that the unlucky Frenchmen began to entertain sweet delusive hopes. At last, after unheard-of efforts, the Saint-Ferdinand sprang forward, Gomez himself directing the shifting of the sheets with voice and gesture, when all at once the man at the tiller, steering at random (purposely, no doubt), swung the vessel round. The wind striking athwart the beam, the sails shivered so unexpectedly that the brig heeled to one side, the booms were carried away, and the vessel was completely out of hand. The captain's face grew whiter than his sails with unutterable rage. He sprang upon the man at the tiller, drove his dagger at him in such blind fury, that he missed him, and hurled the weapon overboard. Gomez took the helm himself, and strove to right the gallant vessel. Tears of despair rose to his eyes, for it is harder to lose the result of our carefully-laid plans through treachery than to face imminent death. But the more the captain swore, the less the men worked, and it was he himself who fired the alarm-gun, hoping to be heard on shore. The privateer, now gaining hopelessly upon them, replied with a cannon-shot, which struck the water ten fathoms away from the Saint-Ferdinand.

"Thunder of heaven!" cried the General, "that was a close shave! They must have guns made on purpose."

"Oh! when that one yonder speaks, look you, you have to hold your tongue," said a sailor. "The Parisian would not be afraid to meet an English man-of-war."

"It is all over with us," the captain cried in desperation; he had pointed his telescope landwards, and saw not a sign from the shore. "We are further from the coast than I thought."

"Why do you despair?" asked the General. "All your passengers are Frenchmen; they have chartered your vessel. The privateer is a Parisian, you say? Well and good, run up the white flag, and—"

"And he would run us down," retorted the captain. "He can be anything he likes when he has a mind to seize on a rich booty!"

"Oh! if he is a pirate—"

"Pirate!" said the ferocious looking sailor. "Oh! he always has the law on his side, or he knows how to be on the same side as the law."

"Very well," said the General, raising his eyes, "let us make up our minds to it," and his remaining fortitude was still sufficient to keep back the tears.

The words were hardly out of his mouth before a second cannon-shot, better aimed, came crashing through the hull of the Saint-Ferdinand.

"Heave to!" cried the captain gloomily.

The sailor who had commended the Parisian's law-abiding proclivities showed himself a clever hand at working a ship after this desperate order was given. The crew waited for half an hour in an agony of suspense and the deepest dismay. The Saint-Ferdinand had four millions of piastres on board, the whole fortunes of the five passengers, and the General's eleven hundred thousand francs. At length the Othello lay not ten gunshots away, so that those on the Saint-Ferdinand could look into the muzzles of her loaded guns. The vessel seemed to be borne along by a breeze sent by the Devil himself, but the eyes of an expert would have discovered the secret of her speed at once. You had but to look for a moment at the rake of her stern, her long, narrow keel, her tall masts, to see the cut of her sails, the wonderful lightness of her rigging, and the ease and perfect seamanship with which her crew trimmed her sails to the wind. Everything about her gave the impression of the security of power in this delicately curved inanimate creature, swift and intelligent as a greyhound or some bird of prey. The privateer crew stood silent, ready in case of resistance to shatter the wretched merchantman, which, luckily for her, remained motionless, like a schoolboy caught in flagrant delict by a master.

"We have guns on board!" cried the General, clutching the Spanish captain's hand. But the courage in Gomez's eyes was the courage of despair.

"Have we men?" he said.

The Marquis looked round at the crew of the Saint-Ferdinand, and a cold chill ran through him. There stood the four merchants, pale and quaking for fear, while the crew gathered about some of their own number who appeared to be arranging to go over in a body to the enemy. They watched the Othello with greed and curiosity in their faces. The captain, the Marquis, and the mate exchanged glances; they were the only three who had a thought for any but themselves.

"Ah! Captain Gomez, when I left my home and country, my heart was half dead with the bitterness of parting, and now must I bid it good-bye once more when I am bringing back happiness and ease for my children?"

The General turned his head away towards the sea, with tears of rage in his eyes—and saw the steersman swimming out to the privateer.

"This time it will be good-bye for good," said the captain by way of answer, and the dazed look in the Frenchman's eyes startled the Spaniard.

By this time the two vessels were almost alongside, and at the first sight of the enemy's crew the General saw that Gomez's gloomy prophecy was only too true. The three men at each gun might have been bronze statues, standing like athletes, with their rugged features, their bare sinewy arms, men whom Death himself had scarcely thrown off their feet.

The rest of the crew, well armed, active, light, and vigorous, also stood motionless. Toil had hardened, and the sun had deeply tanned, those energetic faces; their eyes glittered like sparks of fire with infernal glee and clear-sighted courage. Perfect silence on the upper deck, now black with men, bore abundant testimony to the rigorous discipline and strong will which held these fiends incarnate in check.

The captain of the Othello stood with folded arms at the foot of the main mast; he carried no weapons, but an axe lay on the deck beside him. His face was hidden by the shadow of a broad felt hat.

The men looked like dogs crouching before their master. Gunners, soldiers, and ship's crew turned their eyes first on his face, and then on the merchant vessel.

The two brigs came up alongside, and the shock of contact roused the privateer captain from his musings; he spoke a word in the ear of the lieutenant who stood beside him.

"Grappling-irons!" shouted the latter, and the Othello grappled the Saint-Ferdinand with miraculous quickness. The captain of the privateer gave his orders in a low voice to the lieutenant, who repeated them; the men, told off in succession for each duty, went on the upper deck of the Saint-Ferdinand, like seminarists going to mass. They bound crew and passengers hand and foot and seized the booty. In the twinkling of an eye, provisions and barrels full of piastres were transferred to the Othello; the General thought that he must be dreaming when he himself, likewise bound, was flung down on a bale of goods as if he had been part of the cargo.

A brief conference took place between the captain of the privateer and his lieutenant and a sailor, who seemed to be the mate of the vessel; then the mate gave a whistle, and the men jumped on board the Saint-Ferdinand, and completely dismantled her with the nimble dexterity of a soldier who strips a dead comrade of a coveted overcoat and shoes.

"It is all over with us," said the Spanish captain coolly. He had eyed the three chiefs during their confabulation, and saw that the sailors were proceeding to pull his vessel to pieces.

"Why so?" asked the General.

"What would you have them do with us?" returned the Spaniard. "They have just come to the conclusion that they will scarcely sell the Saint-Ferdinand in any French or Spanish port, so they are going to sink her to be rid of her. As for us, do you suppose that they will put themselves to the expense of feeding us, when they don't know what port they are to put into?"

The words were scarcely out of the captain's mouth before a hideous outcry went up, followed by a dull splashing sound, as several bodies were thrown overboard. He turned, the four merchants were no longer to be seen, but eight ferocious-looking gunners were still standing with their arms raised above their heads. He shuddered.

"What did I tell you?" the Spanish captain asked coolly.

The Marquis rose to his feet with a spring. The surface of the sea was quite smooth again; he could not so much as see the place where his unhappy fellow-passengers had disappeared. By this time they were sinking down, bound hand and foot, below the waves, if, indeed, the fish had not devoured them already.

Only a few paces away, the treacherous steersman and the sailor who had boasted of the Parisian's power were fraternizing with the crew of the Othello, and pointing out those among their own number, who, in their opinion, were worthy to join the crew of the privateer. Then the boys tied the rest together by the feet in spite of frightful oaths. It was soon over; the eight gunners seized the doomed men and flung them overboard without more ado, watching the different ways in which the drowning victims met their death, their contortions, their last agony, with a sort of malignant curiosity, but with no sign of amusement, surprise, or pity. For them it was an ordinary event to which seemingly they were quite accustomed. The older men looked instead with grim, set smiles at the casks of piastres about the main mast.

The General and Captain Gomez, left seated on a bale of goods, consulted each other with well-nigh hopeless looks; they were, in a sense, the sole survivors of the Saint-Ferdinand, for the seven men pointed out by the spies were transformed amid rejoicings into Peruvians.

"What atrocious villains!" the General cried. Loyal and generous indignation silenced prudence and pain on his own account.

"They do it because they must," Gomez answered coolly. "If you came across one of those fellows, you would run him through the body, would you not?"

The lieutenant now came up to the Spaniard.

"Captain," said he, "the Parisian has heard of you. He says that you are the only man who really knows the passages of the Antilles and the Brazilian coast. Will you—"

The captain cut him short with a scornful exclamation.

"I shall die like a sailor," he said, "and a loyal Spaniard and a Christian. Do you hear?"

"Heave him overboard!" shouted the lieutenant, and a couple of gunners seized on Gomez.

"You cowards!" roared the General, seizing hold of the men.

"Don't get too excited, old boy," said the lieutenant. "If your red ribbon has made some impression upon our captain, I myself do not care a rap for it.—You and I will have our little bit of talk together directly."

A smothered sound, with no accompanying cry, told the General that the gallant captain had died "like a sailor," as he had said.

"My money or death!" cried the Marquis, in a fit of rage terrible to see.

"Ah! now you talk sensibly!" sneered the lieutenant. "That is the way to get something out of us——"

Two of the men came up at a sign and hastened to bind the Frenchmen's feet, but with unlooked-for boldness he snatched the lieutenant's cutlass and laid about him like a cavalry officer who knows his business.

"Brigands that you are! You shall not chuck one of Napoleon's troopers over a ship's side like an oyster!"

At the sound of pistol shots fired point blank at the Frenchman, "the Parisian" looked round from his occupation of superintending the transfer of the rigging from the Saint-Ferdinand. He came up behind the brave General, seized him, dragged him to the side, and was about to fling him over with no more concern than if the man had been a broken spar. They were at the very edge when the General looked into the tawny eyes of the man who had stolen his daughter. The recognition was mutual.

The captain of the privateer, his arm still upraised, suddenly swung it in the contrary direction as if his victim was but a feather weight, and set him down at the foot of the main mast. A murmur rose on the upper deck, but the captain glanced round, and there was a sudden silence.

"This is Helene's father," said the captain in a clear, firm voice. "Woe to any one who meddles with him!"

A hurrah of joy went up at the words, a shout rising to the sky like a prayer of the church; a cry like the first high notes of the Te Deum. The lads swung aloft in the rigging, the men below flung up their caps, the gunners pounded away on the deck, there was a general thrill of excitement, an outburst of oaths, yells, and shrill cries in voluble chorus. The men cheered like fanatics, the General's misgivings deepened, and he grew uneasy; it seemed to him that there was some horrible mystery in such wild transports.

"My daughter!" he cried, as soon as he could speak. "Where is my daughter?"

For all answer, the captain of the privateer gave him a searching glance, one of those glances which throw the bravest man into a confusion which no theory can explain. The General was mute, not a little to the satisfaction of the crew; it pleased them to see their leader exercise the strange power which he possessed over all with whom he came in contact. Then the captain led the way down a staircase and flung open the door of a cabin.

"There she is," he said, and disappeared, leaving the General in a stupor of bewilderment at the scene before his eyes.

Helene cried out at the sight of him, and sprang up from the sofa on which she was lying when the door flew open. So changed was she that none but a father's eyes could have recognized her. The sun of the tropics had brought warmer tones into the once pale face, and something of Oriental charm with that wonderful coloring; there was a certain grandeur about her, a majestic firmness, a profound sentiment which impresses itself upon the coarsest nature. Her long, thick hair, falling in large curls about her queenly throat, gave an added idea of power to the proud face. The consciousness of that power shone out from every movement, every line of Helene's form. The rose-tinted nostrils were dilated slightly with the joy of triumph; the serene happiness of her life had left its plain tokens in the full development of her beauty. A certain indefinable virginal grace met in her with the pride of a woman who is loved. This was a slave and a queen, a queen who would fain obey that she might reign.

Her dress was magnificent and elegant in its richness; India muslin was the sole material, but her sofa and cushions were of cashmere. A Persian carpet covered the floor in the large cabin, and her four children playing at her feet were building castles of gems and pearl necklaces and jewels of price. The air was full of the scent of rare flowers in Sevres porcelain vases painted by Madame Jacotot; tiny South American birds, like living rubies, sapphires, and gold, hovered among the Mexican jessamines and camellias. A pianoforte had been fitted into the room, and here and there on the paneled walls, covered with red silk, hung small pictures by great painters—a Sunset by Hippolyte Schinner beside a Terburg, one of Raphael's Madonnas scarcely yielded in charm to a sketch by Gericault, while a Gerard Dow eclipsed the painters of the Empire. On a lacquered table stood a golden plate full of delicious fruit. Indeed, Helene might have been the sovereign lady of some great country, and this cabin of hers a boudoir in which her crowned lover had brought together all earth's treasure to please his consort. The children gazed with bright, keen eyes at their grandfather. Accustomed as they were to a life of battle, storm, and tumult, they recalled the Roman children in David's Brutus, watching the fighting and bloodshed with curious interest.

"What! is it possible?" cried Helene, catching her father's arm as if to assure herself that this was no vision.

"Helene!"

"Father!"

They fell into each other's arms, and the old man's embrace was not so close and warm as Helene's.

"Were you on board that vessel?"

"Yes," he answered sadly, and looking at the little ones, who gathered about him and gazed with wide open eyes.

"I was about to perish, but—"

"But for my husband," she broke in. "I see how it was."

"Ah!" cried the General, "why must I find you again like this, Helene? After all the many tears that I have shed, must I still groan for your fate?"

"And why?" she asked, smiling. "Why should you be sorry to learn that I am the happiest woman under the sun?"

"Happy?" he cried with a start of surprise.

"Yes, happy, my kind father," and she caught his hands in hers and covered them with kisses, and pressed them to her throbbing heart. Her caresses, and a something in the carriage of her head, were interpreted yet more plainly by the joy sparkling in her eyes.

"And how is this?" he asked, wondering at his daughter's life, forgetful now of everything but the bright glowing face before him.

"Listen, father; I have for lover, husband, servant, and master one whose soul is as great as the boundless sea, as infinite in his kindness as heaven, a god on earth! Never during these seven years has a chance look, or word, or gesture jarred in the divine harmony of his talk, his love, his caresses. His eyes have never met mine without a gleam of happiness in them; there has always been a bright smile on his lips for me. On deck, his voice rises above the thunder of storms and the tumult of battle; but here below it is soft and melodious as Rossini's music—for he has Rossini's music sent for me. I have everything that woman's caprice can imagine. My wishes are more than fulfilled. In short, I am a queen on the seas; I am obeyed here as perhaps a queen may be obeyed.—Ah!" she cried, interrupting herself, "happy did I say? Happiness is no word to express such bliss as mine. All the happiness that should have fallen to all the women in the world has been my share. Knowing one's own great love and self-devotion, to find in his heart an infinite love in which a woman's soul is lost, and lost for ever—tell me, is this happiness? I have lived through a thousand lives even now. Here, I am alone; here, I command. No other woman has set foot on this noble vessel, and Victor is never more than a few paces distant from me,—he cannot wander further from me than from stern to prow," she added, with a shade of mischief in her manner. "Seven years! A love that outlasts seven years of continual joy, that endures all the tests brought by all the moments that make up seven years—is this love? Oh, no, no! it is something better than all that I know of life... human language fails to express the bliss of heaven."

A sudden torrent of tears fell from her burning eyes. The four little ones raised a piteous cry at this, and flocked like chickens about their mother. The oldest boy struck the General with a threatening look.

"Abel, darling," said Helene, "I am crying for joy."

Helene took him on her knee, and the child fondled her, putting his arms about her queenly neck, as a lion's whelp might play with the lioness.

"Do you never weary of your life?" asked the General, bewildered by his daughter's enthusiastic language.

"Yes," she said, "sometimes, when we are on land, yet even then I have never parted from my husband."

"But you need to be fond of music and balls and fetes."

"His voice is music for me; and for fetes, I devise new toilettes for him to see. When he likes my dress, it is as if all the world admired me. Simply for that reason I keep the diamonds and jewels, the precious things, the flowers and masterpieces of art that he heaps upon me, saying, 'Helene, as you live out of the world, I will have the world come to you.' But for that I would fling them all overboard."

"But there are others on board, wild, reckless men whose passions—"

"I understand, father," she said smiling. "Do not fear for me. Never was empress encompassed with more observance than I. The men are very superstitious; they look upon me as a sort of tutelary genius, the luck of the vessel. But he is their god; they worship him. Once, and once only, one of the crew showed disrespect, mere words," she added, laughing; "but before Victor knew of it, the others flung the offender overboard, although I forgave him. They love me as their good angel; I nurse them when they are ill; several times I have been so fortunate as to save a life, by constant care such as a woman can give. Poor fellows, they are giants, but they are children at the same time."

"And when there is fighting overhead?"

"I am used to it now; I quaked for fear during the first engagement, but never since.—I am used to such peril, and—I am your daughter," she said; "I love it."

"But how if he should fall?"

"I should die with him."

"And your children?"

"They are children of the sea and of danger; they share the life of their parents. We have but one life, and we do not flinch from it. We have but one life, our names are written on the same page of the book of Fate, one skiff bears us and our fortunes, and we know it."

"Do you so love him that he is more to you than all beside?"

"All beside?" echoed she. "Let us leave that mystery alone. Yet stay! there is this dear little one—well, this too is he," and straining

Abel to her in a tight clasp, she set eager kisses on his cheeks and hair.

"But I can never forget that he has just drowned nine men!" exclaimed the General.

"There was no help for it, doubtless," she said, "for he is generous and humane. He sheds as little blood as may be, and only in the interests of the little world which he defends, and the sacred cause for which he is fighting. Talk to him about anything that seems to you to be wrong, and he will convince you, you will see."

"There was that crime of his," muttered the General to himself.

"But how if that crime was a virtue?" she asked, with cold dignity. "How if man's justice had failed to avenge a great wrong?"

"But a private revenge!" exclaimed her father.

"But what is hell," she cried, "but a revenge through all eternity for the wrong done in a little day?"

"Ah! you are lost! He has bewitched and perverted you. You are talking wildly."

"Stay with us one day, father, and if you will but listen to him, and see him, you will love him."

"Helene, France lies only a few leagues away," he said gravely.

Helene trembled; then she went to the porthole and pointed to the savannas of green water spreading far and wide.

"There lies my country," she said, tapping the carpet with her foot.

"But are you not coming with me to see your mother and your sister and brothers?"

"Oh! yes," she cried, with tears in her voice, "if he is willing, if he will come with me."

"So," the General said sternly, "you have neither country nor kin now, Helene?"

"I am his wife," she answered proudly, and there was something very noble in her tone. "This is the first happiness in seven years that has not come to me through him," she said—then, as she caught her father's hand and kissed it—"and this is the first word of reproach that I have heard."

"And your conscience?"

"My conscience; he is my conscience!" she cried, trembling from head to foot. "Here he is! Even in the thick of a fight I can tell his footstep among all the others on deck," she cried.

A sudden crimson flushed her cheeks and glowed in her features, her eyes lighted up, her complexion changed to velvet whiteness, there was joy and love in every fibre, in the blue veins, in the unconscious trembling of her whole frame. That quiver of the sensitive plant softened the General.

It was as she had said. The captain came in, sat down in an easy-chair, took up his oldest boy, and began to play with him. There was a moment's silence, for the General's deep musing had grown vague and dreamy, and the daintily furnished cabin and the playing children seemed like a nest of halcyons, floating on the waves, between sky and sea, safe in the protection of this man who steered his way amid the perils of war and tempest, as other heads of household guide those in their care among the hazards of common life. He gazed admiringly at Helene—a dreamlike vision of some sea goddess, gracious in her loveliness, rich in happiness; all the treasures about her grown poor in comparison with the wealth of her nature, paling before the brightness of her eyes, the indefinable romance expressed in her and her surroundings.

The strangeness of the situation took the General by surprise; the ideas of ordinary life were thrown into confusion by this lofty passion and reasoning. Chill and narrow social conventions faded away before this picture. All these things the old soldier felt, and saw no less how impossible it was that his daughter should give up so wide a life, a life so variously rich, filled to the full with such passionate love. And Helene had tasted danger without shrinking; how could she return to the pretty stage, the superficial circumscribed life of society?

It was the captain who broke the silence at last.

"Am I in the way?" he asked, looking at his wife.

"No," said the General, answering for her. "Helene has told me all. I see that she is lost to us—"

"No," the captain put in quickly; "in a few years' time the statute of limitations will allow me to go back to France. When the conscience is clear, and a man has broken the law in obedience to——" he stopped short, as if scorning to justify himself.

"How can you commit new murders, such as I have seen with my own eyes, without remorse?"

"We had no provisions," the privateer captain retorted calmly.

"But if you had set the men ashore—"

"They would have given the alarm and sent a man-of-war after us, and we should never have seen Chili again."

"Before France would have given warning to the Spanish admiralty—" began the General.

"But France might take it amiss that a man, with a warrant still out against him, should seize a brig chartered by Bordeaux merchants. And for that matter, have you never fired a shot or so too many in battle?"

The General shrank under the other's eyes. He said no more, and his daughter looked at him half sadly, half triumphant.

"General," the privateer continued, in a deep voice, "I have made it a rule to abstract nothing from booty. But even so, my share will be beyond a doubt far larger than your fortune. Permit me to return it to you in another form—"

He drew a pile of banknotes from the piano, and without counting the packets handed a million of francs to the Marquis.

"You can understand," he said, "that I cannot spend my time in watching vessels pass by to Bordeaux. So unless the dangers of this Bohemian life of ours have some attraction for you, unless you care to see South America and the nights of the tropics, and a bit of fighting now and again for the pleasure of helping to win a triumph for a young nation, or for the name of Simon Bolivar, we must part. The long boat manned with a trustworthy crew is ready for you. And now let us hope that our third meeting will be completely happy."

"Victor," said Helene in a dissatisfied tone, "I should like to see a little more of my father."

"Ten minutes more or less may bring up a French frigate. However, so be it, we shall have a little fun. The men find things dull."

"Oh, father, go!" cried Helene, "and take these keepsakes from me to my sister and brothers and—mother," she added. She caught up a handful of jewels and precious stones, folded them in an Indian shawl, and timidly held it out.

"But what shall I say to them from you?" asked he. Her hesitation on the word "mother" seemed to have struck him.

"Oh! can you doubt me? I pray for their happiness every day."

"Helene," he began, as he watched her closely, "how if we should not meet again? Shall I never know why you left us?"

"That secret is not mine," she answered gravely. "Even if I had the right to tell it, perhaps I should not. For ten years I was more miserable than words can say—"

She broke off, and gave her father the presents for her family. The General had acquired tolerably easy views as to booty in the course of a soldier's career, so he took Helene's gifts and comforted himself with the reflection that the Parisian captain was sure to wage war against the Spaniards as an honorable man, under the influence of Helene's pure and high-minded nature. His passion for courage carried all before it. It was ridiculous, he thought, to be squeamish in the matter; so he shook hands cordially with his captor, and kissed Helene, his only daughter, with a soldier's expansiveness; letting fall a tear on the face with the proud, strong look that once he had loved to see. "The Parisian," deeply moved, brought the children for his blessing. The parting was over, the last good-bye was a long farewell look, with something of tender regret on either side.

A strange sight to seaward met the General's eyes. The Saint-Ferdinand was blazing like a huge bonfire. The men told off to sink the Spanish brig had found a cargo of rum on board; and as the Othello was already amply supplied, had lighted a floating bowl of punch on the high seas, by way of a joke; a pleasantry pardonable enough in sailors, who hail any chance excitement as a relief from the apparent monotony of life at sea. As the General went over the side into the long-boat of the Saint-Ferdinand, manned by six vigorous rowers, he could not help looking at the burning vessel, as well as at the daughter who stood by her husband's side on the stern of the Othello. He saw Helene's white dress flutter like one more sail in the breeze; he saw the tall, noble figure against a background of sea, queenly still even in the presence of Ocean; and so many memories crowded up in his mind, that, with a soldier's recklessness of life, he forgot that he was being borne over the grave of the brave Gomez.

A vast column of smoke rising spread like a brown cloud, pierced here and there by fantastic shafts of sunlight. It was a second sky, a murky dome reflecting the glow of the fire as if the under surface had been burnished; but above it soared the unchanging blue of the firmament, a thousand times fairer for the short-lived contrast. The strange hues of the smoke cloud, black and red, tawny and pale by turns, blurred and blending into each other, shrouded the burning vessel as it flared, crackled and groaned; the hissing tongues of flame licked up the rigging, and flashed across the hull, like a rumor of riot flashing along the streets of a city. The burning rum sent up blue flitting lights. Some sea god might have been stirring the furious liquor as a student stirs the joyous flames of punch in an orgy. But in the overpowering sunlight, jealous of the insolent blaze, the colors were scarcely visible, and the smoke was but a film fluttering like a thin scarf in the noonday torrent of light and heat.

The Othello made the most of the little wind she could gain to fly on her new course. Swaying first to one side, then to the other, like a stag beetle on the wing, the fair vessel beat to windward on her zigzag flight to the south. Sometimes she was hidden from sight by the straight column of smoke that flung fantastic shadows across the water, then gracefully she shot out clear of it, and Helene, catching sight of her father, waved her handkerchief for yet one more farewell greeting.

A few more minutes, and the Saint-Ferdinand went down with a bubbling turmoil, at once effaced by the ocean. Nothing of all that had been was left but a smoke cloud hanging in the breeze. The Othello was far away, the long-boat had almost reached land, the cloud came between the frail skiff and the brig, and it was through a break in the swaying smoke that the General caught the last glimpse of Helene. A prophetic vision! Her dress and her white handkerchief stood out against the murky background. Then the brig was not even visible between the green water and the blue sky, and Helene was nothing but an imperceptible speck, a faint graceful line, an angel in heaven, a mental image, a memory.

The Marquis had retrieved his fortunes, when he died, worn out with toil. A few months after his death, in 1833, the Marquise was obliged to take Moina to a watering-place in the Pyrenees, for the capricious child had a wish to see the beautiful mountain scenery. They left the baths, and the following tragical incident occurred on their way home.

"Dear me, mother," said Moina, "it was very foolish of us not to stay among the mountains a few days longer. It was much nicer there. Did you hear that horrid child moaning all night, and that wretched woman, gabbling away in patois no doubt, for I could not understand a single word she said. What kind of people can they have put in the next room to ours? This is one of the horridest nights I have ever spent in my life."

"I heard nothing," said the Marquise, "but I will see the landlady, darling, and engage the next room, and then we shall have the whole suite of rooms to ourselves, and there will be no more noise. How do you feel this morning? Are you tired?"

As she spoke, the Marquise rose and went to Moina's bedside.

"Let us see," she said, feeling for the girl's hand.

"Oh! let me alone, mother," said Moina; "your fingers are cold."

She turned her head round on the pillow as she spoke, pettishly, but with such engaging grace, that a mother could scarcely have taken it amiss. Just then a wailing cry echoed through the next room, a faint prolonged cry, that must surely have gone to the heart of any woman who heard it.

"Why, if you heard that all night long, why did you not wake me? We should have—"

A deeper moan than any that had gone before it interrupted the Marquise.

"Some one is dying there," she cried, and hurried out of the room.

"Send Pauline to me!" called Moina. "I shall get up and dress."

The Marquise hastened downstairs, and found the landlady in the courtyard with a little group about her, apparently much interested in something that she was telling them.

"Madame, you have put some one in the next room who seems to be very ill indeed—"

"Oh! don't talk to me about it!" cried the mistress of the house. "I have just sent some one for the mayor. Just imagine it; it is a woman, a poor unfortunate creature that came here last night on foot. She comes from Spain; she has no passport and no money; she was carrying her baby on her back, and the child was dying. I could not refuse to take her in. I went up to see her this morning myself; for when she turned up yesterday, it made me feel dreadfully bad to look at her. Poor soul! she and the child were lying in bed, and both of them at death's door. 'Madame,' says she, pulling a gold ring off her finger, 'this is all that I have left; take it in payment, it will be enough; I shall not stay here long. Poor little one! we shall die together soon!' she said, looking at the child. I took her ring, and I asked her who she was, but she never would tell me her name.... I have just sent for the doctor and M. le Maire."

"Why, you must do all that can be done for her," cried the Marquise. "Good heavens! perhaps it is not too late! I will pay for everything that is necessary——"

"Ah! my lady, she looks to me uncommonly proud, and I don't know that she would allow it."

"I will go to see her at once."

The Marquise went up forthwith to the stranger's room, without thinking of the shock that the sight of her widow's weeds might give to a woman who was said to be dying. At the sight of that dying woman the Marquise turned pale. In spite of the changes wrought by fearful suffering in Helene's beautiful face, she recognized her eldest daughter.

But Helene, when she saw a woman dressed in black, sat upright in bed with a shriek of horror. Then she sank back; she knew her mother.

"My daughter," said Mme. d'Aiglemont, "what is to be done? Pauline!... Moina!..."

"Nothing now for me," said Helene faintly. "I had hoped to see my father once more, but your mourning—" she broke off, clutched her child to her heart as if to give it warmth, and kissed its forehead. Then she turned her eyes on her mother, and the Marquise met the old reproach in them, tempered with forgiveness, it is true, but still reproach. She saw it, and would not see it. She forgot that Helene was the child conceived amid tears and despair, the child of duty, the cause of one of the greatest sorrows in her life. She stole to her eldest daughter's side, remembering nothing but that Helene was her firstborn, the child who had taught her to know the joys of motherhood. The mother's eyes were full of tears. "Helene, my child!..." she cried, with her arms about her daughter.

Helene was silent. Her own babe had just drawn its last breath on her breast.

Moina came into the room with Pauline, her maid, and the landlady and the doctor. The Marquise was holding her daughter's ice-cold hand in both of hers, and gazing at her in despair; but the widowed woman, who had escaped shipwreck with but one of all her fair band of children, spoke in a voice that was dreadful to hear. "All this is your work," she said. "If you had but been for me all that—"

"Moina, go! Go out of the room, all of you!" cried Mme. d'Aiglemont, her shrill tones drowning Helene's voice.—"For pity's sake," she continued, "let us not begin these miserable quarrels again now——"

"I will be silent," Helene answered with a preternatural effort. "I am a mother; I know that Moina ought not... Where is my child?"

Moina came back, impelled by curiosity.

"Sister," said the spoiled child, "the doctor—"

"It is all of no use," said Helene. "Oh! why did I not die as a girl of sixteen when I meant to take my own life? There is no happiness outside the laws. Moina... you..."

Her head sank till her face lay against the face of the little one; in her agony she strained her babe to her breast, and died.

"Your sister, Moina," said Mme. d'Aiglemont, bursting into tears when she reached her room, "your sister meant no doubt to tell you that a girl will never find happiness in a romantic life, in living as nobody else does, and, above all things, far away from her mother."

VI

THE OLD AGE OF A GUILTY MOTHER

It was one of the earliest June days of the year 1844. A lady of fifty or thereabouts, for she looked older than her actual age, was pacing up and down one of the sunny paths in the garden of a great mansion in the Rue Plument in Paris. It was noon. The lady took two or three turns along the gently winding garden walk, careful never to lose sight of a certain row of windows, to which she seemed to give her whole attention; then she sat down on a bench, a piece of elegant semi-rusticity made of branches with the bark left on the wood. From the place where she sat she could look through the garden railings along the inner boulevards to the wonderful dome of the Invalides rising above the crests of a forest of elm-trees, and see the less striking view of her own grounds terminating in the gray stone front of one of the finest hotels in the Faubourg Saint-Germain.

Silence lay over the neighboring gardens, and the boulevards stretching away to the Invalides. Day scarcely begins at noon in that aristocratic quarter, and masters and servants are all alike asleep, or just awakening, unless some young lady takes it into her head to go for an early ride, or a gray-headed diplomatist rises betimes to redraft a protocol.

The elderly lady stirring abroad at that hour was the Marquise d'Aiglemont, the mother of Mme. de Saint-Hereen, to whom the great house belonged. The Marquise had made over the mansion and almost her whole fortune to her daughter, reserving only an annuity for herself.

The Comtesse Moina de Saint-Hereen was Mme. d'Aiglemont's youngest child. The Marquise had made every sacrifice to marry her daughter to the eldest son of one of the greatest houses of France; and this was only what might have been expected, for the lady had lost her sons, first one and then the other. Gustave, Marquis d'Aiglemont, had died of the cholera; Abel, the second, had fallen in Algeria. Gustave had left a widow and children, but the dowager's affection for her sons had been only moderately warm, and for the next generation it was decidedly tepid. She was always civil to her daughter-in-law, but her feeling towards the young Marquise was the distinctly conventional affection which good taste and good manners require us to feel for our relatives. The fortunes of her dead children having been settled, she could devote her savings and her own property to her darling Moina.

Moina, beautiful and fascinating from childhood, was Mme. d'Aiglemont's favorite; loved beyond all the others with an instinctive or involuntary love, a fatal drawing of the heart, which sometimes seems inexplicable, sometimes, and to a close observer, only too easy to explain. Her darling's pretty face, the sound of Moina's voice, her ways, her manner, her looks and gestures, roused all the deepest emotions that can stir a mother's heart with trouble, rapture, or delight. The springs of the Marquise's life, of yesterday, to-morrow, and to-day, lay in that young heart. Moina, with better fortune, had survived four older children. As a matter of fact, Mme. d'Aiglemont had lost her eldest daughter, a charming girl, in a most unfortunate manner, said gossip, nobody knew exactly what became of her; and then she lost a little boy of five by a dreadful accident.

The child of her affections had, however, been spared to her, and doubtless the Marquise saw the will of Heaven in that fact; for those who had died, she kept but very shadowy recollections in some far-off corner of her heart; her memories of her dead children were like the headstones on a battlefield, you can scarcely see them for the flowers that have sprung up about them since. Of course, if the world had chosen, it might have said some hard truths about the Marquise, might have taken her to task for shallowness and an overweening preference for one child at the expense of the rest; but the world of Paris is swept along by the full flood of new events, new ideas, and new fashions, and it was inevitable the Mme. d'Aiglemont should be in some sort allowed to drop out of sight. So nobody thought of blaming her for coldness or neglect which concerned no one, whereas her quick, apprehensive tenderness for Moina was found highly interesting by not a few who respected it as a sort of superstition. Besides, the Marquise scarcely went into society at all; and the few families who knew her thought of her as a kindly, gentle, indulgent woman, wholly devoted to her family. What but a curiosity, keen indeed, would seek to pry beneath the surface with which the world is quite satisfied? And what would we not pardon to old people, if only they will efface themselves like shadows, and consent to be regarded as memories and nothing more!

Indeed, Mme. d'Aiglemont became a kind of example complacently held up by the younger generation to fathers of families, and frequently cited to mothers-in-law. She had made over her property to Moina in her own lifetime; the young Countess' happiness was enough for her, she only lived in her daughter. If some cautious old person or morose uncle here and there condemned the course with—"Perhaps Mme. d'Aiglemont may be sorry some day that she gave up her fortune to her daughter; she may be sure of Moina, but how can she be equally sure of her son-in-law?"—these prophets were cried down on all sides, and from all sides a chorus of praise went up for Moina.

"It ought to be said, in justice to Mme. de Saint-Hereen, that her mother cannot feel the slightest difference," remarked a young married woman. "Mme. d'Aiglemont is admirably well housed. She has a carriage at her disposal, and can go everywhere just as she used to do—"

"Except to the Italiens," remarked a low voice. (This was an elderly parasite, one of those persons who show their independence—as they think—by riddling their friends with epigrams.) "Except to the Italiens. And if the dowager cares for anything on this earth but her daughter—it is music. Such a good performer she was in her time! But the Countess' box is always full of young butterflies, and the Countess' mother would be in the way; the young lady is talked about already as a great flirt. So the poor mother never goes to the Italiens."

"Mme. de Saint-Hereen has delightful 'At Homes' for her mother," said a rosebud. "All Paris goes to her salon."

"And no one pays any attention to the Marquise," returned the parasite.

"The fact is that Mme. d'Aiglemont is never alone," remarked a coxcomb, siding with the young women.

"In the morning," the old observer continued in a discreet voice, "in the morning dear Moina is asleep. At four o'clock dear Moina drives in the Bois. In the evening dear Moina goes to a ball or to the Bouffes.—Still, it is certainly true that Mme. d'Aiglemont has the privilege of seeing her dear daughter while she dresses, and again at dinner, if dear Moina happens to dine with her mother. Not a week ago, sir," continued the elderly person, laying his hand on the arm of the shy tutor, a new arrival in the house, "not a week ago, I saw the poor mother, solitary and sad, by her own fireside.—'What is the matter?' I asked. The Marquise looked up smiling, but I am quite sure that she had been crying.—'I was thinking that it is a strange thing that I should be left alone when I have had five children,' she said, 'but that is our destiny! And besides, I am happy when I know that Moina is enjoying herself.'—She could say that to me, for I knew her husband when he was alive. A poor stick he was, and uncommonly lucky to have such a wife; it was certainly owing to her that he was made a peer of France, and had a place at Court under Charles X."

Yet such mistaken ideas get about in social gossip, and such mischief is done by it, that the historian of manners is bound to exercise his discretion, and weigh the assertions so recklessly made. After all, who is to say that either mother or daughter was right or wrong? There is but One who can read and judge their hearts! And how often does He wreak His vengeance in the family circle, using throughout all time children as His instruments against their mothers, and fathers against their sons, raising up peoples against kings, and princes against peoples, sowing strife and division everywhere? And in the world of ideas, are not opinions and feelings expelled by new feelings and opinions, much as withered leaves are thrust forth by the young leaf-buds in the spring?—all in obedience to the immutable Scheme; all to some end which God alone knows. Yet, surely, all things proceed to Him, or rather, to Him all things return.

Such thoughts of religion, the natural thoughts of age, floated up now and again on the current of Mme. d'Aiglemont's thoughts; they were always dimly present in her mind, but sometimes they shone out clearly, sometimes they were carried under, like flowers tossed on the vexed surface of a stormy sea.

She sat on a garden-seat, tired with walking, exhausted with much thinking—with the long thoughts in which a whole lifetime rises up before the mind, and is spread out like a scroll before the eyes of those who feel that Death is near.

If a poet had chanced to pass along the boulevard, he would have found an interesting picture in the face of this woman, grown old before her time. As she sat under the dotted shadow of the acacia, the shadow the acacia casts at noon, a thousand thoughts were written for all the world to see on her features, pale and cold even in the hot, bright sunlight. There was something sadder than the sense of waning life in that expressive face, some trouble that went deeper than the weariness of experience. It was a face of a type that fixes you in a moment among a host of characterless faces that fail to draw a second glance, a face to set you thinking. Among a thousand pictures in a gallery, you are strongly impressed by the sublime anguish on the face of some Madonna of Murillo's; by some Beatrice Cenci in which Guido's art portrays the most touching innocence against a background of horror and crime; by the awe and majesty that should encircle a king, caught once and for ever by Velasquez in the sombre face of a Philip II., and so is it with some living human faces; they are tyrannous pictures which speak to you, submit you to searching scrutiny, and give response to your inmost thoughts, nay, there are faces that set forth a whole drama, and Mme. d'Aiglemont's stony face was one of these awful tragedies, one of such faces as Dante Alighieri saw by thousands in his vision.

For the little season that a woman's beauty is in flower it serves her admirably well in the dissimulation to which her natural weakness and our social laws condemn her. A young face and rich color, and eyes that glow with light, a gracious maze of such subtle, manifold lines and curves, flawless and perfectly traced, is a screen that hides everything that stirs the woman within. A flush tells nothing, it only heightens the coloring so brilliant already; all the fires that burn within can add little light to the flame of life in eyes which only seem the brighter for the flash of a passing pain. Nothing is so discreet as a young face, for nothing is less mobile; it has the serenity, the surface smoothness, and the freshness of a lake. There is not character in women's faces before the age of thirty. The painter discovers nothing there but pink and white, and the smile and expression that repeat the same thought in the same way—a thought of youth and love that goes no further than youth and love. But the face of an old woman has expressed all that lay in her nature; passion has carved lines on her features; love and wifehood and motherhood, and extremes of joy and anguish, having wrung them, and left their traces in a thousand wrinkles, all of which speak a language of their own; then it is that a woman's face becomes sublime in its horror, beautiful in its melancholy, grand in its calm. If it is permissible to carry the strange metaphor still further, it might be said that in the dried-up lake you can see the traces of all the torrents that once poured into it and made it what it is. An old face is nothing to the frivolous world; the frivolous world is shocked by the sight of the destruction of such comeliness as it can understand; a commonplace artist sees nothing there. An old face is the province of the poets among poets of those who can recognize that something which is called Beauty, apart from all the conventions underlying so many superstitions in art and taste.

Though Mme. d'Aiglemont wore a fashionable bonnet, it was easy to see that her once black hair had been bleached by cruel sorrows; yet her good taste and the gracious acquired instincts of a woman of fashion could be seen in the way she wore it, divided into two bandeaux, following the outlines of a forehead that still retained some traces of former dazzling beauty, worn and lined though it was. The contours of her face, the regularity of her features, gave some idea, faint in truth, of that beauty of which surely she had once been proud; but those traces spoke still more plainly of the anguish which had laid it waste, of sharp pain that had withered the temples, and made those hollows in her cheeks, and empurpled the eyelids, and robbed them of their lashes, and the eyes of their charm. She was in every way so noiseless; she moved with a slow, self-contained gravity that showed itself in her whole bearing, and struck a certain awe into others. Her diffident manner had changed to positive shyness, due apparently to a habit now of some years' growth, of effacing herself in her daughter's presence. She spoke very seldom, and in the low tones used by those who perforce must live within themselves a life of reflection and concentration. This demeanor led others to regard her with an indefinable feeling which was neither awe nor compassion, but a mysterious blending of the many ideas awakened in us by compassion and awe. Finally, there was something in her wrinkles, in the lines of her face, in the look of pain in those wan eyes of hers, that bore eloquent testimony to tears that never had fallen, tears that had been absorbed by her heart. Unhappy creatures, accustomed to raise their eyes to heaven, in mute appeal against the bitterness of their lot, would have seen at once from her eyes that she was broken in to the cruel discipline of ceaseless prayer, would have discerned the almost imperceptible symptoms of the secret bruises which destroy all the flowers of the soul, even the sentiment of motherhood.

Painters have colors for these portraits, but words, and the mental images called up by words, fail to reproduce such impressions faithfully; there are mysterious signs and tokens in the tones of the coloring and in the look of human faces, which the mind only seizes through the sense of sight; and the poet is fain to record the tale of the events which wrought the havoc to make their terrible ravages understood.

The face spoke of cold and steady storm, an inward conflict between a mother's long-suffering and the limitations of our nature, for our human affections are bounded by our humanity, and the infinite has no place in finite creatures. Sorrow endured in silence had at last produced an indefinable morbid something in this woman. Doubtless mental anguish had reacted on the physical frame, and some disease, perhaps an aneurism, was undermining Julie's life. Deep-seated grief lies to all appearance very quietly in the depths where it is conceived, yet, so still and apparently dormant as it is, it ceaselessly corrodes the soul, like the terrible acid which eats away crystal.

Two tears made their way down the Marquise's cheeks; she rose to her feet as if some thought more poignant than any that preceded it had cut her to the quick. She had doubtless come to a conclusion as to Moina's future; and now, foreseeing clearly all the troubles in store for her child, the sorrows of her own unhappy life had begun to weigh once more upon her. The key of her position must be sought in her daughter's situation.

The Comte de Saint-Hereen had been away for nearly six months on a political mission. The Countess, whether from sheer giddiness, or in obedience to the countless instincts of woman's coquetry, or to essay its power—with all the vanity of a frivolous fine lady, all the capricious waywardness of a child—was amusing herself, during her husband's absence, by playing with the passion of a clever but heartless man, distracted (so he said) with love, the love that combines readily with every petty social ambition of a self-conceited coxcomb. Mme. d'Aiglemont, whose long experience had given her a knowledge of life, and taught her to judge of men and to dread the world, watched the course of this flirtation, and saw that it could only end in one way, if her daughter should fall into the hands of an utterly unscrupulous intriguer. How could it be other than a terrible thought for her that her daughter listened willingly to this roue? Her darling stood on the brink of a precipice, she felt horribly sure of it, yet dared not hold her back. She was afraid of the Countess. She knew too that Moina would not listen to her wise warnings; she knew that she had no influence over that nature—iron for her, silken-soft for all others. Her mother's tenderness might have led her to sympathize with the troubles of a passion called forth by the nobler qualities of a lover, but this was no passion—it was coquetry, and the Marquise despised Alfred de Vandenesse, knowing that he had entered upon this flirtation with Moina as if it were a game of chess.

But if Alfred de Vandenesse made her shudder with disgust, she was obliged—unhappy mother!—to conceal the strongest reason for her loathing in the deepest recesses of her heart. She was on terms of intimate friendship with the Marquis de Vandenesse, the young man's father; and this friendship, a respectable one in the eyes of the world, excused the son's constant presence in the house, he professing an old attachment, dating from childhood, for Mme. de Saint-Hereen. More than this, in vain did Mme. d'Aiglemont nerve herself to come between Moina and Alfred de Vandenesse with a terrible word, knowing beforehand that she should not succeed; knowing that the strong reason which ought to separate them would carry no weight; that she should humiliate herself vainly in her daughter's eyes. Alfred was too corrupt; Moina too clever to believe the revelation; the young Countess would turn it off and treat it as a piece of maternal strategy. Mme. d'Aiglemont had built her prison walls with her own hands; she had immured herself only to see Moina's happiness ruined thence before she died; she was to look on helplessly at the ruin of the young life which had been her pride and joy and comfort, a life a thousand times dearer to her than her own. What words can describe anguish so hideous beyond belief, such unfathomed depths of pain?

She waited for Moina to rise, with the impatience and sickening dread of a doomed man, who longs to have done with life, and turns cold at the thought of the headsman. She had braced herself for a last effort, but perhaps the prospect of the certain failure of the attempt was less dreadful to her than the fear of receiving yet again one of those thrusts that went to her very heart—before that fear her courage ebbed away. Her mother's love had come to this. To love her child, to be afraid of her, to shrink from the thought of the stab, yet to go forward. So great is a mother's affection in a loving nature, that before it can fade away into indifference the mother herself must die or find support in some great power without her, in religion or another love. Since the Marquise rose that morning, her fatal memory had called up before her some of those things, so slight to all appearance, that make landmarks in a life. Sometimes, indeed, a whole tragedy grows out of a single gesture; the tone in which a few words were spoken rends a whole life in two; a glance into indifferent eyes is the deathblow of the gladdest love; and, unhappily, such gestures and such words were only too familiar to Mme. d'Aiglemont—she had met so many glances that wound the soul. No, there was nothing in those memories to bid her hope. On the contrary, everything went to show that Alfred had destroyed her hold on her daughter's heart, that the thought of her was now associated with duty—not with gladness. In ways innumerable, in things that were mere trifles in themselves, the Countess' detestable conduct rose up before her mother; and the Marquise, it may be, looked on Moina's undutifulness as a punishment, and found excuses for her daughter in the will of Heaven, that so she still might adore the hand that smote her.

All these things passed through her memory that morning, and each recollection wounded her afresh so sorely, that with a very little additional pain her brimming cup of bitterness must have overflowed. A cold look might kill her.

The little details of domestic life are difficult to paint; but one or two perhaps will suffice to give an idea of the rest.

The Marquise d'Aiglemont, for instance, had grown rather deaf, but she could never induce Moina to raise her voice for her. Once, with the naivete of suffering, she had begged Moina to repeat some remark which she had failed to catch, and Moina obeyed, but with so bad a grace, the Mme. d'Aiglemont had never permitted herself to make her modest request again. Ever since that day when Moina was talking or retailing a piece of news, her mother was careful to come near to listen; but this infirmity of deafness appeared to put the Countess out of patience, and she would grumble thoughtlessly about it. This instance is one from among very many that must have gone to the mother's heart; and yet nearly all of them might have escaped a close observer, they consisted in faint shades of manner invisible to any but a woman's eyes. Take another example. Mme. d'Aiglemont happened to say one day that the Princesse de Cadignan had called upon her. "Did she come to see you!" Moina exclaimed. That was all, but the Countess' voice and manner expressed surprise and well-bred contempt in semitones. Any heart, still young and sensitive, might well have applauded the philanthropy of savage tribes who kill off their old people when they grow too feeble to cling to a strongly shaken bough. Mme. d'Aiglemont rose smiling, and went away to weep alone.

Well-bred people, and women especially, only betray their feelings by imperceptible touches; but those who can look back over their own experience on such bruises as this mother's heart received, know also how the heart-strings vibrate to these light touches. Overcome by her memories, Mme. d'Aiglemont recollected one of those microscopically small things, so stinging and so painful was it that never till this moment had she felt all the heartless contempt that lurked beneath smiles.

At the sound of shutters thrown back at her daughter's windows, she dried her tears, and hastened up the pathway by the railings. As she went, it struck her that the gardener had been unusually careful to rake the sand along the walk which had been neglected for some little time. As she stood under her daughter's windows, the shutters were hastily closed.

"Moina, is it you?" she asked.

No answer.

The Marquise went on into the house.

"Mme. la Comtesse is in the little drawing-room," said the maid, when the Marquise asked whether Mme. de Saint-Hereen had finished dressing.

Mme. d'Aiglemont hurried to the little drawing-room; her heart was too full, her brain too busy to notice matters so slight; but there on the sofa sat the Countess in her loose morning-gown, her hair in disorder under the cap tossed carelessly on he head, her feet thrust into slippers. The key of her bedroom hung at her girdle. Her face, aglow with color, bore traces of almost stormy thought.

"What makes people come in!" she cried, crossly. "Oh! it is you, mother," she interrupted herself, with a preoccupied look.

"Yes, child; it is your mother——"

Something in her tone turned those words into an outpouring

of the heart, the cry of some deep inward feeling, only to be described by the word "holy." So thoroughly in truth had she rehabilitated the sacred character of a mother, that her daughter was impressed, and turned towards her, with something of awe, uneasiness, and remorse in her manner. The room was the furthest of a suite, and safe from indiscreet intrusion, for no one could enter it without giving warning of approach through the previous apartments. The Marquise closed the door.

"It is my duty, my child, to warn you in one of the most serious crises in the lives of us women; you have perhaps reached it unconsciously, and I am come to speak to you as a friend rather than as a mother. When you married, you acquired freedom of action; you are only accountable to your husband now; but I asserted my authority so little (perhaps I was wrong), that I think I have a right to expect you to listen to me, for once at least, in a critical position when you must need counsel. Bear in mind, Moina that you are married to a man of high ability, a man of whom you may well be proud, a man who—"

"I know what you are going to say, mother!" Moina broke in pettishly. "I am to be lectured about Alfred—"

"Moina," the Marquise said gravely, as she struggled with her tears, "you would not guess at once if you did not feel—"

"What?" asked Moina, almost haughtily. "Why, really, mother-"

Mme. d'Aiglemont summoned up all her strength. "Moina," she said, "you must attend carefully to this that I ought to tell you—"

"I am attending," returned the Countess, folding her arms, and affecting insolent submission. "Permit me, mother, to ring for Pauline," she added with incredible self-possession; "I will send her away first."

She rang the bell.

"My dear child, Pauline cannot possibly hear—"

"Mamma," interrupted the Countess, with a gravity which must have struck her mother as something unusual, "I must—"

She stopped short, for the woman was in the room.

"Pauline, go yourself to Baudran's, and ask why my hat has not yet been sent."

Then the Countess reseated herself and scrutinized her mother. The Marquise, with a swelling heart and dry eyes, in painful agitation, which none but a mother can fully understand, began to open Moina's eyes to the risk that she was running. But either the Countess felt hurt and indignant at her mother's suspicions of a son of the Marquis de Vandenesse, or she was seized with a sudden fit of inexplicable levity caused by the inexperience of youth. She took advantage of a pause.

"Mamma, I thought you were only jealous of the father—" she said, with a forced laugh.

Mme. d'Aiglemont shut her eyes and bent her head at the words, with a very faint, almost inaudible sigh. She looked up and out into space, as if she felt the common overmastering impulse to appeal to God at the great crises of our lives; then she looked at her daughter, and her eyes were full of awful majesty and the expression of profound sorrow.

"My child," she said, and her voice was hardly recognizable, "you have been less merciful to your mother than he against whom she sinned; less merciful than perhaps God Himself will be!"

Mme. d'Aiglemont rose; at the door she turned; but she saw nothing but surprise in her daughter's face. She went out. Scarcely had she reached the garden when her strength failed her. There was a violent pain at her heart, and she sank down on a bench. As her eyes wandered over the path, she saw fresh marks on the path, a man's footprints were distinctly recognizable. It was too late, then, beyond a doubt. Now she began to understand the reason for that order given to Pauline, and with these torturing thoughts came a revelation more hateful than any that had gone before it. She drew her own inferences—the son of the Marquis de Vandenesse had destroyed all feeling of respect for her in her daughter's mind. The physical pain grew worse; by degrees she lost consciousness, and sat like one asleep upon the garden-seat.

The Countess de Saint-Hereen, left to herself, thought that her mother had given her a somewhat shrewd home-thrust, but a kiss and a few attentions that evening would make all right again.

A shrill cry came from the garden. She leaned carelessly out, as Pauline, not yet departed on her errand, called out for help, holding the Marquise in her arms.

"Do not frighten my daughter!" those were the last words the mother uttered.

Moina saw them carry in a pale and lifeless form that struggled for breath, and arms moving restlessly as in protest or effort to speak; and overcome by the sight, Moina followed in silence, and helped to undress her mother and lay her on her bed. The burden of her fault was greater than she could bear. In that supreme hour she learned to know her mother—too late, she could make no reparation now. She would have them leave her alone with her mother; and when there was no one else in the room, when she felt that the hand which had always been so tender for her was now grown cold to her touch, she broke out into weeping. Her tears aroused the Marquise; she could still look at her darling Moina; and at the sound of sobbing, that seemed as if it must rend the delicate, disheveled breast, could smile back at her daughter. That smile taught the unnatural child that forgiveness is always to be found in the great deep of a mother's heart.

Servants on horseback had been dispatched at once for the physician and surgeon and for Mme. d'Aiglemont's grandchildren. Mme. d'Aiglemont the younger and her little sons arrived with the medical men, a sufficiently impressive, silent, and anxious little group, which the servants of the house came to join. The young Marquise, hearing no sound, tapped gently at the door. That signal, doubtless, roused Moina from her grief, for she flung open the doors and stood before them. No words could have spoken more plainly than that disheveled figure looking out with haggard eyes upon the assembled family. Before that living picture of Remorse the rest were dumb. It was easy to see that the Marquise's feet were stretched out stark and stiff with the agony of death; and Moina, leaning against the door-frame, looking into their faces, spoke in a hollow voice:

"I have lost my mother!"

PARIS, 1828-1844

THE END